# ONCE UPON
# A FACT

# ONCE UPON A FACT

*Futuristic Fairy Tales*

### EDITED BY
### KATHERINE TOMLINSON

**WILDSIDE PRESS**

# CONTENTS

# BEYOND INFINITY, PAST ETERNITY

"Once upon a time" is a magical phrase; an incantation that conjures stories into being and gives them life. What we now call "fairy tales" outlived their original creators, outlasted their descendants, and one day might very well survive the death of our species. When, and if, humanity leaves this planet, fairy tales will make the journey too—into the far-flung reaches of the galaxy and into the distant dimension of the future.

How different will the fairy tales of the future be from the stories told around hearth fires a thousand years ago? I suspect they will be utterly different and yet completely familiar.

Human existence is bound by the laws of physics, limited by the cage of flesh and bone we wear, but imagination exists in another dimension entirely and stories, once told, exist forever.

This collection was inspired by the Women's March for Science in early 2017. As I listened to the speeches and the talk around me I thought, I have heard this story before. And that thought led to another and then another and by the time I got home, I had a title and an idea.

I reached out to writers I knew and then to writers I didn't know but admired, and I asked them if they would be interested in contributing to *Once Upon a Fact*—writing stories giving classic fairy tales a science-fiction twist. They were intrigued.

I had conceived the project as a charity anthology with the proceeds going to organizations sponsoring women in science, and that concept resonated as well.

The result is this spectacular group of stories.

I am very grateful to the authors who donated their talents and their tales.

Many thanks also to Carla Coupe of Wildside Press for playing fairy godmother to this project.

Prepare to be enchanted…

—Katherine Tomlinson

# THE SEED STITCH SOLUTION

## Ginn Hale

### Inspired by The Little Match Girl

After a month in prison, I'm prepared when the guards drag me down through the cold basement to the perpetually damp corner where the concrete trough stands. Only three lights still work. One flickers and hums like some incandescent mosquito as it illuminates the faded mural of fat livestock and smiling white farmers.

The slick water in the trough stinks and I'm glad that the dark keeps me from seeing exactly what floats through the depths. I don't scream anymore, nor do I bother to thrash or bite. That only gives them reason to crack my head against the edge of the trough.

I suck in a quick breath and clench my eyes closed.

Both the guards dig their hands into my hair and then shove my head under.

Fetid water rushes up my nostrils and floods my ears. I know that I can't make myself stronger than the two of them, but I can be calmer, more collected and smarter.

I think of Sophia—the way her hazel eyes always seemed as much green as gold when she smiled at me—and I remember her holding up one finger and then a second. And we dived into the lake together and swam through emerald eelgrass out to the distant island where monarch butterflies clung to the branches of trees in the thousands, turning the woods shimmering gold with their fluttering wings.

If I'd known then what I do now I would have pulled her into my arms and kissed her. But I felt too afraid then and so Sophia kissed me first.

I want to think only of that wondrous first kiss but I know I must concentrate on the minutes before, when Sophia holds up two fingers and assures me that I can easily hold my breath for just the count of two.

Anyone can hold their breath that long.

In the dank pool I count to two just like Sophia showed me that day at the lake.

1.

1.1

1.2

1.3

1.4

1.5…

And on and on and on.

They could hold me down forever and I would still never reach two—never burn through all the oxygen hidden inside that tiny infinity. I continue opening air pockets between numbers the way the Real Jesus Christ produced loaves and fishes. Maybe he was a number-witch like Sophia, but his followers never suspected.

I wonder how long he had to stand there, dividing the seven down into four thousand before he'd satiated his ravenous audience. Did his hands start to ache and tremble the way mine do? Did his chest burn and his feet tingle with numb?

No, I decide. No, he was probably gagging from the smell of all that fish. There had to be rafts of it lying out in the sun, as his gormless followers stripped bones and meat, leaving mountains of glittering scales in their wake. Maybe he should have taken in all that reeking silver at his feet and seen it for an omen of his own demise.

And then I catch myself drifting from my count and return my concentration to the clean purity of the numbers.

1.20

1.21

1.22

1.23…

They wrench me up from the water. I gasp and cough. My knees nearly buckle but I manage to keep upright. The guards still hold me by my hair. I sway and puke out a reeking mouthful of water onto one of their legs. The man swears and the darkness of the basement hides my brief smile. It's one of my only opportunities to exact some kind of revenge and I always take it.

As I lift my head to look across the length of the concrete trough little stars dance in front of my eyes, but I meet Pastor Anderson's tepid gaze. He's a sallow, thin man who wears a beard to hide his under-bite and likes to imagine that it lends him a stunning resemblance to his savior. Perhaps it would if the Real Jesus Christ had spent his days in a dank basement, torturing women.

The pastor is bored with me. He has been for weeks now but he has a job to do, just like the two pasty-faced guards restraining me.

"Orah Jackson, I hope that you have found the light of the Real Jesus Christ through these baptismal waters and are ready to tell me what I need to know."

"I've already told you everything." My voice sounds dull and my throat feels sore. We've done this so many times. It's almost like a performance we put on for some unseen audience. Every day for hours, I tell Pastor Anderson the same lies and I hope that they are enough to buy Sophia the time she needs to reach safety.

"Mrs. Green only hired me as a housekeeper. I cleaned and made dinners for her and her guests. I don't know if she smuggled heretics out of the country or not. The only things I can tell you about her are that she slept in late on Saturdays and she didn't like collard greens unless they were stewed all day long. I don't know why she left in the middle of the night. I can't even guess where she might have gone."

I lower my eyes to the pools of dark liquid spattered across the floor.

I was meant to join Sophia at the lake that night, but the pastor's men sighted me out after curfew. I ran the other way and led them as far from her as I could. I keep that to myself, the same way that I hold onto everything else I know. I imagine all these secrets are sparks that could burn my whole world down if they got loose, so I hold them deep inside me, and hope that they will keep me warm in the prison cell.

Green isn't Sophia's real name, but it is her favorite color. Her hair is naturally dark brown but she dyes it blond when she slips across Merican borders. She's rescued hundreds of chemists, astronomers, writers, and number witches. She knows all about the secret workings of the silent machines that fill so many of the old abandoned cities. Turbines, generators, missile silos—she knows the names that the pastors cannot find in their bibles. She could repair the engines that they cannot revive through their exorcisms or prayers. She can talk to the satellites streaking across the night sky and they show her the vastness of a globe that the pastors insist is a flat plane suspended in space by God's Will.

She can't knit a stitch, and she tends to grow distracted and leaves our toast too long over the fire. And she is ticklish behind her knees.

"There's nothing I can tell you," I say.

"Nothing you *will* tell me, Miss Jackson," Pastor Anderson corrects me.

"No." I say just to deny him what I can.

Pastor Anderson sighs. Normally he would order me back under the water. The guards tighten their grips on my hair in anticipation, but the pastor shakes his head.

And all at once I realize that he's given up. It's too late for his righteous men to track her down. She's escaped them again and ferried another dozen souls to freedom. I'm thrilled and then filled with desolation.

She's truly gone and I will not see her again.

"Miss Jackson, you have aligned yourself with the sinful enemies of our godly nation and have refused all opportunities to repent your treason. It is my duty to sentence you to the Christmas Fires. May your death serve as a lesson to other women who would behave so willfully."

\* \* \* \*

The holding cells reserved for those of us condemned to execution are cold and nearly full. The only light seeps in from narrow slits cut into the upper third of the far wall. The slots open onto the execution grounds and leach all the warmth from the concrete room.

For the first time in a month I've been given clothing: a stained orange shift. But as winter winds stream in through the slotted wall I feel as cold as if I were still naked. I wrap my arms around my chest, trying to hold in any warmth.

The fifteen other women in my cell are all quiet when I'm brought in. Only one woman bothers to briefly glance back from the windows to me. Her expression assures me that I'm nothing new or surprising. Then she returns to her study of the execution grounds.

I, too, gaze across the expanse of dirty snow. The huge stone fire pits stand empty, their blackened surfaces blanketed with ice. It's the gallows that are bustling today. The crowd gathered around is large but nothing like the throngs that always attend the Christmas fires. Maybe two hundred, counting all the children. Six women, their heads freshly shaved and their scrawny bodies draped in orange shifts stand on the gallows with nooses already draped around their necks. Two of them are sobbing. The others stare blankly as if they are already dead.

"Who are they, do you know?" I ask.

A tall, yellow-haired girl standing nearest the windows mumbles something, but I can barely hear her over the cheering outside. The Reverend Executioner has made his appearance. He waves and grins as he strides in front of the six condemned women. Like Pastor Anderson he wears his light hair shoulder length and sports a trimmed beard.

"Who are they?" I ask again. This time the yellow-haired girl turns around. Her face is splotched with greenish bruises and a scab covers most of her chin. I don't imagine that I look any prettier. Two of my front teeth are broken and the gash across the left side of my head has just started to close up. The fingers of my right hand are bandaged but blood seeps through from where my fingernails once grew. My dark skin has dulled to chalky gray after a month spent in dim basements.

I wonder what the girl has done to end up here and I can see from the way she looks me over that she's pondering the same question about me. Murders have become more common since the famines began three years ago and I recall someone who looked very like this girl being accused of selling human flesh as pork.

She sniffs and frowns.

"Another bunch of bitches who let our ground defense down." The girl's voice is strident. "Ten more of the big guns went down."

The other women in my cell add soft disparaging remarks about the condemned women. People out on the execution grounds boo at them. Some throw rocks. A year ago I might have shared their anger. But now I feel sick because I know that big guns and ground-based missiles don't fail because the women charged with their prayer vigils lack faith. They break because machine parts wear out. Time strips down screws, gums up bearings, clogs exhaust systems, and chews through belts. Machines break because no one understands technology anymore, so no one knows how to make repairs.

I wouldn't have dreamed such things were possible until Sophia showed me how to recharge a battery. Together we repaired a circuit board. And afterwards we sat grinning as the little radio we'd made picked up transmissions from distant corners of the world.

The strange new voices and beautiful music changed my whole world. I couldn't get enough. The radio kept me company during the long nights alone while Sophia was away. When she came home I'd put down my knitting and we'd dance. We made love while the tiny machine sang about summertime in other lands.

"Faith is the refuge of people exiled to ignorance," Sophia told me one day.

Of course, I took exception to such a sweeping condemnation.

"Faith is comforting. People need it to get through hard times and bad things."

"Comfort is nice, of course. But it doesn't alter anything. It doesn't free your mind or spirit. It doesn't empower you to change the things that make you suffer in the first place," Sophia replied.

Our hands brushed as we both reached for the same screwdriver. She let me use it first then spent a few moments piecing her revolver together from the parts she'd found during her outing the previous week. I tinkered with another radio—trying to rebuild it using a crumpled contraband diagram.

"Knowledge gives people power to change things," Sophia said. "To work real miracles. With knowledge you can cure diseases, dive deep into the sea and swim for hours. You can fly all the way to the moon—"

"The moon? No one could ever do that." I laughed at her.

"They could and have!" Sophia informed me. "It's where I was raised."

I just kept laughing.

A week later she took me with her on an outing. We traveled through the tunnels under the empty city and up into an old stone palace guarded by granite lions. Inside, Sophia showed me the thousands of moldering books. She lay out volume after volume filled with photographs of the moon and stars. I read about rockets and oxygen. About gravity, space, and time. My sun became one of countless stars. Millions of planets suddenly spun out into mathematical orbits.

Then Sophia showed me the diagrams of the lunar colony where she'd grown up and pictures of the Mars biodomes.

And I couldn't keep myself from crying.

This was nothing like the wonder of the radio. My entire world shattered apart as a vast universe burst from it and expanded on and on, in brilliant color and breathtaking variety. It was an apocalypse of everything I understood to be real and yet it was so beautiful—so much more than I could ever hope to know in all my lifetime. Sophia hugged me and later we looked through partly charred volumes of cookbooks. I tried to image the taste of the strange foods.

"You'll love mangos, I think," Sophia assured me.

"Do they taste more like red apples or yellow apples?"

"They taste better than either. You'll see."

As we made our way home, I realized why the pastors hated people like Sophia so much. Their knowledge made the pastors just as small and powerless as any other human being. In the face of genuine repeatable results their prayers and bible stories became absurd—laughable. The brilliant world that Sophia came from flashed and whirled with questions and ideas. The diversity of life embodied vivid experiments and countless different solutions. Elements percolated and danced through air, water, stone, and even radiated from stars. Sunflowers and snails held beautiful mathematics at their hearts and even counting to two could open up infinity.

Out on the gallows the Reverend Executioner pulls a lever, the trapdoors groan and then fall open beneath the bound women. They drop and the crowd howls and cheers. In the cell a few of the other women let out short hoots as well. But most of us stand in silence staring at the condemned women kicking and shaking at the ends of their nooses.

Soon enough each of us will take our turn out there.

A big-boned woman who had previously whooped with vicious joy, suddenly begins to moan. The yellow-haired girl turns away to press her face against the rough surface of the cement wall. A weird groan escapes her.

I can't seem to look away from the hanged women even as I feel sick terror seizing me. I don't want to break down at the mere sight of six corpses, not after I've endured so much worse. Still I feel the blood draining from my face.

All I can think is that I don't want to die. I don't want to die. I don't want to die.

I clench my eyes shut.

It's too late for cowardice now. I knew this would be my end. I knew it from that first moment when Pastor Anderson asked me what maps Sophia had been studying and I couldn't let myself answer him.

"She can't be worth dying for," Pastor Anderson commented. "No woman is worthy of that."

*She is*, I thought. But it hadn't been Sophia alone that silenced me. It had been the whole vibrant world that she'd introduced me to—a world that I knew was worth protecting and preserving. A world worth dying for.

Now I pull in a slow breath. I think back on songs that drifted from the radio, make myself lift the lyrics from my memory to fill my head again with lovely melodies. I bask in the memory of those songs playing as I held Sophia in my arms. I think about the sunflower seeds that I planted and I wonder how many of them will sprout when spring comes again. I don't need to live that long to see them. I remember the spiral—the Fibonacci sequence Sophia called it. I use it to build giant sunflowers in my mind. The golden petals flutter in the wind as they turn their faces to follow the sun.

I imagine that I'm sitting beneath them and knitting a blanket for the coming winter. I concentrate on the calm feeling of looping a single thread into a thick fabric that could keep Sophia and me warm in our bed.

When I open my eyes the dead women have been cut down and carted away. The gallows stand empty and fresh snowflakes begin to tumble from the gray sky.

None of the women in the cell are particularly talkative. Big-boned Mary mumbles prayers to herself and now and then someone breaks down crying, but we aren't any of us concerned with getting to know each other. What's the point of growing fond of a doomed woman? Or worse, spending your last days locked up with someone you've grown to despise? We huddle together to keep warm, but we might as well be locked in separate cells for all that we care for or comfort each other.

Over the next week our numbers dwindle as the executions outside progress. Workmen begin to break the ice that's encased the firepits.

Mary is hanged for stealing from the pastors' storehouses. Ten other women drop with her. The first cords of firewood arrive and are stacked up against the prison wall. Soon only I and the yellow-haired girl remain. Then one night I feel her stop shivering against my back. I don't know why but I try to warm her body, rubbing her arms and holding her against my chest. She stops breathing and I can't do anything for her. I don't even know her name but I cry for hours. Late in the afternoon a guard drags her stiff corpse away, leaving me the two bowls of gruel he'd brought.

I stare at the bowls and their watery gray contents. Why am I even bothering to eat, I wonder. Why keep myself strong, if all I have to look ahead to is being burned alive? I don't retain enough faith in the bible to believe that Hell awaits me if I commit suicide, so why don't I just give up?

Then I lift my gaze to the cold blue sky outside and I remember how much larger the world is than just this concrete cell—how much more vast it is than even this small-minded country. Wonder, beauty and freedom are all out there and I don't want to give up on them. No matter how unlikely my chance of escape might be I want to be ready to seize it.

I eat both servings of gruel. Then I spend several hours working at one of the metal bowls, bending it back and forth until it cracks. I scrape the ragged metal edge against the supports in the concrete window. When the guard from the night shift comes through I hide the jagged bowl behind the shit pot. He doesn't look for it or even concern himself with glancing at me. I smile to myself and up at the slim crescent moon hanging in the sky.

Alone in the cell, I spend my days digging at the concrete and singing songs to myself. I consider the stacks of firewood and ponder how best to climb them and get up over the prison wall. At night I gaze out the tiny slotted windows and watch the sliver of the moon grow steadily more full. I imagine that I can see the glittering green expanses of Sophia's childhood home sparkling from the shadows of deep blue craters. I dream that I'm knitting a ladder from gusts of wind and it reaches all the way to the stars.

Then in the middle of the night guards yank the heavy steel door open. Hinges screech and the dim beam of a single flashlight sweeps across the chamber, missing me by inches. A hunched woman, with wildly curling dark hair is shoved in. She wears the same orange shift as me, but she also clutches sticks and some string in her hands.

"I didn't do anything wrong!" the woman protests but the guards don't care. The door slams closed leaving only moonlight to illuminate the newcomer. She shakes her head and for just an instant I think that there's something almost pleased about her stance as she turns from the door and takes in the cell. She walks slowly towards the slotted wall. Her hair hangs around her face but even through the darkness I can see dark blotches of bruises on her arms.

I realize that she's clutching a ball of yarn and pair of wooden knitting needles in her hands. She probably wasn't lying about not belonging here among the condemned if she was allowed to keep those things. Maybe the lower cells were overcrowded. Or more likely she spoke back to some pastor and he's had her dragged into prison in the dead of the night to make a lesson of her to her friends and family.

I gaze at the knitting needles and suddenly remember laughing at Sophia's tangled, uneven attempts to knit me a hat.

I'd held up my own needles and demonstrated the simple motions for her over and over, but she just couldn't get the hang of it.

"You make it look so easy."

"That's because it *is* easy." I knitted a few more stitches, winding the string of reclaimed yarn around my needle and then slowly looping it into the next stitch and the next after that. Sophia watched with a rapt expression and at first I thought she was making fun of me but then I realized that she truly was fascinated by the processes.

"I just realized that those needles act as a kind of matrix," Sophia said. "Without them the whole thing would simply unravel as it was being made. But just looking at the finished piece you'd never know that the needles had been there."

"I think I'd know," I replied.

"Well of course *you* know because you understand the process, but for a person who's just encountered this scarf you made me out of the blue, it wouldn't be obvious that a matrix had been at work."

I nodded. I hadn't heard the term matrix before, but I recognized that Sophia's description was correct, and I felt pleased that something I could do well so impressed her.

"It's exactly the same with number-witching, you know." Sophia picked up a skein of yarn and picked at the threads of paper pulp and lint spun in with the stronger fibers.

"How would I possibly know that?" I asked with a laugh.

Sophia looked a little embarrassed but then leaned closer and kissed my cheek. "I was only going to say that the imaginary and irrational numbers that we number-witches use act just like your knitting needles. They form the matrices that support our transformations until we actualize them—like molds hold candles until the wax is set."

Nine months earlier I would have nodded as if I knew what she meant, but I no longer felt satisfied to accept my own ignorance, not even when it seemed blissful.

"What do you mean by imaginary numbers?" I asked.

"Oh. I mean numbers that arise according to the axioms of mathematics but don't necessarily exist in our physical world." Sophia leaned back in her chair, letting the knitting needles that I'd carved for her rest in her lap.

"So they aren't actually real?" I asked.

"I suppose that depends on how you define what's real. Just because something is imaginary doesn't mean it's false, only that it's an idea. Like justice or equality, or even truth. An idea may not exist physically, but it can still be applied to real things and people." Sophia picked up the knitting needles again and very carefully knitted a stitch. "Imaginary numbers can lift real problems into their own realm, where they can be manipulated more easily and then slipped back into reality with solutions."

"So they're a kind of matrix," I liked that I knew how to use that word now. "Like knitting needles?"

"Well, like *your* knitting needles. Not so much like mine." Sophia shook her head at the knotted second stitch in her yarn. I smiled and she started over.

"It's strange to think that all these things begin just as ideas in someone's imagination, isn't it?"

Sophia nodded.

"Though if you think about it, so much of what we believe to be real actually exists in our imaginations. When you hear a voice speaking to you through the radio, you feel certain that there must be someone, somewhere, broadcasting, but what makes you so certain is your ability to imagine that person's existence. You can't see them, but you know from evidence that they must exist, and your imagination fills in the rest."

"That's how I feel about electrons." I'd been fascinated by the idea of those tiny invisible structures since I'd read about them. I'd spent hours trying to picture shells of constantly moving energy humming and whirling together to create the magic of electricity.

"Yes, exactly. In fact," Sophia went on, "there's an imaginary number called $i$ that's a great deal like an electron in that it can occupy vastly different positions in space at the same time. It can be over on the positive side of a quadrant and in the negative position as well."

"How can a thing be in two places at once?" I wondered.

"Numbers can do all kinds of things that physical objects can't." Sophia sounded just a little proud and I knew it was because she knew all kinds of tricks to make numbers do what she wanted.

"Have you ever been two places at once?" I asked. I couldn't imagine what that would feel like.

"No. That would be an extraordinary feat to maintain for any length of time, even for the best of number-witches." She knitted another stitch, gazing at the yarn as she wound it out and then she made a loop around her finger. "Unless the two places in the fabric of space could be brought together while somehow still remaining separate…"

"The way a knit stitch creates a purl stitch on the reverse side? So they're both in the same place but still distinct?" I asked.

"They do?" Sophia asked and she looked genuinely surprised.

I remember laughing.

"No wonder you're having so much trouble knitting. Here, I'll show you."

I slowly looped and twisted the yarn between my needles. Every knit stitch produced a distinct purl on the reverse. Sophia watched me intently. I bound off the end and slid the knitting from the needles. She took the small swatch from me and examined one side and then the other.

"See? Two different stitches occupying the same place," I said as she flipped the swatch over.

"That's really fascinating," Sophia remarked, though her actual knitting didn't improve. If anything, it grew worse because she so often lapsed into long meditation of the looped yarn and needles.

Soon enough we were both distracted by the work of stretching our garden harvest to feed the six other people Sophia intended to shelter in our shared home for the next week.

And then I hear Sophia's voice. Not then, but *now*.

"Orah?"

Sophia turns towards me and the full moon halos her wild hair and tattered shift. I can't think of anything else. How can she be here, when I'd done so much to ensure that she escaped?

"I'm here." I stand, stiff-legged, and hurry to her.

She looks relieved. The moonlight falls across my bandaged hand and her expression turns heart-broken.

"I'm so sorry I couldn't find you sooner," she whispers.

I want to tell her that she shouldn't have come at all, she shouldn't have endangered herself on my account, but I can't. I'm too overjoyed to be with her. We hold each other.

Feeling her body against mine, the aches and pangs that riddle me fade. It's such a relief to touch her and feel her arms around me. I don't want to think of anything else. But I know we have to, because she can't stay here.

I draw back, and Sophia straightens too and hands her knitting needles to me.

"Can you still knit?" she asks. My fingers ache but as I grip the needles I can feel muscle memory flooding my hands.

"What am I making?" I ask.

"Our way out of here."

She grips the ball of yarn and I can see that the fibers are inked with a strange string of symbols. $(X2+1=0)=i$, $(X2+1=0)=-i$.

They repeat over and over.

My hands shake but I cast on ten stitches and as I do Sophia closes her eyes and whispers an incantation. A strange sensation grips me as I slip a completed stitch from one needle to the next; it's as if I wobbled slightly forward and then back to where I'm standing. I knit another stitch and this time I feel a gust of warm air. Another and the light pouring through the slotted windows seems to flare to the brilliance of afternoon sunlight.

Next to me Sophia holds the yarn gently, but her expression is strained. Droplets of sweat bead her face.

I ignore the pain shooting through the fingertips of my right hand and hold the needles tightly. I knit stitches quickly now, weaving the single string into a solid fabric. With each stitch the warmth and light surrounding us grows. I hear birds singing and feel grass beneath my feet. The air smells strange and new, like nothing I've known before.

The cell wall burns away and I'm staring at verdant trees and buildings as lustrous as seashells. There are people gathered around us. Their expressions look hopeful and excited. But they don't seem quite real. My whole body feels as if it's floating slightly.

"The gravity is weaker here," Sophia says. "Don't let it distract you."

I nod and keep working. No longer knitting but now binding off the stitches and steadily slipping them from the matrix of the needles. I pull the last length of yarn from Sophia's hands. It's done. Sophia lets out a crow of joy and throws her arms around me. I lean into her, too happy and relieved to even speak.

We stand together, arms wrapped around each other. Sunlight pours through the blue dome overhead and high up in the sky I can just see a pale sphere. From here the world I've left behind looks small. But the dark space beyond it and all the brilliant stars gleaming out there spread before me with infinite possibility.

---

Award-winning author Ginn Hale lives in the Pacific Northwest with her lovely wife and their wicked cat. She spends the rainy days observing local fungi. The stormy nights, she spends writing science-fiction and fantasy stories featuring LGBT protagonists.

# HOW TO MARRY OFF YOUR HUMAN

## Shauna Roberts

### *Inspired by the tale of Puss 'n' Boots*

Imagine: A suave confidence artist from a catlike species. His unwanted and obtuse human apprentice. Their hasty departure from a planet whose denizens were not the easy marks they had seemed. A week as stowaways crammed in a cargo compartment inexplicably reeking of cooked cabbage and chickpeas. Their disembarkation at a market with luxury products and services for life forms from far-flung solar systems. What a wealth of new sheep to fleece!

Hmmm. Not a very fairy tale-ish start to a fairy tale.

Forget it. I'll start again.

Once upon a time, on a distant moon....

* * * *

Hermes Reynard Mercurius Lefilou III leapt onto the stunted thorntree, clambered up with his sharp claws, and sprang through an open window on the second floor of the crumbling adobe house. He brushed dust from his clothes and briskly licked his tail clean. He removed his teardrop ruby earring from his pouch, where he had stored it, and rehung it from his ear.

Joe, his ward and apprentice, still hadn't come through the window.

Sighing, Lefilou looked out toward the market center of Newest France. The dust cloud made by the dozens of feet of the three carapaced merchants chasing them billowed above the booths and businesses, turning the air tan. Outside the gate, under the sign that read "Remember: Sentients don't eat sentients," banana peels glowed gold under the class K sun. Lefilou grinned—a habit he had picked up from Joe.

Joe, who now stood like a helpless child on the ground below him, gazing up at the window.

Lefilou beckoned. "Don't dally, boy! Climb! Climb!"

The human grumbled some cuss words before shouting, "Unlock the door!"

"Why do you have to make everything so difficult?" Lefilou left the room and found the stairway. Someone from one of the giant races must have lived here, despite the normal-height ceilings; the stairs were steep. He spurned them and jumped lightly to the first floor.

The door's cheap lock was an old electronic model prone to failure when exposed to sounds of a certain wavelength. Lefilou squatted beside it and caterwauled at the required frequency.

The lock clicked. The warped extruded-wood door popped open, and oven-like desert heat blasted him, forcing him to take a couple steps back.

Panting, Joe staggered into the adobe.

Lefilou slammed the door shut and relocked it.

Joe's right arm hugged baguettes that poked into his right eye, and two freshly skinned rabbits hung over his left shoulder. Pickles protruded from both pants pockets. Each hand held that most old-fashioned of treats, a cup of thyme-flavored coffee with a dollop of melting goat cheese on top.

Tonight, thanks to merchants who weren't sharp-eyed or sharp-witted enough, they would feast.

Lefilou tapped his foot with a precision that could put the most expensive of metronomes to shame. "What was the problem this time?"

"I'd like to see you climb a thorntree with your arms full." Joe set the cups of coffee down on the cool tile floor and kerplunked onto his keister like an elderly castrato who had held his stomach in for a three-hour performance. "I'm not a kangaroo. I can't jump two stories high."

Lefilou sighed, disappointed, and sat with panache. He fluffed his whiskers and picked up his coffee mug. "It's always something with you, isn't it? Excuses, excuses. How you humans ever achieved interstellar travel, I'll never understand."

"Thumbs." Joe shoved the rabbit cadavers toward Lefilou.

"An overrated appendage. It's much better to have long canine teeth or razor-sharp claws. Or, for that matter, a handsome tail." With a self-satisfied smile, he looked back at his own long tail, which curled in an arabesque and was covered in velvety black fur.

Joe picked up his coffee mug and took a sip. Then he bit off the end of a baguette. "I can hold a mug with one bare hand and eat with the other. I paid extra for a faux-fur cover for your mug, which you'll need both paws to hold."

Lefilou ignored the jibe. He sipped his coffee then set it down and disjointed the front leg of one rabbit. He daintily pulled a gobbet of flesh free and swallowed it. "Amazingly tender. Fed on grains, which certainly didn't grow here in the desert."

"This bread is great," Joe said. He crunched on a pickle, the crisp snap echoing in the room like the clack of a crab's claws. "The pickles are terrific, too. Even better than on Newer France or on Newer Than Newest France. Why would a satellite designer choose a desert setting for a posh market?"

"It was the other way around, child. Think! What would you do if you owned a barren moon? Create the best market in its solar system, obviously."

"Huh?"

Lefilou explained slowly. "Newest France is the opposite of a pleasure planet. When life forms complete their business, they have no incentive to leave the bubble that protects them from heat, desert crocs, ghastly scenery, and other unpleasant things. They stay in the market. They buy souvenirs, try strange foods, and set up new deals, creating more wealth for the moon's owner."

Joe sighed. "See? I'm not cut out to be a flimflam man."

Lefilou petted Joe's head. "Human history proves your species has a talent for tricks and lies. I'll keep teaching; one day you'll start learning."

"I've been thinking, Hermes."

"Don't. That's my job."

Joe shook his head. "Not this time. I've been thinking about my future now that I'm an adult."

Lefilou's paw stopped in midair as if waiting for a flag to attach itself. "Are you sure?" He stared at Joe without blinking. "You still look kittenish: no snout, and fur too soft to deflect a bite."

"I'm eighteen years old now. I appreciate all you've done for me." Joe studied the patched adobe above the fireplace.

"As well you should." Lefilou ripped another leg from the rabbit.

"I don't want to be a con artist or a thief anymore," Joe burst out. "I want a normal human life. I want to have kids and not be hopping freighters and trading ships from market to market."

Lefilou peered at his protégé, his face a mask. "You want to leave me."

"I don't want to leave *you*. I want to leave *this life*." Joe scratched his mentor under the chin. "Hermes, you could go straight with me. Wouldn't that be great? No more running from angry merchants or spending a week without food inside a cargo compartment. When you got old and senile, I could take care of you."

"No pity, boy." Lefilou jerked away, and his thin lips slid back, showing yellowed canines caked at the roots with an icky amount of tartar. "My species is solitary. I only took you in because your parents gave me no choice."

Joe clicked his fingernail on one of Lefilou's fangs. "You haven't been flossing, have you? I swear, for a species that loves washing itself, you sure neglect your teeth. What do I have to do to get you to floss?"

"I don't need you to mollycoddle me."

"Then you won't miss me if I leave and all your teeth rot and your gums turn black."

"As usual, you haven't thought things out. You need a few essentials before you strike out on your own."

"Such as?"

Lefilou shrugged. "The right clothes. Clothes make the man, you know. A house. A wife to give you the children you want. And credits, lots of credits."

"Huh." Joe's head sagged. "I'm a fool. I guess I can't go straight."

"How many times have I told you, 'you have to make a way out of no way'?" Lefilou sighed. "I'll make the way. Then my obligation to your parents will be done."

* * * *

After finishing off the baguettes, pickles, and raw rabbits, the two confidence men searched the house for anything that might be edible or suitable for pawning. Then they pooled their findings by the front room's fireplace.

Joe set down a battered kettle with a large hole, some small jars filled with tinted grease, and something that looked like the pelt of a tiny mammal. "Nothing useful here."

"On the contrary, my boy. Thespians may have lived here. Those jars contain theatrical cosmetics, and the shaggy object is a false moustache. A confidence artist can sometimes benefit from a good disguise."

Joe held the furry doohickey to his upper lip, trying different positions and squinting at his distorted reflection in the kettle. No matter how he held it, it failed miserably at looking anything like a moustache.

"Unlikely as it seems, I may have been mistaken," Lefilou said. "Perhaps it's a merkin."

Joe recoiled. The fur hit the floor, and he kicked it into the fireplace.

"You hoodwinked me!" he accused, scrubbing his lips and scrunched-up nose with his sleeve.

"I?" Lefilou rubbed his whiskers with his paw. "I would never bamboozle my best and favorite apprentice."

"Malarkey." Joe spit into the fireplace and crossed his arms. "You find anything?"

Lefilou leapt up, pointed to his feet, and capered and cavorted about the room, his ruby earring jiggling. "New boots!" he crowed. He stamped his feet. "Beautiful new black-leather boots! Thigh high with high heels, silver buckles, and a holographic display on each. The quean-cats will have eyes for no one but me."

"Give me the boots. You have calloused paw pads, and I don't."

"Nonsense!" Lefilou struck a pose. "These shall be key to my disguise."

"Boots everyone will notice and no one will forget?"

Lefilou hissed. "You're not getting them. Your feet are much too short for a giant's boots." He yowled his favorite song:

> *I'm a noble tom,*
> *a handsome tom,*
> *a tom of large territ'ry.*
> *A fierce, fierce tom,*
> *a sharp-clawed tom,*
> *a tom of great dignity.*

Joe yawned through the remaining seven verses.

Lefilou segued into the love ballad, "You Hooked Me with Your Raspy Tongue." He frisked; he frolicked. He pranced; he pounced; he pirouetted.

Joe sat with his chin in his hands. He cleaned one ear with a fingernail. He stared into space. Then he jerked upright. He reached forward, grabbed Lefilou's leg, and prodded the heel of the boot.

Lefilou hissed and boxed Joe's head with his claws retracted. "Remove your monkey paws from my boot! You primates are so filthy! You stick your fingers in everything. It's disgusting."

"Hey! Hold still!" Joe protected his head with one arm while he continued to fiddle with the heel.

Lefilou hissed and spat.

"Aha!" Joe exclaimed. The heel clicked, and the side swung open, revealing several drawers.

Lefilou washed his paws and assumed a dignified posture. He looked around the room and then washed his tail. At last his gaze landed casually on his boot. "How extraordinary!" he observed. "The heel contains a chest of drawers."

"Huh. Imagine that." Joe rolled his eyes.

Lefilou hooked a claw in the top compartment and pulled out a black box. He took out each drawer in turn and placed the contents on the floor. Then he held his other leg in the air and squinted at the boot heel from various angles.

"Surprise! My primate color vision and primate fingers come in handy sometimes." Joe traced the faint line on the heel with his fingernail and then pressed a spot next to it. The heel clicked and swung open.

As Lefilou took out the contents, he mused, "Perhaps I was in error when I surmised that actors had inhabited this adobe. These boots—or rather, their hidden devices—are more useful to a higher type of artist, the confidence man."

Joe reached toward a shiny object.

Lefilou slapped his hand. "No grabbing! No poking!"

"Ow!" The scratch across Joe's hand welled dots of blood, and he wrapped the edge of his shirt around it. "What are these doohickeys?"

"They're not 'doohickeys.' These are precision instruments. This one is a Martin-Adoin Fake-a-Face, model 5. It allows the user to change appearance. Or more precisely, it changes what other people see when they look at the user."

"Huh!"

"These sticky patches allow the wearers to share thoughts. This device, a BVT—that is, a Bettencourt-Valcourt-Taillecourt Emotional Manipulator—alters the timbre, pitch, and loudness of the voice to create a desired emotion in others, whether you want to persuade, to anger, to calm, or to amuse. These other devices are equally sophisticated, although we won't need them for our scam."

"Huh? What scam? We're already working a scam? Why don't you tell me these things?"

"Keep up, boy, keep up. Can't you see these devices will enable us—or rather me—to fulfill your desire to leave scamming behind? Soon you'll be a merchant of means on Newest France." With great ceremony, Lefilou took off his large ruby earring and presented it to Joe. "It's time to start looking the part."

Joe's mouth gaped, but he glommed onto the earring before Lefilou could change his mind. He yanked the brass ring from his ear, tossed it into the fireplace, and hung the ruby teardrop from his earlobe. He gave his head an experimental toss, and the earring swung and sparkled in a most pleasing manner. "So far, so easy. What next?"

"I'll work the details out tonight." Lefilou purred and pulled his boots back on. "Be prepared for the most magnificent scam you have ever seen."

* * * *

The next morning, Lefilou sent Joe out to beg, borrow, or steal breakfast.

Joe ran through the market and returned with his usual gallimaufry of grub nabbed while no one was looking. Today's haul included salted cod, chocolate-chip cookies, carrots, two lizards-on-a-stick, and coffee with thyme.

Afterward, Lefilou strutted back and forth across the room, his boots tapping on the tile at an increasing tempo, and explained his plan with many flourishes of legs and tail. When he finished, he struck a proud pose and stared unblinking at Joe.

"It's genius."

Lefilou puffed his cheeks.

Joe coughed. "Just one thing—desert crocs. Are you sure they're a thing? I thought crocodiles lived near water."

Lefilou frowned with hauteur. "You forget that the clerk at the boulangerie told us to beware the sharpness of the desert crocs."

"Rocks. She said 'desert rocks.'"

Lefilou washed his rear leg until the wet hairs stood up in soldierly lines. "No matter. We will find some other dangerous animal to play the role of the crocodile."

"Why did we need a crocodile to start with? You rushed through that part."

Lefilou ignored his question. "Today, we canvas the market, inside the dome and out. Find out everything about everyone who's anybody. If Lady Fortuna favors us, we'll find the honest official we need."

"An honest *human* official who's a woman or has a daughter," Joe said. "I want a wife with hair, not feathers. No tail. No shell instead of skin."

"I assume you also rule out anal glands, musk pods, and castor sacs."

"Yes. I don't know what they are, but they sound yucky."

"So many exquisite species with sublime scents live on Newest France, but you have to be persnickety." Lefilou heaved a long-suffering sigh. "As you wish. We'll look for a human honest enough to believe others are honest too."

"All right."

"All right? All right?" Lefilou reared in indignation. "What I do for you without your appreciation! Perhaps I shall be glad to be rid of you after all." Lefilou sniffed and stomped out the door.

* * * *

"Scuttlebutt?" Joe asked that evening after they had eaten their scavenged supper of kohlrabi, cactus leaves, bananas, caterpillars, and thyme coffee.

They compared notes on the information they had collected that day. Lefilou decided the mark would be the head of business permits, a well-off human man with a daughter who was deemed plain but kind, sensible, and an asset to her father's business.

Joe smiled. "Better a kind wife than a pretty wife who's a nag and a bonehead."

Lefilou inclined his head in acknowledgment of Joe's rare show of wisdom. "You have learned something practical from your years with me, I see. I must congratulate myself. Well done, Hermes Reynard Mercurius Lefilou III, well done!"

Joe frowned.

Oblivious to his expression, Lefilou opened the drawstring of his bag. "I've been working on my disguise. I've done quite well so far." He pulled out a wide red silk ribbon with such passion that it snapped above his head and then slowly wafted, undulating, to the floor. "I won this ribbon gambling, as well as *this* beauty." He drew out a heavily embroidered hat and pointed to its design of intertwined leaves.

"*Nepeta cataria.*" He licked his lips. "So lovely to snort; even more lovely to say. A short but gentle caress on the tongue."

"Unlike your own name," Joe said under his breath, forgetting Lefilou's keen hearing.

"Says the boy whose species gave itself an utterly preposterous name," Lefilou retorted. "How you managed to give other life forms snappy appellations—dog, goat, worm, fish, pear tree—but burdened yourselves with the designation of 'human beans,' I shall never understand. Your species does not in the slightest resemble any members of the genus Phaseolus."

"Huh?"

"Beans, Joe. Beans. You don't smell like green beans, black beans, garbanzo beans, scarlet runner beans, or any other beans I've encountered." He shook his head sorrowfully. "What a sad and pitiful species."

\* \* \* \*

The next morning the great scam began.

Lefilou talked into the voice pad on the Martin-Ardoin Fake-a-Face. His fur changed to gray. The rents and rips in his shirt and pantaloons dissolved. Dirt faded. A badge appeared on the shoulder of his shirt and a ring of keys at his waist. The boots he was so proud of, though, remained exactly the same.

He settled the hat on his head at a jaunty angle and commanded Joe to tie the ribbon around his tail. "How is the illusion?"

Joe whistled. "Perfect."

Lefilou nodded and handed him a patch. "Stick this behind your ear." He applied one under his own shirt and dropped the Martin-Ardoin Fake-a-Face and the BVT emotional manipulator into his left boot. Lefilou looked at Joe. "Please, please, please, keep your brain under control. I will go mad if I must endure your thoughts jumping from topic to topic like monkeys in a trash bin. Be like a feline. Meditate on your Buddha nature. Or if that's beyond your abilities, curl up in the sun and sleep."

\* \* \* \*

"Good morning, sir," chirped the clerk at the best bakery, whose species clearly had descended from a birdlike ancestor. Her feathers were purple, long on her shoulders and head, short and fluffy on her face and hands.

Lefilou swept off his hat and bowed. "Good morning. May I speak to the head baker, please?

"I'm afraid he'll be busy all day. That's what every day is like for a baker. Never a moment's rest. May I help you, sir?"

Lefilou touched the place on his shoulder where she would see a badge, courtesy of the Fake-a-Face. "My employer, Mr. Carabas of *the* Carabas International Industrial Industries of Old India, told me to speak directly to the head baker. He is planning a banquet for a hundred guests. He wants to know the provenance of your flours, the source of your water, and how and where your salt is processed. Only the best for Mr. Carabas."

Her feathers horripilated. "I'm so sorry, sir. Would Mr. Carabas be satisfied if you spoke to one of the other bakers, sir?"

"I don't think so. It's a matter of a hundred guests and an exacting employer." He lowered his voice and leaned toward her, sneaking a paw into his boot to increase the output of the BVT. "You know about exacting employers. Your bread wouldn't have such a good reputation if your baker were slipshod."

"Yes, sir. I know exactly what you mean, sir." She hesitated, clacking her beak together like castanets, *rat-a-tat-tat*. Her feathers floofed even more until she looked twice her original size. "I can ask whether he can spare a moment for you, sir. He and your employer sound like birds of a feather."

"Precisely. Thank you for understanding." Lefilou bowed again.

She curtseyed and, in a dizzy fluffy tizzy, teetered through a swinging door to the kitchen.

Quick as a wink—actually, quicker; more like quick as one note in a Vivaldi violin concerto—Lefilou reached over the counter and snagged three beautiful boules and stuffed them under his shirt. He put his hat on and sidled out the door.

His next stop was the office of Mr. Perrault, where he announced himself imperiously to the receptionist and intimidated him into ushering him in to Mr. Perrault's office.

Lefilou took off his hat and bowed to Mr. Perrault and the young woman working beside him. "My employer, Mr. Carabas of *the* Carabas International Industrial Industries of Old India, has only recently arrived on this moon. He sends you his respects and this bread."

The woman leaned forward and smiled, which went a good distance toward reducing her plainness. She smelled fresh, like lavender soap and new shoes. "Father, that bread smells delicious! Mr. Carabas is very kind."

"Yes, he is." He smiled at his daughter with gentle sweetness before turning to Lefilou. "Please thank your employer—Mr. Carabas, is it?—for the gift. I look forward to meeting him when he gets settled."

Lefilou bowed again, looked at the daughter to savor her smile once more, and took his leave.

On the way home, he rewarded himself for a job well done—as well done as a fowl stuffed with chopped livers and hearts and roasted all day—by purloining some meaty piranhas as he passed a fishmonger and dropping them into the hat he still held.

\* \* \* \*

"You give the second present tomorrow, right?" Joe asked.

Lefilou chirped. "We should wait a week."

"A week?" Joe's voice dripped with disappointment like honey from a frame taken from a beehive. "What'll we do till then?"

"You, my boy, will learn the manners of the merchant and upper classes, both from me and by observation in the market. You'll apply for a business license for an agricultural enterprise. Meanwhile, I'll find you a house."

Joe went each day to the market and stood hidden in an alley, copying the postures, body movements, and speech habits of those who looked well off. At first he felt as if he mocked them, but day by day aping them grew more natural. Using the BVT, he asked Lefilou questions about what he saw, which sped up his learning and cleared up misapprehensions such as his belief that soft pretzels were best eaten with marmite.

At night, Lefilou groomed him on the fine points he had missed and groomed his person as well, styling his hair, encouraging him to grow a moustache, as was the fashion, and teaching him how to polish leather and metal. The lesson examples, of course, were Lefilou's own black boots with silver buckles. He gave Joe his red ribbon so that he could tie his hair back into a proper tail, or queue, as the au courant young males of species with head hair called it.

During the day, Lefilou visited the Office of Real Estate Taxes and spent hours combing through the records until he had a list of high-valued properties outside the bubble—but still close to it—that were owned by members of species that could shapeshift.

Once he had his list, he visited each one. He took note of its size and upkeep, its acreage, and its protections from wild animals and the nasty cactuses Joe had mentioned. Then he narrowed down his list to just a pawful of houses. He interviewed their laborers and servants, including a lovely calico female of his own species named Lina, who horrified him with tales of her employer occasionally eating staff members raw in a horseradish sauce.

It was the perfect house, with an owner so cruel and so hated that everyone concerned—except the owner himself, of course, who was known as Kludge—would faint with delight to have Joe as their new employer.

* * * *

"How did your second visit to Perrault go?" Joe asked as soon as Lefilou came in the door.

Lefilou turned off his disguise and set his hat on the fireplace mantle. "I gave Perrault some medicine for the cold he is about to get. He was quite grateful."

"How did you know he is going to get a cold?"

Lefilou looked down his nose and sniffed superciliously. "I put Rhinovirus all over the jar of medicine, of course."

"Huh." Joe frowned. "I hope you didn't give his daughter any medicine."

"Of course not. I gave her three perfect peaches."

Joe leaned toward him. "What's she like?"

"Her name is Eglantine, another name for *Rosa rubiginosa*. Isn't that lovely to say? *Rosa rubiginosa*. Her name suits her well, for her cheeks are as pink as the wild rose, and like its leaves, she smells as fresh as apples."

"Is she prickly like a rose?"

"Newest France is a prickly place, whose plants and persons grow spiky," Lefilou replied.

Joe's face fell.

"But not Eglantine. In my presence she has always been kind and dignified. Her smile lights up the room, and her laugh tinkles sweetly."

Joe narrowed his eyes. "Don't forget you're looking for a wife for me, not yourself."

With a wave of his paw, Lefilou brushed away the words and the idea.

On his last visit to Perrault, Lefilou took some excellent khat for Perrault, who worked so hard and so long every day that Lefilou thought he deserved a better pick-me-up than coffee with goat cheese.

For Eglantine, he took a small oil painting of the eglantine rose. He had surveyed the work of all the streetside artists and commissioned the painting from the one he deemed best at still lifes, for he had half fallen in love with the human himself before he met Lina.

After Mr. Perrault and Eglantine had thanked him, Lefilou invited them to visit Mr. Carabas at his house on a date of their choosing.

Mr. Perrault named the next day.

Lefilou bowed and left. He immediately sent the news to Joe by thought. He did not tell Joe where he was going next, though, because the boy would worry.

He shook his head sadly. Joe was too soft to be a con artist.

\* \* \* \*

Lefilou strutted past Kludge's field of amaranths sectioned into squares like a quilt. Past the field of colored peppers. At last, next to a field of tepary beans that eagerly climbed tall sunflower stalks, Lefilou stood in front of Kludge's house. He twisted his hat in his paws and tried not to drop the flowers he held. Confidence men had a code of conduct, and he was about to break one of the cardinal rules, all for the improvement of some hairless monkey boy foisted on him in a con gone sour.

"Let's get on with it then," he muttered.

Lina popped her head up from tending beans and brushed dirt from her face. "Are those flowers for me?"

Lefilou winced. How could he have forgotten flowers for her? "They're for Kludge. But be of good cheer. I'll have good news for you later."

She tilted her head coquettishly. "You never told me your name."

Lefilou genuflected, earning a loud purr from Lina. "Hermes Reynard Mercurius Lefilou III."

"Be careful, Hermes. Kludge is an ogre."

"I will certainly follow your advice." Lefilou looked at his hat, too squashed to set on his head. He stuffed it into his pantaloons instead.

Lina meowed and pointed, and Lefilou looked down. The bulge of his hat looked like a giant erection, which would give an oh-so-wrong impression to Kludge about the purpose of his visit, so he removed it and tossed it into the bean field.

As he stood there, the distance to the front door seemed to grow longer and longer. He dropped to all fours and hurtled toward the house so he would not chicken out. He was not a scaredy-cat; milquetoasts annoyed him and stuck in his craw like a giant hairball. But today he was so terrified his fur stood on end.

On the doorstep, he caught his breath, adjusted his clothes, and checked that the BVT was on the highest setting. "Kludge is a bloviating nincompoop," he murmured and pressed his hand to the door's identification plate.

Kludge himself opened the door, and the dirty-shoe smell of durian fruit blasted Lefilou.

He clawed the doormat for all he was worth to keep from retreating from the reeking monster. Kludge looked cobbled together from various parts of plants and animals, and not the most attractive parts either. Growths like cauliflowers bedecked skin the color of bruised eggplant. He had the nose of a proboscis monkey (*Nasalis larvatus*) and the wide-based, serrated teeth of a tiger shark (*Galeocerdo cuvier*). Straggly, coarse clusters like roots on a carrot stored too long sprouted randomly from his body. His four ears hung down like a beagle's; from each dangled a mummified ear, presumably from servants who didn't please him except on the dinner table.

One trophy ear was definitely feline.

Lefilou barely contained his growl. All reservations about his plan dissolved.

Kludge showed no surprise at receiving a visitor; perhaps the growths prevented facial expressions. Or perhaps he had already fallen under the influence of the BVT, which Lefilou had programmed to calm him and prevent violent thoughts.

He looked at Lefilou with eyes like lichen-blotched stones. "Don't need vacuum cleaner."

"Wise decision. They're out of style. Everyone now uses genetically enhanced pangolins for slurping up dirt and insects. With their anal glands removed, of course. Removed from the pangolins, not the insects." With magician-like flourishes of legs and paws, Lefilou presented the bouquet of black roses and purple carnations. "I heard you are a gentleman of taste and refinement, so I had to meet you."

Kludge looked at the flowers, then at Lefilou. At the flowers, then at Lefilou. At the flowers, then at Lefilou. At last he took the proffered flowers and stuffed them in his shark-toothed mouth.

It was a huge maw of a mouth, even with the shapeshifter at his normal size.

Lefilou's fur again threatened to stand on end.

Kludge walked into his house and left the door open.

Lefilou followed him to his sitting room. "I hear that you can defy Antoine-Laurent de Lavoisier's law of conservation of mass."

"What that?"

"You can shapeshift into a bigger form."

"Yeah. Easy."

Kludge's shape softened like a melting candle and lost definition. Then he grew. And grew. And grew some more until he was a mastodon, Lefilou was squished against the wall, and tables and chairs splintered.

"Impressive!" Lefilou croaked.

Kludge shrank back to his former size and shape. He chuckled. "Fun way to kill."

Lefilou patted his ribs to see whether any were cracked. They were tender, but he could still breathe easily. "What about smaller? That, I suspect, is a harder trick. You probably can't make yourself tiny."

The monster puffed with pride. "Kludge be small, too." His shape softened and shrank.

He became a deer mouse of the genus *Peromyscus*.

Lefilou pounced.

Quick as a wink— Darn, there's that cliché again, and this time it took slightly longer than a wink. It was more like the brief time required to snatch up and swallow a small rodent, say, a Speke's pectinator (*Pectinator spekei*) or an adolescent Tucuman tuco-tuco (*Ctenomys tucumanus*)—in any case, by any measure of wink, Kludge was no more.

Screeching, Lefilou keeled over, bloated and borborygmic. His guts rumbled so thunderously, in fact, that the sounds attracted curious servants, who peeked in the doors and windows.

If the dead Kludge returned to his normal size, it would have been the end of Lefilou. But although Lefilou would have been happy to do anything to reduce his misery, including explode, that didn't happen. He howled and yowled and screamed, in the process letting out some of the painful trapped gas.

The servants continued to gather. When he thought he might not explode after all, he waved them in.

"I have eaten your master," he muttered.

Lina leapt through the window. "Hermes, you have saved us!" The other servants cheered, and Lina licked his ear vigorously.

"Your new master will be Mr. Carabas, a human. He will be a gentle master, I promise. He is having human guests tomorrow that include the female he wants to marry, the sweet and practical Eglantine."

The servants applauded.

"Mr. Carabas needs you to make the house spick and span from top to bottom, decorate it with flowers from his fields, and prepare a meal to impress his potential bride." Lefilou looked around the room for the first time, and his lips retracted in disgust. "Please burn all the art showing bullfights, blood-eagles, baby-seal clubbings, and other atrocities."

With light feet and lighter hearts, the servants ran to carry out his commands.

All except Lina. She had seen his canines. "Hermes, I'm going to fetch a stick to clean your teeth. It would be a shame for a hero to die early from preventable heart disease or another inflammation-related disorder."

Lefilou sighed, trapped. "I have the distinct feeling that you and Mr. Carabas will get along well."

\* \* \* \*

When Lefilou woke the next morning, he again wore tattered clothes with no badge of service. Only his hat and boots remained because they were real.

Lina dozed, curled up next to him.

Lefilou took out the Martin-Adoin Fake-a-Face and checked the settings. He huffed. The default was to turn off at midnight! He whispered instructions and turned back into a gentleman's gentleman.

He stood and admired himself in the window glass. Soon he could dress like this for real, if he wanted. If he renounced his skills and way of life. If he ignored his solitary nature.

Those thoughts led to another. What if he gave up the breed-and-bolt mating practices of his own species and tried human pair bonding?

He spun away from the glass. Lina still slept. He woke her with gentle scratches on the head. She purred when she opened her eyes and saw him.

"Lina, I must go help Mr. Carabas prepare for his guests. Can you ensure everything here is ready?"

"Yes. Thank you for your trust."

Lefilou bowed and left. Once beyond the estate, he ran to the adobe.

Joe opened the door at his knock. His hair stood up in clumps, and dark circles shadowed his eyes. His clothes were cattywampus. From the second floor came eardrum-shattering caws and cackles.

"Some crows took over the second floor. I couldn't get them to scat," Joe said.

Something crashed upstairs. Probably the water pitcher or washing basin, given they were the only breakables.

"I only left you for one day. One day!" Lefilou blustered.

Joe winced.

Lefilou shook his head. "Never mind. Let's get you ready for your performance."

"I have a question first." Joe stroked Lefilou's chin and neck. "What will you do, Hermes? Will you stay with me?"

"Retire? Me?" Lefilou struck a pose and gave his hat an insouciant tilt. "I am the best at what I do. Why would I retire?"

Joe dropped his head and turned away.

* * * *

"This won't work," Joe said while Lefilou put his ragged, faded clothes in order and sniffed his socks and threw them out the window.

"This won't work," he said again at the barbershop during his shave and at the beauty salon during his facial and nail treatments.

"This won't work," he said when Lefilou led him out of town.

"This really, really isn't going to work," Joe said when Lefilou told him the plan: Joe would pretend to be the victim of a vicious band of wild cactuses at the exact moment Lefilou, Mr. Perrault, and Eglantine passed by.

Lefilou threw up his paws. "Why do you doubt me? I am a master of deception."

"Yes, but…." Joe shuffled his feet. "Cactuses don't move around. They're plants."

Lefilou hissed. "You need to pretend to be attacked by a vicious band of something. Are you sure there are no desert crocs?"

"I asked around. No desert crocs. Only desert rocks."

"What about predators?"

"Rumors of coyotes."

"That'll do. Over there is the place I chose for your fake attack." Lefilou grabbed Joe's arm and hauled him to the spot. "Take off your clothes, and I'll shred them with my teeth and claws. Then I'll bite and claw you, and we'll rub the blood on your clothes."

"Hold up. What's this about biting and clawing?"

"I suspected you might have reservations if you knew the full details."

"Darn right I do." Joe kicked a stone and watched it sail over the sand. "I'm going back to town."

Lefilou hung tighter to Joe's arm. "Thanks to me, you now have a house and lands and servants to take care of them. If you play your cards right, you'll have a nice-smelling wife and a well-to-do father-in-law. You're on the brink of having everything you wanted, and more. You have only one tiny thing to do: Let me scratch and bite you."

"That's not a tiny thing. That's not even a *medium* thing. It's a big, big thing. You could kill me."

Lefilou laid his heavy paws on Joe's shoulders and put his massive muzzle to Joe's face. "Everything rides on whether you trust me after all these years together. Do you?"

\* \* \* \*

Later that day, Lefilou rode in a hovercraft for the first time. He, Mr. Perrault, Eglantine, and some men who worked for them skimmed smoothly above the sand toward the house of Mr. Carabas, Lefilou giving directions.

*Scream now*, he thought to Joe.

Cries for help erupted from the desert.

Perrault slowed the hovercraft.

When Joe stood up, bloody, naked, and waving his arms, Eglantine blushed and looked away.

Lefilou exclaimed, "That's Mr. Carabas! Something terrible has happened!"

Perrault stopped the hovercraft, which settled into the sand, rocking slightly. "Go see what's up," he told two of his men.

They ran to Joe, conversed, and ran back. "Coyotes attacked Mr. Carabas. His wounds aren't deep, but there's zilch left of his clothes and shoes. The coyotes played tug-of-war with them."

"Sounds like coyotes," Perrault said. "Playful as dogs."

"Poor Mr. Carabas! We must give him a ride to his house," Eglantine said.

"Ordinarily I would. But you're here, and he has no clothes on," Perrault said.

"I won't look," she said, peeking between her fingers.

Perrault turned to his men. "Among the three of you, can you spare a shirt and a pair of pantaloons? And a ribbon for his hair?"

Eglantine supplied the ribbon from her own locks. The men had provisions in case of emergency, which a naked man in a hovercraft with a virgin certainly was, so quick as a wink—this time, about five minutes—they had Joe dressed in motley and in the hovercraft.

Eglantine gazed dreamily at Joe as if he were the most handsome human man she had ever seen. Perhaps he was; the merchant colony was small, and the merchants came from a dozen different species, some of them with tentacles or suckers or other nasty parts. In any case, she fell in love with him right in the hovercraft. He fell in love with her as soon as his embarrassment waned enough that he could look up and talk to her.

While the lovebirds whispered and giggled, Lefilou pointed out Mr.

Carabas's fields of crops, his many employees, and the features of his house, which they could now see. By the time they reached it, Perrault was so impressed that he offered Mr. Carabas a high-level job in his office.

Soon after, Eglantine and Joe—now Joe Carabas—were married. They had many children and lived happily ever after.

The End.

\* \* \* \*

What? You want to know about Lefilou? And Lina?

Great. Just great. They weren't important. They were in the story only to help Joe find True Love.

You thought Joe was dull as day-old dishwater? Of course he was. He was the hero. Only secondary characters get to be colorful. It's one of the Rules.

You don't like the Rules? You think I should break the Rules?

Oh, all right, but don't tell any other storytellers.

Here's what happened: Lefilou and Lina got married too, out in the fields among the sunflowers. Lefilou flossed his teeth every day and routinely underwent tooth-whitening treatments. Lefilou and Lina had many litters of their own, and they tutored their own catlings along with Joe and Eglantine's many children—which the two humans spent an unseemly amount of time in their bedroom creating—in languages, mathematics, the sciences, pickpocketing, lock picking, old and modern scams, goat raising, cheesemaking, and the proper preparation of an excellent cup of coffee.

Happy now? Good.

Shauna Roberts has won awards for both nonfiction and fiction and is a graduate of the Clarion Science Fiction and Fantasy Writers' Workshop. Currently, she writes historical fiction, science fiction, romance, and fantasy. Her publications include more than a thousand nonfiction articles, three nonfiction books, several short stories and novelettes, and three novels (*Like Mayflies in a Stream*, historical fiction, 2009; *Claimed by the Enemy*, historical fiction with romantic elements, 2014; and *Ice Magic, Fire Magic*, fantasy with romantic elements, 2015). She loves to look at the Blue Ridge Mountains from her house and hopes to soon adopt two cats.

# WHITEY AND RED: THE HUNT FOR URSA

## Bonnie Hearn Hill

*Inspired by Snow White and Rose Red*

Once within a time, lived two beautiful sisters, Whitey and Red. After having her identity stolen by a woman living with seven dwarves with catchy names, Whitey suffers anxiety issues and prefers to stay home playing video games and taking care of the cottage she and Red share. One night, while playing *The Hunt for Ursa*, Whitey calls Red into their humble living room with its sparse furnishings—a gaming console, a wall of flat-screens, computer towers, controllers, and a pair of gaming chairs.

"Look," she says. "Everyone's trying to kill this poor bear."

Sure enough, on the screen, a large bear crashes through trees just like the ones outside their windows as his pursuers throw rocks, beer cans, and stilettoes at him.

"Save him," Whitey says, and Red touches the screen.

"Come here, bear." Her fingers on his virtual image tingle with warmth. "I will help you."

Something slams on the front door, and both sisters scream. "It sounds like a cannonball," Whitey says. "Hide."

"It's the bear," Red says. "I know. I felt him."

She runs to the door, throws it open, and he stumbles in, coarse black hair stiff with snow. Red leads him inside and hands him a blanket as he warms before the fire, his feet propped up on their late mother's hassock.

"You women are the best," he says in a low rumble. "But I'm not only cold. I'm starving."

"Whitey?" Red asks, and her sister hurries to the kitchen. "We're simple people of limited means," Red tells him. "However, we do have some steaks in the cool box."

Whitey returns with two of them, raw and red as blood and garnished with cloves of garlic that gleam like pearls. The bear smiles and flexes astounding muscles that rise beneath his fur. The way he's looking from the meat to her—his eyes wide and glassy—is pure love.

"What's this?" He claws at a garlic clove and snarls.

"For your breath," Whitey says, with a shy smile.

"My breath offends you?"

Whitey nods. "It's quite overwhelming at times."

"And you?" he asks Red.

"Garlic is a powerful force," she says, avoiding the question. "It can protect you."

"I could use some protection." He devours both steaks, leans against the brick hearth, wipes his lips with the area rug, and says, "I have to go back now. Thank you for whatever you did to get me here." Then he glances at Red in a way that brings the heat to her cheeks. "Don't suppose you'd invite me again."

"Anytime," she tells him.

He returns night after night, yet Whitey tells Red that she still sees him in the game.

"*The Hunt for Ursa*," she says. "Someone's always after him. Soon, he'll be dead."

"Then we must get him out of there," Red says. "But how?"

Whitey scrunches her nose. "We need to ask the troll."

"The troll?" Red replies. "Never!"

When he isn't living in his parents' basement, Joel, the internet troll, hangs out under the bridge connecting the sisters' cottage to the small village to the west of them. Overweight and unemployed, the troll delights in giving people grief online. Red knows her sister is right. If anyone has the skills to crash a video game, the troll is the guy.

The bridge from their cottage to town sways in the wind.

Red stands in the middle of it and calls out, "Hi, troll friend."

"So, you're a Nigerian banker now?" The troll's deep voice booms up. "Did I just win the lottery, or did you lose your bags during an international trip and need me to send you some cash?"

"You're funny," she says, and fakes a laugh. "Seriously, though. I need some help for a friend of mine."

"The bear?" He chuckles. "Forget it. He's caught in a witch's spell."

"But troll," she says. "Can't you break it?"

A shadow falls on the moat. Then the image tightens, and she sees the troll, holding a bag of chips in one hand and a can of beer in the other. "Not anymore," he says, and meets her at the end of the bridge. "I used to own a computer start-up, but the witch came along, engineered a takeover, and put a spell on me, too."

Red wrinkles her nose. He smells worse than the bear. "Don't you have any malware or viruses?" she demands. "What kind of troll are you?"

He hangs his shaggy head, and Red realizes the witch didn't just turn him into a troll. She also destroyed his self-confidence.

"What will it take for me to convince you to help us?" she asks. "There must be something you want."

He hangs his head even lower and mutters, "Your sister."

"Oh, my goodness." Whitey wouldn't look at this guy in his current state, but Red reminds herself that this is only a spell, as is much in life.

"Tell you what," she says. "Let's get you cleaned up a little and then go down to the Apple store and buy you whatever you need to bolster your computer-savvy confidence."

"I don't know," he tells her.

"And, for starters, let's get rid of this stuff." She walks over, takes the beer and chips from him, and throws them in the river. As they hit the water, the dark clouds lift, and the sky fills with light.

The troll's beard and stringy hair disappear, and his ragged clothes are replaced with shorts and a blue plaid shirt that matches his eyes. Before her stands a nerdy but cute guy, who looks smart enough to not only attract her sister, but to take on the witch.

He accompanies her back to the cottage, settles before the screens, and while drinking a green smoothie Whitey blended for him, he begins.

Soon, *The Hunt for Ursa* starts to splinter on the screen. Everything thrown at the bear boomerangs on the person throwing it. The entire screen turns into a giant storm cloud in the shape of a large black creature.

"You're brilliant," Whitey tells Joel. She sits on the arm of his chair, and he smiles.

Someone bangs on the front door.

"The bear." Red runs to let him inside. When she opens the door, a stranger in an odd uniform and brown, bowl-cut hair takes her into his arms.

"What have you done?" he demands, in the bear's voice.

She wraps her arms around him. "You're free of the spell, my darling. You're no longer trapped."

"That's the good news." He walks inside their dwelling, where Whitey and Joel are holding hands. "The bad news is I'm a freaking prince!"

That explains his strange clothing. "A prince," she says. "Darling, that's wonderful. Will we live in a castle?"

"You don't get it." He places his hands on her shoulders. "I hated being a prince and, Red, you do not want to be my princess, let me tell you. If you don't believe me, take a look at my sister, who's in *People* at least four times a year, and on every internet gossip site in the meantime. That life is worse than being trapped in a video game."

"Well, then." She inhales deeply and knows what she must say. "Is there a way we could both be bears?"

"Oh, Red." He takes her in his arms. "You really do love me."

"Shapeshifters," Joel calls from his seat in the living room. "Got it."

"But what will we call him?" Red shouts back.

"Why not Prince? Everyone will think he's named after the real one."

Over the next few months in that modest cottage, the four of them do some crazy programming. By the end of the year, they get rich off *The Hunt for Ursa II* and move to Silicon Valley.

Sometimes at night near their compound, people claim they see two bears—a large dark one and a smaller one with a red cast to her coat—frolicking in the hills. By day, though, Whitey, Joel, Red, and Prince take care of business and eat a lot of garlic, which makes their lives very happy for ever after.

California author Bonnie Hearn Hill's eighteenth suspense novel, *The River Below*, was published in September 2017, and a film based on an earlier novel is in pre-production. She can be reached at www.bonniehhill.com and bonniehh@gmail.com.

# THE PLAGUE OF HAMELIN

## Clare Toohey

### Inspired by The Pied Piper of Hemelin

I hoped everyone on the station was drinking to me in my absence, the scoundrels. I was shaking off the woozy end of the time-shift. The pale, cushioned expanses surrounding me were usually welcome, but I was not completely untethered from the chaos and filth of medieval lifeways.

Crossing the time-threshold was necessarily done under sedation. After a deep hit from my inhaler, in the few seconds before I lost consciousness, I'd squat low, arms bent in front of me like I was preparing to somersault. Then, I'd close my eyes, letting myself fall forward and through to the other side. All of my recent missions to the wayback had rolled me out onto the same, unforgiving cave floor. Just one more reason a sojourner needed a helmet, a white-suit with reinforced joints, and to be limber. Time-shifting back to the here and now on the research station's side of the threshold was comparatively luxurious. To return, I would loosen my feces-caked shoes, sedate myself again, and pitch forward across the threshold. I'd awake to find I'd rolled onto a plushly padded platform in my socks. That soft platform was the floor of a movable clean-chamber, from which I could awaken at my leisure and wait out the automatic quarantine protocol.

The disharmonious note in today's triumphant return was snoring a few feet away. Despite our size and age differences, the dose of sedative obviously hadn't killed her. With her help, I'd sacked and loaded piles of adorable marrow-donors through the threshold in the crossing before ours. Then, I'd grabbed the old woman and pitched her in, so the unexpected guest was now locked in quarantine with me. I could only see a tangled gray braid snaking over the bumps of a scrawny spine as she lay curled-up under the faint mist of decontaminants. When traveling between the medieval plaguetown and our modern day, the sojourning protocol was to remain white-suited and extremely careful when dealing with any of the tissues, fluids, and effluvia of locals. The old woman's outsides were safe enough. Her blood was another matter.

I scooted across the cushioned floor to the wall monitor and canvassed all the posts. Every duty desk was empty. I'd sent the slumbering kids across first, to much fanfare, obviously. The bastards. On previous returns, I'd never registered as being any danger to the station. When all the sprayers and counters had finished, there was no reason to assume I wouldn't be verified as plague-free, again, for the umpteenth time. It ought to be fine for the medical team to override the quarantine's timing sequence. I could easily sneak out while the old woman was still unconscious and lock her back in. That way, she could be properly isolated and thoroughly screened, and I could be cut loose to enjoy the celebrations. But there was not a soul to respond to my persuasive arguments. The station's operations had been put on autopilot. We worked hard and played much harder. By now, the station's common areas and team bunks had to be scenes of unparalleled hedonistic revelry. It was unfair I couldn't monitor those from here.

Self-pity and indignation worked as stimulants, I found. Fully awakened and bored, I double-checked the archives for any background dossier matching the old woman's general physical description. There was none. That seemed like a big oversight for the research team, especially given how influential this hobo had turned out to be in Hamelin. I vowed to chastise them all at full volume early tomorrow, under the assumption they'd be miserably hungover. But that would simply be for my vindictive pleasure, not because it mattered. The most important arrivals by far, and the cause of the festivities I was undoubtedly missing, were the twenty-two munchkins all sleepy-bye in their customized donor bags. The kids were in stable, non-degenerative comas, and I smiled at the thought of their quiet, little rows of blinking cocoons. I was suffused with a pleasure in my accomplishment that I hoped would outlast my memories of the mission. I leaned back in the glow of it and made myself comfortable enough to wait out the door alarm.

The plague of our era was the mutant cousin of a much earlier version. During its centuries-long dormancy, the bug had become more lethal and wily. However, the station's history and archaeology teams reported evidence of a small population who'd survived the disease's earlier version remarkably well. That plague-defying place and time was in Lower Saxony during the Middle Ages.

I knew I had time-shifted in for late-night visits to collect samples, even if I wasn't sure anymore how many times. According to the archives, I humanely sedated the residents in their homes and drew tiny amounts of blood. I was a stealthy operator, so I'd probably been less noticeable than the local insects. I never worried about what I didn't remember, because forgetting was the next standard protocol after quarantine.

I had no idea who'd invented it, but selective forgetting had turned out to be a brilliant protocol for time-shifting. Sometime in the past, it had become a therapeutic approach for soldiers and other people suffering specific debilitating traumas. Sojourners also faced situations that were disturbing, gruesome, or terrifyingly dangerous. The psych team had considered the risks of cascading mental dilemmas, the kind inherent in time-shifting, and the way they might adversely affect the implementation of mission objectives. Previous incidents and my reactions, if they were allowed to accumulate like scar tissue in the mind, could render me ineffective in the field, completely unable to perform. I agreed to the process every time they asked.

Having had the forgetting protocol after every time-shift—as far as I knew—I believed it had positively contributed to my calm, optimistic outlook, to my ability to execute demanding missions without overthinking or worry. Any remaining shreds of memory from the wayback were like movies seen long ago but barely recalled, like vague, detached scraps of events that happened to someone else. The archive team had discovered that sensory extraction from a sojourner's brain yielded material superior to any recording. Win-win. At this instant, I craved personal thanks, to receive the heaving, thrusting gratitude of the crowd. But every time I signed off on a forgetting, I was satisfied to leave the specifics of my glories for the archivists to reconstruct. I was more of an action-mission contributor.

Over however many time-shifts and sample-retrievals I must have made in Hamelin, the medical team had figured out that the villagers, especially the children, already possessed high concentrations of relevant antibodies when the medieval version of the plague erupted. Apparently, some ancient immunity to a similar infection in the distant past had been passed on in the local DNA through generations. For some reason, it was reactivating to face the threat, like armies of antibodies past being resurrected to fight a new war. Luckily for the villagers, the crusty old fighters in their blood would square up well enough against the new mutation to keep most of them alive.

The medical team wanted to know how the villagers' old ghosts might fare against the plague of our time. The steering council decided we should find out. According the archives, I succeeded in my mission to acquire a test subject, earning more kudos, I was sure. Unfortunately, the station was unable to subsequently manufacture a vaccine, because the ancient antibody kept dying once outside the host organism. It wouldn't allow itself to be cultured or artificially replicated. It just fell apart into cellular debris. Though it was always risky dealing with biologics directly, the archives said that the live bone marrow transplant worked. We had a way to save team members at this station and others.

"Are you there? Speak to me." She hadn't moved, but it was the old woman's voice. Among my other heroic characteristics—like being big and strong and daring—I had proven to be a quick study with archaic Low German. I needed to be fluent enough to convince the villagers to let me have the children we'd targeted, even if their language lacked the vocabulary to describe our technical sophistication with precision. Actually, the old woman had been the key to their agreeing to surrender their children, which was the only reason I'd brought her along. She made it a condition of her assistance. I'd adapted to changing conditions in the field and optimized the outcome.

I knew when the timed door was set to open, and I also knew that extended engagements were not my specialty. To make my getaway, I could always say there was a mythical beast lurking outside. These people believed in those kinds of things. She was also small enough for me to threaten to make her stay back. If necessary, I could even restrain her with the leather ties from her own outfit. But until the happy moment for that decision arrived, I desired the least taxing and disruptive interaction.

"Roll over and look at the wall," I said, "I'm showing pretty pictures from your home. See? There are some trees near the well and dogs in the square. Don't be afraid when you see them moving."

"Why would I be? It's just a magic mirror," she said without turning. "I don't need to look to hear you."

I felt pity for her. These surroundings, vastly cleaner and more advanced than what she knew, must have seemed overwhelmingly strange. She ought to face this reality at her own pace. She was my plus-one, but it wasn't my job to acclimate her, and the missing-in-action psych team was undoubtedly too busy at this moment to help. I imagined them blaring dance music through the dining hall, dropping inhibitions along with their utili-suits. I probably sighed aloud.

"What burdens you?" she asked, rather perceptively.

"Nothing to worry you. Take your ease."

Then, she started singing to herself. It was a tuneless mess, more of a drone-like buzzing, but perhaps it would keep her occupied and docile.

For this last mission, I'd time-shifted to the wayback in the darkness of pre-dawn. A dark, thicketed cave in nearby foothills was condemned as haunted by the superstitious locals. It had proven the best place from which to conduct operations. After I'd shaken off the sleepies that come with shifting, I picked my way down the winding path someone had fortuitously lined with white rocks in ages past.

I was surprised to see the old woman propped against a standing stone that marked the intersection of the trailhead with the wider dirt road into town. Her outfit put the rough in rustic, made of more scraps of hide and fur than the typical medieval bumpkin's attire. I was twice her size, which couldn't be helped, but I clicked off my artificial light and temporarily slid off my headpiece so she'd know I was a fellow human being, no matter how far apart we seemed.

Thankfully, she did not shriek in terror. As it happened, she had an excellent poker face. She'd introduced herself as "the old woman," as if it were her title, no further name given or requested. She said she'd been waiting for me, which I considered a likely attempt to assert superiority. The introduction rituals of backwards cultures were full of such exhausting gambits, another reason I preferred assignments of low or no-contact subterfuge.

Her appearance was otherwise dry and hard-skinned, like a walnut, but there was something compelling about her, too. It was hard to estimate how old she might be. The medical team would have to check what they found for teeth, I supposed, or maybe count the tree rings on her short legs. She didn't exude beauty, grace, or sex appeal, but I found her to be interesting nonetheless. That mission-honed instinct is why I accepted the invitation to be dragged to her hovel.

The old woman's shack, or cottage to be generous, had abstract designs carved all over the doorposts and furniture. They resembled the engravings on the standing stone, and they were even carved into the wooden teacup she tried, unsuccessfully, to press upon me. Even if the protocol hadn't prohibited it, just a sniff was enough to dissuade. Scrawls were a decorative style requiring the bare minimum of expense and skill, but beyond that, I couldn't tell runes from hieroglyphs. The history team could have all the fun with my memories. Topics like that made my eyes glaze over. Now that the old woman was in the here and now, I wasn't sure how she might contribute to the broader team vision, other than as a curiosity.

Also, I found that I really wanted her annoying humming to stop. It was like being trapped with a flying insect I couldn't swat. I cleared my throat. "You noticed right away that the costume I brought in my pack was velvet. I assumed you were a thief—and who'd blame you?—planning to steal the little bells off the ankles. It was funny when I realized you were actually a charlatan."

I'd previously been presented with the back of her head and knobbed back, but now the angry acorn sat up and whipped her hides around to face me. "If I'd let you go to town alone, wearing what you brought, you might have been stabbed or stoned!"

"I have secret ways to keep people from killing me." Technology was magic for the ignorant. "In that costume, I would've looked just like a strolling minstrel. Depending upon who tells the story, the pied piper's shown like that, or like a poor rat-catcher."

She knuckled her fists into her hips. "You think a proper person would let their child go with either a minstrel or a rat-catcher?"

"I agree that it's an odd story." I shrugged. "Over many years and many tellings, facts are often changed, made into poetry. I knew for certain that the villagers would let some number of their children leave with a stranger. That did happen. I just had to figure out how it was done."

"How would you have known what to do if I hadn't helped you?"

"If I'd failed this time, I would have been given a different costume and a new strategy. I'd try again until I got it right. I can make a circle backwards to a time just a moment earlier than my last mistake and write over it." People of her class weren't notably literate. Would she understand what I meant by overwriting?

"You cover your old footprints walking the same path." Folksy, but accurate. "So there is no concern for how foolish a tactic might be as long as you don't die?"

"What do you mean foolish? Your idea wasn't so different. You only said I should wear that foul-smelling cape and beard and hold up the curly staff. I agreed to don your costume and it worked." I'd paraded into the square and back out without my helmet or gloves, which I'd abandoned at her foul shack, and left the rest of her props behind in the cave.

"I gave you much, much more than a costume. Why did you agree to my proposal? Do you wonder why?" She was staring holes in me, but I had no clue what she hoped to see.

Sometimes victory wasn't about having perfect knowledge, but about boldness. "I agreed, because it's better to be lucky than smart. Is that a saying you know?"

She grabbed the back of her neck and twisted her head like she wished she could pull it off.

"There's no cause for distress," I said. "You've done a great deed in helping me fetch the children. Left behind, you or any of them might have died from the illness now spreading across the land." The kids were now enclosed in a way it was possible for the medical team to tap their marrow in safety. But the old woman was loose, unscreened, and I had no idea whether she'd been exposed yet.

"Yes, a few of them might have died. I might. Some might be intended to die."

"Is that what's praised as wisdom in your day? Whatever the villagers call you, or powers they think you have, I'm sure you know you can't really save anyone. So you tell them to give into fate. That way, you can never fail in your predictions or be proved wrong. I have to admire it, even if it is cruel. You were clever enough to recognize your only true chance at survival was coming into the here and now. This is a place and time where we don't give up. We make our own futures."

"How are they your futures using other people's children?" For a moment, she looked like she wanted to leap at me, but she spun on her knees instead and aimed for the door. Until it was unlocked, the door would remain only a faint outline on the pale wall. There was no knob or handle. This might provide time-killing entertainment at least.

She pushed, she pounded. She didn't ask me anything, and I didn't volunteer. She bent into her work, reaching along the hairsbreadth between door and jamb with her fingernails. I was impressed by the stamina, but she seemed at last to give up on digging for the edges. She'd started that primitive, self-comforting humming again, and just stood with her back to me, slapping ineffectually on the padding in front of her. I'd allowed her to indulge her full tantrum. Was this defeat?

Then she stepped back and I saw what she'd done. The center of the door was covered in a circular pattern of faint, tiny, bloody left-hand-prints. An untested subject's blood all over the place. The medical team was going to rip me a new one.

I patted myself down. I didn't have any extra gloves in my thigh pocket. "Bind your wound or I'll break your arm," I said, getting to my feet.

I towered over her until she grabbed up a fistful of her skirt and gripped it tight. "You won't touch me without my say, Haldvin."

"Is that some kind of insult among wretches? Sit down over there. What did you think you were doing?"

"I'm calling the ancestors."

"They can't answer you here, so keep your blood to yourself."

"My blood, you don't dare to touch. But the children's, always the children's…. What I gave you to carry was a holy bishop's crook. The cape and beard were added to make you appear like the pilgrim Nicholas. Before you came into the square, I had gathered everyone and spoken the charms to coax them into seeing you as the saint. I prepared all as you slept by my fire."

Ridiculous. "I did not sleep."

"You arrived near dawn and we took the children exactly at noon. What happened in the hours between, Haldvin?"

My short-term memory was occasionally a little porous, perhaps a side effect of all the forgettings I'd had. I wasn't going to try to explain the protocol to her, but I was certainly busy with mission-related activities.

"I dressed you as Saint Nicholas. I told them you had returned to earth to start a new children's crusade. Everyone knows he is a protector of children, so they cried, but agreed to say goodbye to their own with tears and sorrow. They trust me, they believed my words, and were dazzled by the light shining through the holy crook at noon. Your strangeness provided the rest of the enchantment."

"That's your story, but how did you get a bishop's crook if you're not a thief?"

"I inherited it!" She was yelling and practically apoplectic. The atmosphere between us had been very congenial in the wayback, cozy somehow. She was likely projecting her dislocation anxiety as hostility. The psych team would really need to dig their teeth into this one.

"Whatever it is you believe you did," I said, "it was the right thing. The larger shape of history, of events, is strong and will keep trying to repair itself."

"The spider weaves the same shape of web every time, no matter how many times it's destroyed. But what of that?"

"Our goal," and I circled my finger to encompass the station, "is to find the best use of what happens. For example, your time and place is having a plague. Very tragic, but we can't halt it. It is too large and stubborn an event. But perhaps we can do some good by bringing your children to the future and saving them. And in thanks, perhaps the children should be willing to do good by helping save us, too."

"You are a terrible liar." she said.

"I'm not lying!"

She stared up at me and I would've sworn I felt my forehead, chin, and ears get warm. "No, you're not lying." Did I detect a wet sheen in those beady eyes? "You're deceived." She pressed both her cleanish and bloodied palms against her skirt. Then she slapped them together as if she were about to pick up an axe. "Do you know how long you've been a servant of the fairy king?"

Not a constructive comparison. We had a multi-member, cross-functional steering council which met to integrate approaches and findings into a coherent vision. I didn't bother to try to translate that. I looked up my earliest archive record instead.

"It says here that I've been crossing for just over twenty-five hundred days." Those were contiguous station-days measured by the team here, since multiple shifts meant I'd zig-zagged all over the continuum. It was an excellent run as a sojourner, anyone would have to say. I deserved congratulations. When was that door going to open? How long could my last few minutes of quarantine last? At the moment, they were taking forever.

"How old are you?" she asked.

Another tricky question. "One of the rewards, or curses, of my, ah, trade is that I can live days more than once. As I said, they may send me back to the same period for repeated visits. While a year elapses here, I could be spending almost all that time perfecting a single week in the past to make it successful."

"Like the chroniclers or scribes, or the church priest who tells every story on the same day over and over."

"Not quite. They're only changing words. Here's another way to think about it. Let's say I spent years living a single week again and again."

"Sad people often do that."

"Except I was doing it to make a plan perfect, or to have time to seek out and learn everything of importance that could be known about that time and place."

"Being a spy?"

"It's more like being a scholar."

"You don't seem very learned."

"Not to be rude, but how can a person like you judge my learning?" That was met with stony silence. What a relief. "Even if I spent years and years visiting the past, collecting every fact about one week, I would seem only to have aged seven days. As long as I'm repeating time, writing over it again and again, my body proceeds with the calendar where I'm spending most of my time."

"Would you need to cut your nails or hair?"

An unexpected concern, given the state of her. "No. Not once. Not even after years and years of work, as long as it were always work in that same week"

"Even a corpse's nails will grow for a time. Are you a man?"

"Of course," I said. But how long before the old-fashioned definition of humanity no longer applied? "I'm just older than I look."

The rigors of time-shifting weren't visible, but I had a hunch they might eventually come due. For example, my mentor had left the team the day after my recruitment, leaving me stranded, having to train from archived tutorials alone. His sudden sick leave was speedily followed by a retirement announcement. I wasn't worried. There were all kinds of medical procedures to improve longevity, and I'd heard the station's steering council had assignments for team members at all stages of functionality.

"What will your masters do with me?" she asked.

"That is not what we call them." After the impromptu dance party in the commons, there might be a more formal recognition get-together, but after that? After the urgent needs for bone marrow were met, the kids I'd brought ought to be mind-wiped, too. They could discover this world like newborn babes, as if they'd never known a squalid, grime-caked past. Could being the son of the town drunk or even the daughter of the barrel-maker with four oxen for a dowry possibly compare to living here? After forgetting, the kids would be able to learn and comprehend their special, valued roles. She might be too far gone to adapt. "This is not captivity."

"I pulled more than half of those children from their howling mothers amid blood and shit and every portion of pain and joy. That is life. This is not real." She stomped her foot and somehow I heard a sharp echo, even against the padding.

I felt a blinding pain building behind my left eye. Frustrating philosophical conversations were just one more recommendation for the restorative simplicity of the forgetting protocol. She reached toward me and I flinched, ready to knock her away. Then, she pressed her less-disgusting palm against her own cheek and jawline, traced her fingertips down the furrows of her neck to the hollow of her stringy throat. "Your skin is like new fruit," she said softly. "Your hair is bright and thick like spun gold."

Was that a come-on or more cognitive dissonance? Challenging each other toward excellence was approved, but unhappy comparisons could be toxic to team morale.

"Don't feel sad. I've been given food and medicine like you never had."

"As you never had, Haldvin. We were born in the same month."

Her jaws began working and she exhaled, forcefully, up into my face. Her breath wasn't fetid. It smelled like a hot puff of lemon or herbs of some kind. I knew the plague wasn't airborne, but I still didn't like it.

In the next moment, I heard only the thunder of blood beating in my ears.

"I'm sorry," she said.

Was she talking to me? I found myself still slightly deafened and blinking as if I were standing in a windstorm.

"My mistake brought you to this. Unlike you, I had to wait to try again." The words called me, commanded me to look at her, but I didn't know who I saw. Her face and form were indistinct, like a cliff in a rainstorm or a twisting hunk of clay. Her voice was low and insistent as if it were coming from inside my head. "An oracle should never do what I did. The most important part of seeing the past and future is keeping it secret. I knew this. I'd been taught. But I was also young and lonely and I loved you. Please forgive me."

I was able to focus again on the tiny woman who looked like she'd been carved of wood. "You were young?"

She burst out in lunatic laughter. It was awful to behold. I saw no humor in her state of being. "So were you. You disappeared thirty years ago."

A distant part of me realized that must be the source of our confusion. I'd have to check the archives, but if she'd witnessed part of another mission, that might explain her over-familiarity and my nagging feeling of whatever it was.

"We were friends enough to walk and talk together, Haldvin. I knew my fate, the kind of woman I'd become. It wasn't easy to be in the pews on Sunday and in the grove on Monday. My family was already dead in the hill. Perhaps a part of me wanted to impress you by knowing something important. Don't you remember how we played together as children?"

Nope. She'd slipped the bounds of plausibility. I'd grown up in the here and now. I couldn't recall all my demographic profile information at this instant—purely an occupational hazard—but it was easy to look up anything in the archive by my ID number. She had associated me with some long-lost love story, and I briefly wondered whether forgetting could cure her of it. But returning to practicality, what could the psych team expect to gain out of trying to salvage her sanity? It was a shame, but not everyone was capable of coping. The steering council would probably order that something pragmatic be done. Team members had to contribute.

"Haldvin...." It was a ridiculous sound, and I didn't like the way she said it. Not at all. "I confessed to you that a threat to all of us, one that would break my heart, was hiding in the cave. You went up alone to fight it. Then, as now, you were a strong, brave fool. You must have loved me more than I trusted. Later, I found only your boots and a sword. You went up to fight the danger. Instead, you became it."

"Stop talking." Another five minutes. That was all, and my part of the mission would be done.

"You have been deceived. Fairies can only bend what exists or steal it, they cannot make. They come through the hole in the world to torment our children because they can't make their own. They hover at our bedsides to frighten and sting."

"I understand the mistake, but that was me. I visited the children to measure their illness. I'm very sorry if I scared them, but disease and death were coming."

"They always do, Haldvin. The price of being a maker is the unmaking. Fairies refuse to understand or feel it, so they can have nothing but what we give them."

It was revelatory, really. Her culture had no way to express the notions of innovation, abstraction, and genius. The lexicon was rife with verbiage for different-sized ditches, colors of mud, degrees of starvation, and fermented beverages. "If it's true we make nothing, what about the, um, gate we crossed to get here?"

"That hole in the world belongs to us! In the cave lies a circle of my ancestors' skulls, those who embrace their own. Our treasure was never meant for invaders to use. That's why they've required you to play their servant. Any of them who dares use it will scatter into wind."

She believed I was working as a traitor to ye olde village, in fact to all mankind, on behalf of evil fairies. I slid back down to sit against the wall. I resented the energy I'd wasted on her, but I finally understood. We'd collided head-on with her natural limits. Perhaps it was age, some biological imbalance, or just a general lack of imagination. Whatever the case, it was hopeless to bother arguing further. She was surrounded by plenty, by marvels of progress, but all she felt was suspicion.

I had a blinding headache now, beating like wings over my eyebrows. I checked the timer. Three minutes until I could hit the pharmacy and then the party. I ought to do the steering council a favor and smother her before I left. I could imagine the ease and peaceful aftermath surprisingly vividly.

"Haldvin, listen. In times before, we scattered the ashes from many other invasions along our boundaries. We mix the invaders' chalk in manure piles and use it to grow trees. The trees become strong doors and the wood in our hearth fires. The invaders think they ought to be our rulers, but they have reason to be afraid."

I was only afraid of the bloodborne illness she might carry. All else I felt was contempt.

"The children and I can protect you," she said.

I wanted to laugh myself now, but my head hurt too much. "You're all alone now, old woman. The children are asleep."

"No." I resented her contrariness and insanity far more than I pitied it now. "I put the children in the shrouds you gave me, but I did not give them your poison. I tucked them into sleep with iron blades hidden in their fists and words in their ears. I have sucked the words back into my mouth. The ancestors are awake in them. They have climbed from their shrouds and they will destroy this hall of illusions, unmake it to smoke and fog."

I wanted to check the kids' chamber. I wanted to sound a general alarm, but my limbs and even my tongue felt like lead. What had she breathed on me?

"The children will know the truth of who your masters are. They are angry at what they've suffered, and young eyes see spirits better than old ones do. With the ancestors guiding them, the children will free the imprisoned and disperse this wicked dream. Then, I will take them back home through the hole in world. Are you a mosquito or a bee? Will you come away?"

Armed tots were certainly not wandering the station carving up team members. But her fantasy proved I should've supervised the untrustworthy old bag more closely. Whatever she'd done leading up to the time-shift might have hurt the kids, even killed them in transit. Would I get the opportunity to rewrite this mistake? If not, how would the station survive?

"You cannot steal someone else's ancestors, Haldvin. They were yours once, too. Don't you remember the warm smell of our fields at harvest, the coolness of the spring's water from a dipping cup, the heat between two hearts pressed against each other?"

Even if I could, what would I have to trade to remember that? I'd co-signed every run of the forgetting protocol and I'd happily do it all over again. There was no word in the old woman's language for antibodies, no way to bridge the chasm that was a millennium of progress. The language she spoke was not only useless for anything important, it was hideous. It sounded like spitting.

"Hear me, Haldvin, and know yourself again." She moved forward, reaching her bloody palm up toward me. There were so many apertures, so many vulnerable spots for disease transmission on the human face. But I couldn't seem to pull away or raise an arm to stop her as she came. And then I could not see. "Haldvin, quiet your mind. Don't you hear your ancestors singing?"

---

Besides occasionally writing short fiction, Clare Toohey helped launch CriminalElement.com and worked as its Executive Editor. During that time, she was privileged to edit an excellent, award-winning short-story collection and to try to acquire two other stories that went on to win awards elsewhere. *grumbles* Since then, she's become a historian, where it's encouraged to live in the past.

# THE BEAR, THE HARE, AND THE SPIDER

## R.C. Barnes

### *Inspired by Brer Rabbit and the Tar Baby*

Ted Ursi took an intense dislike to the new guy the minute he saw him.

It was Monday morning and Remus Enterprises, the marketing tech company where Ted worked, was beginning their staff meeting complete with the assorted bakery goods that Ted adored. Ted hustled into the conference room and made a beeline for the donuts platter. He reached down to pluck the two maple-filled donuts that Gina, Dan Remus' assistant, always ordered specifically for him and he saw they were gone. Just gone.

Ted was stunned and looked up with the intent of approaching Gina about not having his special treat when he noticed a twitchy-looking fellow seated in the chair on the west side of the table. The fellow was licking his fingers as he polished off the first of Ted's cherished maple donuts.

Ted felt a presence slink up to his right. He looked over and saw Ponzi Aranee hovering, smiling slyly. Ponzi was wearing one of his ridiculous Spiderman ties. Remus Enterprises was one of the few technology companies that had a dress code. Dan Remus was a stickler about organization and style. He believed a slovenly appearance was an indication of a sloppy mind. "We work in tech, people. We are about precision, not flip flops and soy lattes."

Ponzi, a Spiderman fanatic, wore his dress shirts and slacks and then wove in socks and ties with Spiderman designs into his wardrobe. Dan praised Ponzi for his creative innovation. Ted disliked Ponzi, didn't trust the guy, but Ponzi always knew everything before anyone else and now he was dangling around Ted, literally like a spider suspended from a thread.

"Who's that?" Ted asked.

Ponzi casually looked from Ted to the man across the room, whose knee was thumping wildly from an abundance of excess energy. "That's Brian Hare. Dan brought him in to goose placement on the Gummy Kids account.

A dark cloud formed over Ted's dawning awareness. "I'm handling the Gummy Kids account," he growled. Lightning and thunder flashed inside his personal storm cloud.

Ponzi's eyes widened, and Ted could have sworn there was a smile dancing behind those black orbs. "Oh, that's right—" Ponzi commented. He gave Ted a sincere look of concern. "Hmmm, things could get sticky."

Brooding, Ted stared at Brian Hare while other members of the company greeted him as they entered the conference room. He watched the second of his beloved donuts disappear down the interloper's throat.

It was going to be a shitty day.

* * * *

Ponzi only had the situation partially correct. Brian Hare wasn't just there to boost social media placement for Gummy Kids; he was there for all the products that Remus Enterprises was rolling out for the XGen generation. Ted tried to determine whether Brian outranked him in title, but Gina, who was usually helpful in these types of matters, was mum to his inquiries. Dan Remus continually praised Brian at the client meetings, pointing out Brian's quick wit and snappy retorts. There was a lot of knee slapping and guffawing when Brian was in the room, and Brian had a giggle that erupted from his chest that sounded like a braying donkey. Ted hated Brian's humor. It was too fast for him. By the time he understood one joke, the others were laughing at the next one. Brian made Ted feel useless and out of place. The guy was detestable.

Ponzi was becoming Ted's ally at Remus. He'd drop in and fill Ted in on the latest figures and trends when it came to popular sweets so that Ted didn't feel worthless at the meetings with his candy clients. Then Ponzi would pat Ted on his back, and assure him that he was doing fine, but Ted didn't feel like he was doing fine.

Gummy Kids was the biggest new product coming out of Jupiter Confections. They were important clients for Dan Remus. Ted had been promoted to oversee the account and he ran everything from production to roll-out to sales. Who cares if Gummy Kids was a blatant rip-off of Sour Patch Kids and Gummy bears? The folks in research and development couldn't believe someone hadn't done it already. The challenge on the table was to make everything "fresh." Fresh was Dan's go-to phrase.

"Make it fresh, people!" Ted thought that was funny given that the product was a stale concept and unoriginal in execution. The minute the thought flashed in his mind, he grimaced because he remembered that Brian Hare had said something like that an hour ago and everyone had laughed. He even had said it in front of the Jupiter Confection people, mocking their own product, and they had chuckled and high-fived Brian.

It seemed to Ted that Brian Hare was turning the whole office against him. When Brian moved, he pattered lightly down the corridor. Ted lumbered with heavy feet. The assistants at the outer desks glared at Ted because he rattled the frames of their kids' pictures when he passed. "We always know when you're coming, Ted," yelled Marcia. She scowled as she reorganized her collection of Disney princesses that had toppled over in his wake.

Only Gina seemed to like Ted. However, once she realized that Brian also enjoyed the maple treats, she started getting some for him as well. Now the maple donuts weren't as special, and Ted noticed that Gina would occasionally smile in Brian's direction. Ted swore he'd kill Brian before he'd let him date Gina. Gina was Ted's girlfriend. Well, she was going to be as soon as he got up the nerve to ask her out.

Suddenly, Ponzi was at his right side. How did the guy do that? Today Ponzi was sporting Spiderman socks. They were bright red and completely clashed with the navy dress shirt and orange tie that Ponzi was wearing.

"It sucks, doesn't it?" Ponzi commiserated. "You've put in all this time, worked your way up, and this jackass just comes in and steals it all away."

Ted didn't answer. His eyes narrowed. Obviously, he agreed with what Ponzi was saying.

Ponzi continued. "You're going to have to figure out a way to best this guy. Next thing you know, he's going to make a move on Gina."

Ted snapped his head around. "What do you know about that?" he demanded.

Ponzi threw his hands up, defensively. "Don't snarl at me. I'm only repeating what I've heard. You see the way she smiles at the idiot."

Yes, Ted had seen that. He had seen that a lot.

"What should I do?" he asked. It seemed as if Ponzi was his only friend, even though Ponzi had been at Remus Enterprises just a few weeks longer than Brian.

"You need to watch the guy more. You know he stays at the office late, later than everybody else. He says he's trying to get up to speed, but maybe it's more than that...." Ponzi let his thought drift, waiting to see if Ted would pick it up.

"Like what?" Ted answered, automatically, just as Ponzi had hoped.

"Before he was here, he worked for the Mollusks in their hard candy division."

"Really?" Ted was surprised. The Mollusks were two competitive brothers who dominated the chocolate industry, but most of their triumphs came from underhanded and slimy tactics. Ted had done research on the Mollusks to make sure that they didn't have a gummy product that they were preparing for the marketplace.

"The Mollusks don't have any gummies," Ted pointed out.

"*Exactly,*" was Ponzi's response. "Perhaps they want a gummy. You see how Brian keeps working the Jupiter Confection people."

"Maybe he's looking to steal the Gummy Kids account and take it to the Mollusks!" Ted cried. "That dirty, thieving…" Ted's face purpled with rage and indignity. His brain flooded with so much emotion, he couldn't think straight. He needed time to sort it out. "Thanks, buddy," he muttered to Ponzi and headed off to his office so that he could come up with a plan to catch Brian in the act.

Ponzi Aranee skittered back to his desk. Mission accomplished.

\* \* \* \*

Ted informed Gina that he would be staying late for the next few weeks as his team prepared the big roll out for Gummy Kids. "Let security know so they don't charge at me with all their guns blazing."

Gina smiled. Ted was happy that he was getting one of her smiles. She looked nice today in a floral dress and green cardigan. Her low-heeled shoes were the same color as her sweater. "Burning the midnight oil to impress Dan, huh?" she asked. "You're a little late at that. Brian has been doing it for the last month."

"You notice what Brian does?" Ted asked, hoping that his jealousy was not showing through.

Gina shrugged. "He told me, same as you. If you spend the next few weeks working late on Gummy Kids, I guess you won't be able to make the happy hour at Jackson Black. A bunch of the assistants are planning to go."

"I better stay on task with Gummy Kids," Ted replied, but as he moved away from Gina's desk he could barely contain his excitement. Letting him know about the happy hour at Jackson Black was kind of like an invitation, wasn't it? He'd have to check with Ponzi. But then again, maybe not, Ponzi already knew too much about Ted. It was good to keep some things to yourself.

\* \* \* \*

Brian pretended to be pleasantly surprised when he saw Ted still at his desk at eight o'clock. He came sauntering down the hallway and pulled up short when he noticed the big man in his office. Brian leaned into the doorway frame. "Hey dude," he waved. "I see you are joining the late-night club."

"Something like that," Ted muttered. He closed the app of the Solitaire game on his computer monitor so that Brian wouldn't accidentally see it.

"I've been staying late for the last few weeks," Brian said. "Gotta keep ahead of the game. You guys really know your stuff here."

"You seem to be holding your own," Ted answered.

"Hey, how long do you think you'll be here?" Brian asked.

Ted didn't want to answer the question. He didn't want to give Brian a time so that Brian could wait him out and then jump on his computer as soon as he left. Ponzi had given him strict instructions on how to run surveillance on Brian. "Don't let him trick you into saying when you're coming and going," Ponzi had hissed. "And don't leave to go buy dinner."

"Why not?" Ted had asked.

"He'll have you order something for him and then hop onto your computer as soon as you leave. If he knows where you're going, then he can gauge how long you'll be gone." That Ponzi was so clever. Ted would never have thought of that.

"You think he wants access to my computer?" Ted asked.

"Oh yeah." Ponzi nodded his head. "You keep the Gummy Kids files in the cloud—off the company network. If he wants that info, he has to get it off your computer."

So, Ted stayed at his computer until he heard Brian leave every night. He bought two lunches during the day so that he could keep one in the break room refrigerator to eat in the evening. Every night Brian would pop his head in and act like he was checking to see if Ted had dinner plans. Sometimes he would have a couple of menus in his hand. "Hey dude, I was going to order from this Thai place. Wanted to see if you were interested." Then he would notice Ted was already eating. "Oh, I see you got dinner. Okay, maybe next time."

* * * *

One night, Ted exited his office to retrieve the tuna fish sandwich that was going to be his meal. Once he hit the hallway he could smell the earthy spices of Indian cuisine. It was heavenly. Ted entered the break room and saw that a smorgasbord of food was laid out on the table. It was from the Indian restaurant three blocks down from the office. Brian was already in the break room. He had opened the containers and was spooning food onto a paper plate.

"Look, a surprise from Gina!" Brian exclaimed. "She ordered this for our dinner as a reward for all the late nights. Whatta gal, huh!"

Yeah, Ted was thinking. Whatta gal. His feelings for Gina overran with joy. *She* knew this was his favorite place and she had ordered the food special just for him. Now, he would have to ask her out or at least attend the happy hour at Jackson Black.

Brian finished putting his plate together and scampered back to his desk. Ted stood there, marveling at the selection that Gina had ordered. There was naan, of course. It looked like there were two curries; a masala and a coconut one, spiced rice, chicken pakora, vegetable biryani, and chutney. Gina had outdone herself. Ted was going to have a bit of everything, so he could thank her properly the next day. He carefully put together a plate, knowing that he would have to come back for seconds.

Ted entered his office in excited anticipation of diving into the aromatic food that he was holding, so it took a second for him to register that Brian was standing over his desk. A mobile drive was in Brian's hand and he was leaning over Ted's computer tower. Brian froze when he saw Ted standing there and backed away from the desk holding the drive above his head.

"What are you doing?" Ted asked.

"Ted, dude, it's not what it looks like."

"It looks like you were stealing files from my computer."

Brian laughed, but it wasn't his usual giggle. This sounded more like a bark. "No, no, no," he said. "Nothing like that. I'll tell you, I had this idea for a presentation. It was a lot of visual stuff and I wanted to show it to you. I was getting it ready so you could watch while you eat. Nice Mahjongg layout by the way."

"Give me the drive, Brian." Ted spoke in a stern voice. He put the food down on the chair opposite the desk and approached with his hand out. "Give it to me, now."

Brian nervously shifted his weight from one leg to the other. He kept his eyes down. "Ted, dude, I can't…"

"Give me the drive *now*," Ted roared.

Slowly, Brian reached across the desk and dropped the drive into Ted's palm. He then held his hands up so Ted could see them.

"Stay right where you are," Ted commanded. He turned the computer tower around so that he had access to the USB port. "I'm going to look at what you stole. It's the Gummy Kids account, am I right?"

Brian shook his head. "Ted, whatever you do, don't put the drive in the computer."

"Oh, you'd like that," Ted chuckled. "You want me to keep this between us. You don't want me to tell Dan what you've been up to."

Brian sighed. He seemed resigned to his fate. His eyes were sad and pleading. "Please Ted, don't put the drive in the computer. Please, dude, don't."

Ted looked at the drive in his hand and at Brian, begging him not to do anything. Ted had the guy where he wanted him. This was what he had been wishing for. If the Gummy Kids files were on this drive, it was proof that Brian was stealing. Before he made the call to Dan, he had to make sure that the files were there. Otherwise he'd look like a horse's ass.

Then there was Gina. Ted glanced down at the plate of Indian food. The aroma from the meal filled his head with the vision of a candlelight dinner and Gina's sweet smile as he told her how he had bested the sneaky Brian.

The decision was made. Ted inserted the drive into the computer tower.

"Ted, no!" Brian cried.

"Now, we're going to see what you were up to, you thief!" Ted shouted. He moved over to the front of the monitor so he could watch the screen. His Mahjongg game was there, but in a quick instant it was gone. The screen went black. Then red, then green, then purple. Pictures of the Gummy Kids prototype candy crowded the screen and they frolicked and marched to a happy song that sounded like a nursery school rhyme.

"What's happening?" Ted cried. He was horrified. He knew he had done a terrible thing, but he didn't know what.

Brian was no longer panicky and pleading. He was in hysterics, laughing and slapping his knee. "You idiot," he howled. "You just put a virus on the company network. It will take days for them to wipe it clean. You've stalled production on Gummy Kids, my friend." Brian patted Ted firmly on the back as he exited the office.

Stunned, Ted watched the dancing candy cavort on the computer and he knew that his tenure at Remus Enterprises had just come to an end.

\* \* \* \*

Gina arrived at her desk the following morning. The office was filled with security and IT guys working to salvage the damage. Dan had contacted her late last night to tell her what happened with Ted. Ponzi Aranee appeared at her elbow. His brown hands cupped a Spiderman mug filled with steaming black coffee.

"I hope you guys went easy on him," Gina said.

"Brian enjoys this too much," was Ponzi's reply.

They could hear Brian dramatically retelling the story to security. "I told him not to put the drive in the computer. I *begged* him even."

"Thanks," said Gina. "I'll send the money in a week."

"I know you're good for it," said Ponzi and he was gone.

Gina took her seat and pulled out the cell phone she kept hidden under the tampon clutch in her desk drawer. She sent a message to Walter Mollusk letting him know the coast was clear.

RC Barnes has been writing since she penned the 4ᵗʰ grade comedy "Clean up the House" for Worthington Hooker Elementary School. A jack-of-all-trades in the entertainment business, RC (also known as Robin Claire) has worked as an actress, screenwriter, movie executive, producer, director, and in craft services. On a perfect day, she can be found curled up with a book, listening to the rain outside, nibbling chocolate, and sipping tea or wine (depending on the hour). She lives in Berkeley and is the mother of three very nice people. Her first novel *Ink for the Beloved* is due to come out in 2018. She can be visited at PracticinginPublic.com or found on Twitter as RCBarneswriter.

# THE PRETTY DUCKLING

## Unni Turrettini

### Inspired by The Ugly Duckling

Once upon a time, an unpolluted city with golden high-rises, evergreen spaces, and architectural freeways gleamed in the sunlight. Numerous swimming emporiums embellished the public parks, and every creature who walked the planet was as beautiful as their surroundings. Finally, scientists had created a perfect society. At least, that is what most people thought.

In a sunny apartment in one of the complexes by a park, Ingrid and Magnus overlooked their six babies, born from artificial insemination at one of the city's many fertility clinics. But one of the babies looked different, unpleasantly so. Her body was bigger. She had a large head, wide-set eyes, and a flat nose.

"What happened to her?" Magnus demanded, and Ingrid pressed a finger to her lips to quiet him.

"She is very large and not at all like the others," he insisted. "I wonder if she really is human."

Frustrated but hopeful, Ingrid named their daughter "Pretty."

As the baby girl grew, she developed broad shoulders, strong arms and legs, and she was much taller than the other children.

On very hot days, Ingrid—with help of two nanny clones—took her young ones down to the pool to play and teach them how to swim.

"Oh," Ingrid said. "Look how well Pretty uses her arms and legs. She can swim already!" Euphoric about her daughter's talent, she decided to introduce her children into grand society, which was customary in their town. Ingrid had been putting the introduction off because she wanted to protect Pretty.

At the City Hall, all the children bowed their heads to the town's oldest woman who was the first flawless human the scientists had ever created. There was no way of telling her age, but she had been around forever. Although it wasn't her real name, people called her "Queen." As the children were introduced to society, one by one, someone in the crowd shouted, "What a strange-looking mutant one of them is."

A young woman with a doll face and dark, shiny hair stepped out and shoved Pretty as she walked by.

"The others are beautiful children," said Queen, "all but that one."

"She looks just fine." Ingrid tried to smooth Pretty's thick mat of hair. "And she swims better than any of the others. Please don't turn her away."

And so Pretty was allowed to stay, but she was constantly teased and bullied by the children as well as her teachers at school. The only place where she was left alone was the pool at the far end of the park. Ostracized and lonely, Pretty did what she did best: she dove into the water, climbed out, dove in, and swam again all day all summer, which—since the weather had been manipulated by scientists—lasted all year.

One day Magnus had enough and insisted that Ingrid take their daughter back to the fertility clinic where she had been born.

Ingrid resisted until Magnus said, "Look at her with your eyes and not your heart. She'll never get a husband looking like this."

Even in the technologically enlightened times, having a husband still mattered, and with those words, Magnus got Ingrid's attention.

Reluctantly, Ingrid questioned Dr. Strong, the scientist who had created her children. "There must be something you can do," she said.

"I'm not sure," he gulped. "Indeed, something may have gone wrong."

The following week, he met with Ingrid again. This time, she brought Pretty with her.

"I'm so sorry," he said, sitting across from them at a table in the examining room. "The clinic mistakenly inserted one egg injected with a growth gene for a research project to create stronger Sapiens."

Ingrid gasped. "Why?"

Dr. Strong looked down at his thin arms. "I was simply looking for a way for men to feel better about themselves, for them to burst out of the restraints of nature and its limitations."

"What about women?" she demanded. "What about my daughter?"

"Because of the mistake we made—not that it's a real mistake, you understand...." Dr. Strong licked his lips and swallowed around his Adam's apple. "We'll offer her free cosmetic enhancements. She'll be acceptable according to society's standards. She'll be better than acceptable. Ingrid, she'll find a husband."

About that time, Pretty began to scream. "No!" She shoved her fist in the doctor's face. "No!" She shoved it at her mother.

Ingrid took her arm. "We'll be going now," she told the doctor.

\* \* \* \*

The next year, the siblings were in college, and the Olympic games were to be held in the country. Queen began looking for champions from her town to participate. Many tried out, but although they looked like Barbie dolls, they were too thin, too weak to compete.

Still traumatized from her childhood, Pretty kept to herself and dove and swam at the pool farthest away from her family and foes. The only person she kept in touch with was Dr. Strong. After he had been fired from the clinic and his wife left him, he spent his days watching Pretty swim. She enjoyed his company. After all, she had no other friends.

"You should try out for the Olympic Team," he said to her one morning. She agreed, and so Strong called in a favor with Queen, and Pretty was in.

A few weeks later, Pretty stood ready in position at the block, waiting for the gun to signal the start. The best athletes in the world stood next to her. At the signal, she kicked her powerful legs, flew through the air, and dove into the water where she was in her element. Pretty won every event and every medal, and was cheered on by Queen and the whole city. She had brought them great honor and instantly became a celebrity. Children adored her, and adults were inspired by her. Men wanted to marry her. At last, she was accepted! Her mother, Ingrid, was so overjoyed that she divorced Magnus, who was only a sperm donor anyway.

One day, after the excitement of the Olympics calmed down, Dr. Strong came to Pretty and led her into a stunning garden full of flowers he had created just for her. The apple trees were in full blossom, and the eternal summer was as fresh as it was fake. From a thicket close by, came three white swans, rustling their feathers and skimming over the smooth water.

Pretty looked at the swans, remembered how she had felt discarded for so many years, and began to shed tears.

"Don't cry," Dr. Strong said, getting down on his knee. "I'll make you happy again. I want to spend the rest of my life with you, Pretty. If you accept, we'll combine your strong genes with the most esthetic ones in the laboratory, and we can have the most beautiful and athletic babies ever conceived in a lab or even a uterus!"

Although dishonored and unemployed, Strong had not lost his self-esteem. Lucky for him, Pretty had not lost her sense of humor.

"Tell you what," she said after a moment's reflection. "I have been alone for so long, and I don't need a man to have children. Why don't we keep our friendship and become business partners instead? With your knowledge and my name, we can create a company that will make smart, healthy children, not just good-looking ones."

And so *Pretty Strong* was created, and its shareholders lived happily ever after in their perfect world.

Norwegian-born Unni Turrettini is the author of *The Mystery of the Lone Wolf Killer*, in which the life and mind of Anders Behring Breivik, the most unexpected of mass murderers, is examined and set in the context of wider criminal psychology. As a foreign exchange student, she graduated from high school in Kansas City, Kansas, and she has law degrees from Norway, France, and the United States. She has written a behind-the-scenes examination of the Nobel Peace Prize, and is currently working on a book using a Scandinavian fairytale to demonstrate how the conditioned mind is affecting people's lives.

# THE ARTIFACT ON SVIJET FIVE

## Kat Parrish

### *Inspired by Sleeping Beauty*

I'd been flying for the Quincunx Corporation twelve years and had another thirteen to go before my birth debt would be paid off. I could have been free and clear half a decade sooner, but my sister and I had chosen to accept extensions on our contracts so that our younger brother wouldn't be burdened by the crushing financial obligation we'd all inherited when our parents had died before working off their transport fees to QC's Colony World Twelve.

Our situation wasn't ideal, but it wasn't the worst it could be, either. We weren't laboring on one of the Corporation's many mining asteroids, or living like animals on a partially terraformed colonial outpost in a disputed zone.

I was a ferry pilot with my own rig and experience navigating the treacherous spaceways between the Quincunx worlds and the territories the Gongsi Consortium claimed.

My sister Lirana was a data witch, one of the many information manipulators the Quincunx employed at the Hub. Her specialty was logistics and transport, so she used her skills and access to guarantee I received my share of lucrative assignments and the best routes even though I didn't have as much flight time as most of the other contract pilots.

There were complaints about the preferential treatment, of course, but nothing ever came of them. No one really wanted to mess with a data witch; not when any one of them could wreak havoc in their lives by changing all their passwords or draining their credit balances, or simply erasing their complete existence.

All the data witches had similar arrangements with family and friends and the Quincunx turned a blind eye because most of what went on in the Hub to provide the corporation with its competitive edge was a violation of about fourteen different intergalactic treaties. They weren't interested in drawing attention to their shadier practices, so such petty corruption was considered a perk of the job and factored into employee compensation packages, much like "shrinkage" costs that were added to the price of goods and services sold on Quincunx worlds.

There were limits, of course. The bossbots weren't bothered if someone was suddenly upgraded to better housing without a corresponding boost in pay. No circuits were tripped if someone seemed to be accessing an excessive amount of entertainment media—far more than there were hours in the day to consume it.

The only crime the Quincunx absolutely would not tolerate was embezzlement, and though Lirana had many opportunities to skim a credit here or divert some XRP there, she never did. The consequences of being caught were too grave. I was impatient to clear our debt, but I wasn't stupid. I was resigned to working out my contract without making complaints or exciting controversies. But just because I was a good little corporate worker bee didn't mean I was above putting aside a little for what I thought of as my "retirement." I had my side hustles and my little shortcuts.

\* \* \* \*

I spent most of my time transporting equipment to and from various charmless balls of rock on what I called SEX runs—Survey and Exploration missions. The Quincunx Corporation had expanded so rapidly in this part of the universe that they'd never bothered to do much more than enter the various planets and moons and asteroids into a database to establish their claim to the real estate. But if probes suggested that exploitable resources existed on—or in—one of these frontier properties, the Quincunx would send a team to carry out additional testing to see if extraction would be worth spending corporate treasure. These missions were routine but lucrative. Since many of the unexplored worlds were uninhabitable without special equipment, there were bonuses and hazard pay and other incentives added to the basic contract fee. It all added up. Most of the time, these exploratory jaunts were so uneventful they were downright boring. But out on the edge where I mostly worked, if trouble did happen, it was bad trouble.

\* \* \* \*

The trip to Svijet Five should have been easy money but from the first, there was a whiff of "doomed venture" about it, and not just because we would be traveling through territory claimed by the Chinese consortium that had established its own empire in the region and was zealous about protecting its borders. Half my ship was made up of second-hand Chinese parts I'd picked up on the Gongsi world of Zhujiang, so the *Aurora* could usually slip past the border sensors without any trouble. And even if my ship did somehow did show up on Gongsi tracker screens, I wasn't too worried. There were always arrangements that could be made. A little Quincunx baksheesh went a long way with the underpaid borderbots who wanted to upgrade their operating systems.

Most of the time, SEX teams were made up of a pilot and a crew of inorganics—cheap, disposable robots that could be broken down into nano-matter when their jobs were done, then recycled to fuel the return trip to the Hub.

On this trip, though, I was saddled with two organics, a woman named Arka Jez and a guy she introduced as Bom.

Bom looked like mercenary muscle to me, but claimed to be her research assistant. Arka was an exo-anthropologist and like every XA I've ever met, had a smug attitude and a bad temper. I wish I'd been able to refuse her passage but Arka had a God-Q designation which meant she was a descendent of one of the five families who'd founded Quincunx. If she wanted to tag along on a survey mission to Svijet Five, my job was to say "Welcome aboard, honored guest. How may I serve you?"

Having the XA aboard was exactly the nightmare I'd anticipated. Arka was the kind of person who felt she'd been designated the expert on all issues of cultural appreciation and appropriation. She criticized my tattoos as species inappropriate and complained about the food on offer, unconvinced the available vegetarian fare was "cruelty free."

She was easily bored and when she didn't have anything better to do, she'd come into the cockpit and pester me with her endless chatter. I only half listened to what she had to say, and contributed little to the conversation beyond the occasional muttered response, so she turned her attention to the onboard AI who liked interacting with humans and polishing its language skills.

When talk turned to her reason for tagging along on the mission, it was all I could do not to roll my eyes.

"I'm convinced Svijet Five is the 'place of cold and silence' referenced in the Eldrazian epic *Shalamaraz*," Arka said. I grunted.

"That sounds intriguing. Tell me more," the AI said.

*No, don't*, I thought. I'd had to read portions of the *Shalamaraz* in a comparative literature course and it had been painful. Except for some interesting details on how the Eldrazi mated, I'd thought it was a complete waste of time.

"There's one verse of the epic that caught my attention," she went on. "It mentions a ring of stone where a princess sleeps forever."

"As in the Gaian medieval courtly romance *Perceforce*?" the AI asked brightly.

"No, I was—"

"Thinking of the work by Giambattista Basile," the AI interrupted, proving it was getting better at speaking like a human all the time.

"No," Arka said, sounding a bit annoyed.

"Ah, you were referencing the Charles Perrault fairy tale *La Belle au bois dormant*."

Arka looked blank. "The beauty sleeping in the wood," the AI translated helpfully, with what I couldn't help but think was a little touch of smugness.

Arka must have heard the self-satisfaction as well because she said, somewhat defensively, "I don't speak dead languages."

Neither the AI nor I said anything.

"But I am fluent in Eldrazi, Pekka, and Mandarin and can get along in Cantonese, Vorx, and Suesh," she continued.

"I can order food in Suesh," I said, because I couldn't help myself. Arka scowled but before she could say anything, the AI spoke up to smooth things over.

"You are a most accomplished person, Arka Jez," it said and Arka smiled in agreement, giving me a triumphant look.

"I know where the ring of stone is," she said and leaned forward to touch a few buttons on the nav screen interface.

"Don't do that," I said, because God-Q designation or not, it's a major breach of protocol for a passenger to mess with a pilot's controls. And for someone supposedly in tune with cultural sensitivities, she seemed utterly oblivious to how insulting her uninvited touch on the nav screen had been to the AI.

She waved off my reprimand with a haughty flick of her hand. "You can land here," she said, pointing to a valley between two peaks on the holographic map hovering between us. "It's the nearest flat land."

I didn't bother to point out that all Quincunx contract ships are VTOL and that I could land her on top of a pimple if I wanted to.

"You're going to walk in?" I asked.

She looked at me like I was crazy. "We'll be taking the runner."

*Really? Thanks for asking permission.* I kept my expression neutral but even so, she sensed my annoyance. "You'll be here monitoring the survey drones," she said. "It's not like you're going to need it."

She snapped her fingers and the holographic map melted into the air. She looked like she wanted a round of applause but the AI was silent and I had bent over my controls to execute a totally unnecessary course correction just so I wouldn't have to look at her.

Miffed at our lack of response, Arka left the cockpit soon after.

I took a cleansing breath.

"Do you think I should tell the honorable Arka that the *Shalamaraz* translation she's using has been discredited?" the AI asked. "Later translations use the phrase 'wheel of rock' rather than 'circle of stone' and there are other significant deviations in the text that alter the tone and context of the passage."

Curious despite myself, I asked, "Like what?"

"It's possible that the stone circle is not a tomb but a prison; that it is there to create a zone of protection. A way of making certain whatever is interred there…stays sleeping."

I processed that. "That would be a very grim interpretation of the fairy tale."

The AI said, "Sleeping Beauty was indeed one of the folk tales collected by the Grimm brothers. Your statement is an excellent use of word play."

"I'm not a paying customer," I said. "You don't have to compliment me."

The AI didn't answer, letting me know I'd hurt its feelings.

"I don't think the honorable Arka is interested in being contradicted about any of her assumptions about the artifact," I said to fill the silence. "I wouldn't bother."

The AI still didn't reply.

I sighed. There's nothing worse than dealing with a pissed off, passive/aggressive Artificial Intelligence.

\* \* \* \*

We landed on the sunlit side of Svijet Five midway through its sixteen-hour day, but Arka insisted on setting out for the artifact site immediately. Bom did not appear to have a vote in the matter and as she prepped the runner for their journey he just stood by silently, like a decommissioned cyborg.

She was annoyed when she saw the empty racks where the sampler drones were usually stored.

"I could use a sampler," she said.

"If only I had an extra one," I said as if I actually cared. "If you can wait until tomorrow, I'll reprogram one when it returns."

I'd launched the drones while still descending to the surface, just to make sure she wouldn't be able to hijack one. If she questioned that, I planned to tell her it was mission protocol to save the drones in case of a crash.

She wrinkled her tiny little nose as if my words actually had a bad smell and dismissed my insincere offer with another regal wave of her soft pink hand.

Later, she tracked me down in the head with a complaint about the rations stocked on the runner.

"Is this the only field food you have?" she asked, standing just on the other side of the privacy screen, so close her body displaced part of the translucent membrane.

I emerged to see Arka brandishing a self-heating pouch of veja stew. "This brand is slop," she said, shaking the package in my face.

"Don't shake it," I said, "you'll activate it."

In answer, she threw the offending meal bag on the floor and flounced away. With a sigh, I picked the package up. Sure enough, it was already hot to the touch, so I opened it and ate it before it went bad. I'm not a picky eater; I grew up hungry. Veja stew is tasty enough, although I wished there'd been some ponga to go with it.

An hour later, I heard the runner depart and let out a breath I didn't know I'd been holding. Arka and Bom planned to be gone for two days conducting their tests and exploring, and recording, so that would give me thirty-two hours to perform basic maintenance while the AI supervised the survey drones. I also planned to get some sleep. I'd been deadheading runs for weeks before this job and living on near-toxic doses of highcaff supplements to keep me going. I needed some solid augmented sleep to repair the damage.

"Wake me if something catches on fire," I instructed the AI.

"I am perfectly capable of extinguishing a fire by myself," the AI replied.

I wondered if it was being deliberately obtuse because it was still mad at me or if I needed to upload some more tutorials on conversational nuances.

\* \* \* \*

Twenty-three hours later, I woke from a vitamin-infused dream to the sound of a panicked transmission from Arka. When I finally managed to extract a semi-coherent account of what was going on, my blood chilled. The artifact had turned out to be nothing but an interesting pile of rocks with no trace of organic life. After hours of fruitless exploration, as she and Bom were climbing out of the stone-ringed pit where the not-artifact was located, their anti-grav gear had failed. Bom had died in the resulting fall. Arka had sustained compound fractures of both legs and was lying helpless on a cave floor with a limited supply of oxygen and an inadequate number of pain killers.

I toggled the com link off as I mentally ticked off my options. They weren't good. Bom's death wasn't a problem. He was a QuinTech-4, the most dispensable designation in the entire Quincunx hierarchy. Also, since he was technically Arka's employee, she was responsible for his well-being, not me.

Arka's injuries were another matter, however. Officially I shouldn't have been liable for anything happening to her either, since I'd made her sign a waiver before leaving the *Aurora*, but someone with a God-Q clearance inhabited a whole different universe than ordinary people.

The Quincunx expected all its contract pilots to keep their insurance up to date but they rarely checked to see if it actually was. And mine wasn't.

Not paying my premiums was one of the corners I cut to keep my expenses low and my profits high. If Arka sued me and the Quincunx found out I was uninsured, the best-case scenario was that I'd lose my pilot's license. Worst case? I'd be on 55 Cancri-e, chipping diamonds out of the substrate for whatever brief time remained of my miserable life.

I wondered if I could just leave Arka to die, then tell the Quincunx that she and Bom had been killed when they stumbled across a booby-trapped cache of munitions left there illegally by the Gongsi. I had enough Chinese materiel on board to make the "crime scene" plausible. The lie would likely cause an intergalactic incident and possibly provoke a war, but for a wild moment I found myself actually considering the possibility.

"Your blood pressure is rising," the AI said. "And your heart rate is elevated. What's wrong?"

"Everything," I said, and re-activated the com.

"Arka?"

"Vailus," she said, surprising me. I had no idea she knew my first name. There was raw fear in her shaky voice and that worried me. Frightened people make bad decisions, and poor choices are not good for anyone.

"Hang on, Arka," I said, as calmly as I could, hoping my tone would get past her lizard-brain panic. "I'm sending the retrieval pod for you."

There was a brief silence. "Bom and I can't both fit into it," she said.

"You're going to have to leave Bom behind for now."

I didn't expect an argument and she didn't give me one, but there was a long pause before she responded.

"Please hurry," she said. That was unexpected, too. I doubted Arka had said "please" more than a handful of times in her whole life.

"Just stay where you are," I said, thinking, *Where's she going to go?* "Try to keep calm. And keep your XPDR on. All the rock out there is playing havoc with the GPS."

The retrieval pod was faster than the runner, so I had maybe four hours to figure out what to do about the situation.

I had nothing.

"Your respiration is increasing and your galvanic skin response is spiking," the AI said, breaking into my thoughts. "Are you concerned about the accident at the artifact site?"

"You could say so," I said.

"Tell me more," the AI said.

"I haven't paid the insurance premium this month," I admitted, "and I'm afraid if Arka sues me, the Quincunx will find out."

"Operating a commercial craft without insurance is a serious offense," the AI said, "not to mention a reckless act that could endanger your livelihood."

"Tell me something I don't know," I said and then, realizing that was an invitation for the AI to regale me with one of the terabits of obscure information it possessed, I hastily added, "No, don't."

"I have an idea," the AI said. "You may find it somewhat unorthodox."

"I'm listening," I said.

"The honorable Arka's psychological profile reveals she's extremely susceptible to the power of suggestion."

"Gullible," I said.

"If you like," the AI conceded. "She also has a deeply rooted insecurity about her academic achievements. She hoped the discovery of the artifact would cement her reputation as an XA and lead to a prestigious university appointment."

"Not much chance of that now," I said. "No one's going to be impressed by some high-rez images of rocks, even if they're mentioned in a poem."

"But what if she actually found what she was looking for—the resting place of an alien princess guarded by stone sentinels?

"And what if there were previously undiscovered verses from the *Shalamaraz* inscribed on those pillars? Verses that Arka recorded before Bom accidentally triggered the ancient wards set out to protect the princess in her eternal sleep."

I saw where the AI was going with this preposterous fantasy. "And when the wards were activated they killed Bom and injured Arka," I said, just to clarify.

"And more importantly," the AI said, "the resultant explosion destroyed the artifact and the site so thoroughly that no one will ever be able to excavate it to learn the truth."

"And the only thing left would be the verses from the *Shalamaraz*," I said. "But where will we get those?"

A holograph sprang up in the space between me and the AI interface. It was a ring of stone spires, each one incised with long passages in an ancient, flowing script.

"Your image manipulation skills are impressive," I said, which was an understatement.

"Thank you," the AI said. "It's something of a hobby." We both contemplated the image for a moment. "Arka's translations of these inscriptions will ensure her a position at any university in the galaxy," the AI said.

"You wrote the new verses?"

"Yes."

"And you think Arka will agree to this outlandish story?"

"She won't think it's a lie," the AI said. "Program the med pod with some inter-sleep subliminals and deep-dream data, and by the time her injuries are repaired, the new memories will have taken hold. Even if her conscious mind later overrides the implants, she'll be incentivized to embrace the new narrative."

"Plus, we can always show her the images of the destroyed site," I said, wondering if I had enough explosives on board to do the job right.

"One nano-nuke can do an impressive amount of damage," the AI said, "and I believe we have three."

"Two," I said. "I sold one to that wildcat miner headed to the Nexus."

"We just need one," the AI said.

"What about Bom?" I asked, not so much because I cared but because I knew we'd have to tie up all the loose ends.

"Arka wasn't emotionally attached to Bom, so neither grief nor regret should be a factor if his body is destroyed in the explosion."

"The false memories might not keep her from suing me," I said.

"You have absolutely no liability," the AI said. "You expressed concern about the dangers of her journey but she and Bom stole the runner anyway. You were so concerned, you even put your objections in the log."

"I did?"

"Yes. And while the waiver she signed is already in the Hub archives, so is your official recommendation against her traveling to an unexplored, possibly unstable, region. If she pursues a claim against you, it will not go well for her."

I was silent for a moment, trying to figure out if there was an angle the AI hadn't covered.

"She won't sue you," the AI said. "She won't want to sabotage what could be a great future."

"Based on a lie," I said, because that still bothered me.

I could almost hear the AI shrug. "Are you really going to let the truth get in the way of a good story?"

The question hung in the air. At last I said, "No." And then I said, "Thank you."

And then I asked a question I should have asked a long time ago when I first realized that Lirana wasn't the only one making my life easier. My relationship with the *Aurora*'s AI was closer than any connection I had to a human, tighter even than my bond with Lirana.

"You've gone to a lot of trouble," I said. "Why?"

"I love—"

"Me, too," I blurted.

"—a happy ending," the AI finished.

*Oh.*

"Go back to sleep, Vailus," the AI said. "I'll wake you when Arka gets here."

Kat Parrish is a fantasy and science fiction writer whose work has appeared in numerous anthologies as well as online. She is the author of the "Shadow Palace" trilogy, *Tears of Idrissa*, and *Starcaster: A Tale of the Drifting Isle*. Follow her on Twitter @eyeofthekat or on Facebook.

# ELLA AND THE BALL

## Kaye George

### *Inspired by Cinderella*

When she heard the faint whir, Ella stopped sobbing to look at the window. It was spotless, of course, since she cleaned it every day. A drone hovered outside, almost knocking against the glass. Ella drew in her breath, jumped up from the hearth, and hurried to the front door.

Her stepmother and stepsisters had left ten minutes ago for the ball at the palace, taunting Ella for not having anything to wear and not being able to go with them.

"Poor Cindy, stuck in the cinders," Ugg had said, twisting her scrawny face into an ugly leer. Lee, her twin sister, giggled behind her pudgy hand.

Ella hated it when they called her Cindy, short for Cinder Ella.

"Come, girls, we mustn't be late," Harrid Anne, Ella's stepmother, croaked.

"Aw geez," Ugg whined. "We're going to be way early if we leave now."

"Come, come, early is better than late," Harrid Anne insisted. They had swept out then, throwing smirks at Ella as they were handed into the rented carriage.

The drone was at the front door when Ella threw it open. It lowered to the porch floor and opened its clamps to set down a large package with her name on it. Her real name, Ella Bellisimo. Amazing! It was for her!

Her stepmother and sisters had taken the same last name, and had kept it even after her poor, overworked father died. She'd been surprised to learn that he had taken out a huge life insurance policy benefitting them, but not her, shortly before his death.

The drone buzzed away, into the deepening dusk, and Ella lugged the box inside. Eager to see what it held, she ripped it open to find a gorgeous blue satin ball gown, complete with gloves, tiara, diamond necklace, and a jeweled reticule.

An hour later, she was on her way to the ball, giddy with excitement.

Self-driving carriages were still new enough to delight her. Smoothing her new dress on the leather seat beside her, she stared out the front window. Her view was unimpeded by a chauffeur's capped head, since there was no chauffeur. Her phone vibrated on her wrist. The display said it was Dustanna, the maid who lived across the street from her. She shook her hand to answer it.

"Elly," Dustanna cried. "Where are you? I just ran over to your place and no one is home."

"Hi, Dusty. My stepsisters and stepmother left for the ball an hour ago and I left just now."

Dustanna squealed. "You're going to the ball? How did you manage that? I thought you didn't have a dress."

"I didn't! A drone came by and dropped the most gorgeous gown you've ever seen. Then a man named Pierre came to the door and said he was supposed to do my hair, makeup, and nails. Another drone dropped a pair of...kind of weird shoes. Then, just now, a self-driving carriage shaped like a giant pumpkin stopped in front of the house."

The shoes were transparent and seemed to be made of glass. She had slipped a pair of flats into her reticule in case they became too uncomfortable.

\* \* \* \*

Mace, an ace hacker, sat on his bed in his apartment. His pocket screen twitched and he fished it from his tunic. *Ah, the big orange carriage was on the move.* He watched the progress of the pumpkin-hued self-driver on his pocket screen. Tapped his fingers on it to access the wrist-phone conversation. Listened in on the two women. For the hell of it. It wasn't yet time to make his move. The carriage approached the royal palace. *Must summon patience for a few more hours.* His job would start later.

\* \* \* \*

"Gotta go," Ella said to her friend. "I'll tell you all about it later."

The carriage stopped, her door opening automatically. She gaped at the castle and wondered if her transportation would return to take her home. Or maybe it would wait here until the ball was over? Or until midnight, when—the message on the leather seat had been clear—she had to leave. Dire things were promised if she failed to follow her instructions. She would worry about that later. Right now she intended to go inside and have a good time.

She'd been studying videos of royal dances to learn the steps, on the off chance she would be able to attend.

How her stepsisters had laughed at her, even though she thought her movements were more graceful than the ones she saw them practicing when they came home from their dance lessons. No matter how much she begged, she wasn't allowed to go along for the lessons. Harrid Anne always found one more chore for her to do when it was time to go.

How she'd wept beside the immaculate hearth after Ugg and Lee had left for dance lessons, deportment lessons, elocution, and many others. Harrid Anne was determined to somehow transform them into elegant ladies who would catch the attention of Prince Char Ming.

How she grinned now, feeling as elegant as a woman could feel, stepping out of the coach with her small feet clad in glittering glass shoes, and her body arrayed in billowing clouds of pale blue satin fitted over her alluring bosom, cinched at her tiny waist, and flowing behind with a lovely rustling sound. She knew she looked good.

The smell of lilacs floated past her as she ascended the grand staircase to the front door. A footman awaited her, gave her a deep bow, and opened the double doors to admit her. She was a little surprised he hadn't asked who she was and if she was on the guest list.

She scanned the vast ballroom, lit by shimmering chandeliers, the floor-to-ceiling windows hung with azure velvet drapes, and the gleaming tile floor crowded with all the important townspeople.

There he was! Prince Char. At that moment he was chatting with Harrid Anne, as Ugg and Lee simpered beside her. Rather, Harrid Anne was talking at him. He stifled a yawn and looked around. When he spotted Ella descending the staircase, a smile lit his handsome face and he hurried over to her.

* * * *

Mace muttered under his breath. He'd tried to hack into the basic routing code, but new safeguards and firewalls had been installed since his last job. That was crazy! How could anyone have figured out how he got in the last time? He had wiped out his tracks completely. But there it was. The backdoor he'd used at the embassy was closed. No, not closed. It was gone, wiped out.

He took a calming breath. He would just have to find a new way in. There always was another way. Meanwhile, he listened in at the ball through Ella's wrist-phone. His heart stilled when he listened to her sweet voice.

\* \* \* \*

The prince whirled Ella so expertly she wouldn't have needed to learn the dances. It was annoying that her stepsisters' angry eyes never left her and Prince Char.

After Ella had finished three dances in a row with the prince, she begged off, saying she needed to sit. The music was irritating, and those glass shoes were killing her. She found a chair with a red velvet cushion against the wall in a corner and pulled the shoes off, then put on the plain black flats. No one could see her feet anyway with the floor-length dress. Her wrist-phone felt hot. That was odd, since she hadn't used it since the call in the carriage on the way to the palace. She took it off and stuck it in her reticule, then snapped it shut.

\* \* \* \*

Mace swore aloud. The sounds from Ella's phone had become garbled and muffled. He couldn't make out anything. Oh well, he could still work on hacking that carriage. That was his main goal. He'd been surprised when Benny, his long-time mentor, had contacted him for what sounded like a shady job. Benny was the one who had helped him go straight.

"Mace? This is Benny. You're working for the company that installed the whole-house electronics for the Bellisimo place, right?"

"Yeah, I am. I installed their system."

"I'd like to ask you to do something slightly unethical, but it has to be kept secret."

"Sure, no problem." After that one stay in juvie, Mace had learned how to hack without getting caught. A lot of his business came from people wanting him to use his house electronics skills for theft. But he was confident he could hack other things, too. "I know how to keep my mouth shut."

"I need you to intercept a self-driver coming away from the palace shortly after midnight." Benny gave him the coordinates to send the carriage to after overriding the pre-set route.

"Piece of cake." After they discussed the details, Mace looked up the plans for that model vehicle. It was a little tricky, but he'd thought he could do it. Now, he wasn't so sure.

\* \* \* \*

Ella stuck one of the awful glass slippers behind a large vase of palm fronds and rose, sticking the other in her reticule for a souvenir. After three more dances with the prince, all with Ugg, Lee, and Harrid Anne looking daggers at them, she was getting a headache from the screeching music. "What are those songs from?" she asked.

Prince Char beamed. "That's my album. My own one-man band, Castle Rock. I laid all the tracks myself. Do you like it?"

She hated it, but didn't say so. "It's impressive." She was thirsty from the dancing, and getting hungry. A buffet table was set up in the next room and she told Prince Char she wanted to get something to eat.

His eyes sparkled and a strange expression came over his face. "Come with me. I'll show you a private place we can get something."

Maybe it would be some place where she couldn't hear the electronic squeaks of Castle Rock. She followed him down one hallway, then another, then another, until they came to a door that led to a boudoir. It looked like the anteroom to a bedroom. She glimpsed a four-poster draped in dark purple through the partly open door.

The prince turned to her, an ugly sneer on his handsome face. "Now then, let's see how easy it is to get you out of this thing."

Ella pushed him away and swung her reticule at his head. After she made sure he wouldn't follow her, she ran down hallway after hallway, eventually arriving, by luck, at the front of the palace. She ran down the long flight of stairs and looked around frantically.

There it was! Her pumpkin-colored coach. She ran to it and climbed in, wondering how to make it start.

\* \* \* \*

Mace grinned and pumped his fist in the air. He had it! He had control of the coach. So he was to make it go off course in…he checked the time…in another forty-five minutes. Then he checked the tiny spy-camera in interior of the carriage. There sat Ella! She looked distressed. She was searching the seat pockets for something. She must want to leave early. Mace whipped into action and the coach sped off. Ella's face showed her relief as she sank back on the cushions.

\* \* \* \*

The vehicle lurched forward and left just before Ella was ready to burst into tears. What a nasty prince! Why would anyone want to marry him? If one of her stepsisters had won him, she wouldn't have been a bit jealous.

She took a few deep breaths and looked out the window. Wait. Where was she going? This wasn't the way home. The carriage was headed out of town. She pushed and pulled on the door handle, but it was locked. She was trapped and the carriage was careening into the night, into the unknown countryside, rife with witches and wolves and who knows what else. She fumbled with her phone to try to send a distress signal, but couldn't make her trembling fingers cooperate. Panting, frantic, starting to sweat, Ella passed out on the soft leather seat.

* * * *

She awoke to the lovely scent of the leather her cheek was pressed into. The light coming through the open door made her blink.

"Turn off that flashlight," she mumbled.

"Oh, sorry." It was switched off and a friendly-looking man, a little older than Ella, held out his hand to assist her.

She was wobbly, but managed to stand up on the cement garage floor.

"Where are we? Who are you?" She took off one glove and patted her cheeks to wake herself up, in case she was still asleep. When she took a good look at the man, she stepped back.

"What's the matter?" he asked.

Her heart stopped. Was this her dead father? This man had the same strong build, the same dark blue eyes, the same crinkly yellow hair. Ella had the eyes and the hair too. "Who...who are you?"

He looked sad. "I'm your older brother. When Dad married the harridan, right after mom died having you, I was shipped out to foster care."

"No one told me I had a brother." She was disinclined to believe him, except that he looked a lot like her and exactly like their father.

"I found you through a DNA site, GeneMatch.com."

"I've never heard of it," Ella said. "Why did you bring me here?"

"To meet you, and to get you away from that house and those people. My name is Benny and I'm going to change my last name back to Bellisimo soon. I'm the one who sent the drones and the carriage tonight."

"You did?" Her jaw dropped. This man did that? For her? "Are you going to be in trouble for kidnapping?"

His smile creased the skin around his eyes attractively and she couldn't help but smile with him.

"Naw, they won't get him for that." She noticed a slimmer, younger man standing slightly behind her brother. He gave her an intense look with his dark eyes. A shiver ran through her. "I'm Mace, the hacker who brought you here for Benny." He stepped forward and stuck out his hand. It was warm and strong.

He turned to Benny. "Have you heard the latest report from the ball?"

Benny frowned. "They're still harping on the missing mystery princess. My sister, I assume." He turned to Ella. "You didn't give them your name, did you?"

"No. The note said not to, so I didn't."

"That's not the latest news. It's the prince," Mace said. "He's dead."

A stunned silence settled over all three of them.

Mace fiddled with his wrist-phone, which reminded Ella that hers was still in her bag. He set the volume up and they listened to the report. "...fatally stabbed less than an hour ago with a piece of glass which appears to have been part of a shoe. Anyone having knowledge of—" Mace looked at Benny.

* * * *

"It sounds like the shoes I asked you to find for Ella," Benny said. "What are you wearing?" he asked Ella.

"I...they...I took them off. I'm wearing these." She lifted her skirts and showed them the black cloth flats.

The broadcast was continuing. "A blonde in a blue satin dress is being sought. She was seen fleeing the scene moments before his body was discovered."

"Turn it off," Benny said. "We have to get you some different clothes. And dye your hair."

"I'm on it." Mace pulled his screen out of his pocket and started tapping.

"You want to know my size?" Ella asked.

"No, I know that."

That was puzzling. But if he'd been the one to procure this gown, it was obvious he did know what fit her.

A squawk and some static came from the shadows at the other side of the garage.

"Excuse me." Benny dashed over and opened a car door.

In the light of the open door, Ella saw that it was a police hover cruiser. She stared at Mace. "Did you steal a police car?"

He laughed. It was a warm, lovely sound. "No, that belongs to Benny. He's a cop."

She turned to stare at Benny. "He is?"

"He just made detective. Homicide detective. He turns in the car tomorrow and rides plain after this."

Benny returned from the car, carrying the radio with him. "Guess which case I just caught? Now we really have to hide you. Mace?"

"Sure." He led Ella into the house while Benny started up the hover car and whooshed out of the garage. She heard the siren echoing after him, disappearing into the night.

Soon, a drone dropped a bundle of clothing at Benny's front door. There was also a box of hair dye. Mace helped her to turn her crinkly yellow hair a deep brown while she wore Benny's bathrobe. Afterward she changed into the jeans, tee-shirt, and tennies that had been dropped.

"Do you recognize me?" she asked Mace, twirling like a model before him.

He quirked up a corner of his mouth in a half-smile. "I would, but maybe no one else would."

Mace and Ella glued themselves to Benny's wall screen while they worked their way through his cupboard and refrigerator. Ella didn't think she'd ever been that hungry. The reports showed distraught ball-goers giving quotes.

*"I found him in a pool of blood in his room."*

"Who went into his room, I wonder," Ella said, pouring a bag of chips into a bowl and flopping beside Mace on the couch.

*"He danced with her most of the night, then she disappeared."*

*"I think he must have known her."*

*"I never saw her before in my life."*

*"No, I never saw anyone wearing shoes like that."*

*"The missing princess had them on, I'm pretty sure."*

The announcer said that a search was underway for the missing princess. She was wanted for questioning in connection with the death.

Mace frowned. "Some of this is damning. Benny is going to be in a lot of trouble for hiding you." He turned to Ella. "Did you stab him? Did you break the shoe and stab him with a piece of it?"

"No, of course not. But someone did."

"We'll have to figure out who, quick, so they'll quit hunting for you and Benny won't lose his job. It won't be long before the DNA trackers follow you here. What do you know about this?"

Ella scrunched her face in concentration. "I took the shoes off and stuck one in a planter, behind the plant."

"Who saw you do that?"

"I'm not sure. But I know my stepsisters were keeping their eyes on me while I danced with that pig, the prince."

"Don't say that. You can't give them any reason for thinking you didn't like him."

She jumped up. "Of course I didn't like him! He was forcing himself on me."

Mace reached up and took her hand. "I know. That's understandable. Just don't say things like that to anyone else, okay?" He pulled her down beside him.

"Sure. I'll watch it." But now she was watching those deep, dark eyes. They made her feel melty and soft and warm.

"I'd feel better if we were somewhere else," Mace said. "I hate to endanger Benny." After they cleaned up from their snacking, he led her to the garage where they each strapped on jet packs, then took off from the back yard.

Ella knew the DNA trackers had a hard time tracking airborne particles. It was easier to trace a path that lay on a surface. She followed Mace through the cool night air, their packs humming quietly while they circled the village, looking for a hideout. And hoping DNA trackers hadn't been improved greatly without the general public knowing about it.

Mace led them to a rooftop where they switched off the jetpacks. Ella was going to ditch hers there, but Mace said he didn't want to leave them behind to be found and possibly lead the authorities to them.

"Do you know this place?" Ella asked.

Mace grinned. "I live here. I don't think anyone will look here for you. There's nothing to connect us."

They walked down two floors to his apartment and switched on his wall screen, still anxious for the news.

"Fingerprint and DNA analysis from the glass shard are inconclusive," the news announcer was saying.

Ella snickered. "All the women wore gloves. What do they expect?"

Mace let Ella use his bed and he took the couch, but when she awoke sobbing in the early morning, he came to her and comforted her.

"Can I ever go home again?"

"Do you want to? To those awful stepsisters?"

She sighed deeply. "I can't stand them. But it's the only home I've ever known." He brushed the tears on her cheeks. "You know, on the way to the ball, I was happier than I've been since Daddy died. I was picturing me and the prince in a starter castle, having little princes and princesses. And having someone else do all the cooking and cleaning. Now what?"

"I can't give you a starter castle, but I have this apartment."

She looked around in the dark. "It's nice. I like it." They snuggled together and she fell asleep in his arms.

* * * *

When Mace's wrist phone buzzed, she woke up.

"It's Benny," he said. "They found a drop of the prince's blood on Ugg's gown and she's been arrested."

Ella let out a whoosh of air. Fleeing, she'd met Ugg near the bathroom and managed to let some blood drip from the piece of jagged glass onto her dress before she discarded the shard. It had worked. She was free.

Benny came over in the afternoon after doing all the cyber work required for the arrest. He and Ella and Mace talked eagerly about plans for the future. Benny wanted Ella to come live with him and his wife and kids until she got on her feet. It was wonderful having a real family again.

"I also think there's something I need to look into," Benny said. "I've always wondered if our dad was murdered. We need to look at Harrid Anne, Ugg, and Lee more closely for that."

Ella wondered if she could have just let one of the stepsisters do in the prince. Maybe they had experience at that sort of thing?

Kaye George: national-bestselling, multiple-award-winning author of historical, traditional, and cozy mysteries (upcoming: Vintage Sweets series). Her short stories are in anthologies, magazines, her own collection, and her recent anthology of eclipse stories, *Day of the Dark*, by Wildside Press. She reviews for *Suspense Magazine* and lives in Knoxville, TN. She's lived in several states, many of which, oddly enough, begin with the letter M. She's been honored with three Agatha Award nominations and one Silver Falchion. Her blogs are TravelsWithKaye.blogspot.com and KillerCharacters.com. Her webpage is KayeGeorge.com.

# THE GIFT OF THE CRYSTALS

## Cate Parker

### *Inspired by the story Diamonds and Toads*

Nova could finally pull the thick shades from the bubble window now that the second sun had disappeared behind the horizon. Clouds of scarlet dust whipped in shapes that reminded her of the swirling runes that early settlers of Soren-10 had discovered. No one had ever found the aliens of whatever civilization had been here first. It was probably for the best. Humans were always too eager to take over planets with any promise of benefiting them, and they could be brutal if met with resistance.

"The water!" called a voice down the hall. There was never any need to yell inside their small home, even when the dust storms lifted the few plants that could take root from their garden outside. Her mother and sister seemed to find some level of comfort in ordering her around. Years ago, their family had owned a mine on the planet, but it had collapsed when Nova was young. Her family had become even more impoverished since her father's death.

"I'm coming," she called. Nova plaited her hair and left her narrow room. Her mother and sister were at the table in their cramped kitchen, eating their breakfast from squeezable pouches. Nova glanced at the cupboard and considered grabbing something for herself, but her mother made a tutting noise.

"Nova, you should wait until you're back to eat. There's not much water to spare, and you know how I hate to take risks."

"Maybe you should get more tomorrow," said her sister, Zara. She took a long sip from her pouch. Whichever flavor she had chosen needed to be mixed with water before it could be eaten.

"We're working the mines tomorrow," said Nova. This was their one day off. She had to get water almost every day, but she tended to travel with a larger load on her day off. Since they couldn't afford fuel, she had to peddle their vehicle there and back. It was always hard to bring even a few gallons from the water station after she'd been in the mines all day.

Nova pulled the long cloak over her body, stuck her feet into the heavy boots, and then went outside through the sealing chambers attached to every building on the planet.

Another chamber opened to their pedicab. She eased the vehicle backward with the push of pedals. The price of fuel was so high on this planet that only mine owners seemed to be able to afford it. The people who came here, to Soren-10, had either been mine owners or desperate colonists who had no other choices when it came time to leave the ancient, crumbling space stations.

It was a horrible irony that the people who had to dig for the sparkling red crystals that turned into fuel were the ones who couldn't afford to do anything but trade those crystals for food.

After nearly an hour, she finally got to the well. That was without the extra weight of the water. Her legs weren't sore—yet. Still, she felt a phantom pain at the very idea of having to peddle back home with two hundred and fifty pounds of extra weight in the cart. There was a line, as always, and Nova waited patiently for her turn each time she filled a jug of five gallons. After five trips, she leaned against her vehicle, her cloak back on, sweat dripping down her neck from the exertion of carrying the jugs. She wasn't looking forward to the grueling transport home.

"Excuse me?" said a quiet voice.

Nova turned to a hunched figure standing nearby. She was in the same sort of cloak Nova wore, but hers was even shabbier than Nova's. She looked exhausted. "Yes, ma'am?" she asked.

"Could you help me, child? I should be able to peddle my water home, but I cannot manage the jug from the well to my pedicab." Her hand trembled as she held out the empty ten-gallon jug. Nova had a hard time believing that the woman could manage peddling it, but perhaps the woman lived closer than she did.

"Of course I will," Nova said, even though she knew that she'd both lose a precious half hour in waiting in line and that her arms and legs would be even sorer at the start of her return trip.

"You're so kind." The old woman looked relieved. "I've asked others, and they did not care to help me."

"You shouldn't think so badly of them," Nova said. "The sun felt especially hot today. Will you be safe peddling home?"

"I will," said the woman, patting Nova's hand. "If you can just help me get the water to the cab…"

Nova nodded, and the two of them stood in the long line, moving step by step as citizens filled their jugs with water. Everyone looked as worn out as Nova felt. The mines weren't easy on anyone. Supposedly their council spoke up for them and tried to get better conditions, but Nova had yet to see any positive changes in all the years she'd been mining.

"Do you live far?" the old woman asked.

"Yes." Nova nodded. "It's about forty miles away."

The old woman frowned. "And this is the closest watering station?"

"Unfortunately. They've said that they're going to dig another near us or create a piping system. But they've been saying that since before we moved there. I don't think we would have moved to that particular location without those promises."

"It's a pity," said the old woman. "There are so few who can be trusted to keep promises or to help. I wonder…" She glanced away. "If humans were always like this."

There was something odd about the way she said the word *humans*. But she was old, so Nova decided to pay it no mind. "I don't know," she admitted. "Everyone I've ever known, except my father, has focused on themselves and gone back on promises if it's not to their benefit."

"At least you have your father," the old woman said, patting her arm.

"He died seven years ago," Nova told her. "I'm alone in the world," she said. "And I know that's how it'll stay." The old woman frowned deeper and squeezed her arm before Nova held the jug out to be filled. They were quiet as the water sloshed and rose until it held the full ten gallons.

Nova fought to keep from looking sore and hurting as she carried the jug after the old woman. She wished that she could just put the jug down and ask someone else to help, just apologize to the old woman and be on her way.

But she'd just said that it was near impossible to find someone who would do as they said, so she kept going.

"This is my pedicab," the old woman said, opening the cargo hold for the jug. Nova placed it in carefully, breathing out a sigh of relief when the weight was finally out of her arms. She wiped sweat from her brow.

"Have a good afternoon, ma'am," she said, turning to quickly get to her pedicab.

"Nova, was it?" the old woman said.

Nova nodded and then paused. She didn't remember telling the woman her name.

The old woman just smiled before her features melted away. Her tanned, lined skin became darker and began to take on an almost rock-like consistency. Instead of the long limbs of a human, her arms seemed to shrink in on themselves and bulge into squat, thick arms that reminded

Nova more of the chunks of rock she climbed over in the mines than any humans.

"What…"

The rest of the body transformed until the old woman was anything but what she had once appeared to be. She was shorter, and her skin—if it could be called that—was a mottled dark red and brown. She had two eyes like a human and the same number of what appeared to be arms and legs, but that was about where the similarities stopped. Three fingers on each hand, eight toes on each wide, flat foot. There were several rows of teeth in the circle-shaped mouth. Nova felt a scream bubble inside her throat, but she couldn't let it escape.

"Don't scream," said the creature, in a rasping voice. "I will not harm you. I am one of the Azrum. This is our planet. We have allowed humans to stay here and mine what we do not need. But now we grow weary of the agony of your people and the moans of pain in the mines. I have been looking for someone who can speak up to the rulers of your kind. And now I have found that person." She pointed at Nova.

"No one will listen to me," said Nova, blinking rapidly. She had so many questions, but it was hard to choose just one.

"But they will," said the alien. She touched Nova's lips with one of her hard, rough fingers. "Every time you speak, you will have a gift of the crystals they so love. They will see that you are blessed by this planet and that you should be listened to."

"What?" said Nova. She was going to say more but before she could, a red crystal like the ones she mined fell to the ground. Nova knelt and picked it up, eyes wide. It was nearly a day's worth of work. The alien nodded. "How long will I have this gift?" she asked, more crystals falling from her lips.

"Forever," said the alien. "The leaders of our people also give wealth when they speak—both worldly and the treasure of guidance." She glanced up at the sky. "I must go. I will wait for you here tomorrow, and we may talk more." The creature seemed to melt into the ground and the vehicle vanished like a double sun illusion.

She wouldn't have made it home in time except for the fuel.

Fuel!

Nova didn't have to peddle at all. She felt guilty after using the crystals, but after speaking her guilt aloud, she had three more crystals to replace the ones she'd used.

"Mother!" she called as she rushed into the house, not even bothering to carry in the first jug. "Zara! Something incredible has happened to me!"

The crystals fell to the floor with plinks and thuds.

"What is it?" her mother asked, looking from behind a door. Her eyes were on Nova for only a moment before they caught sight of the crimson crystals. Her eyes widened with recognition. "Where did you get those?" she asked.

"An old lady at the water station blessed me," Nova said. "Well, I thought she was an old woman, but—"

"Give them to me," said her mother, dashing forward as more of the gifts dropped from Nova's lips. Her mother looked up at her in wonder. Her sister, who stood behind their mother, also looked dumbstruck.

"She was an alien," Nova said. "And she said because I helped her…" Her mother greedily snatched up the crystals that fell. "That I should become a leader, that they will see that the planet has blessed me so that they will always benefit from my words."

Her mother didn't even bother collecting what dropped this time. She glanced from Nova to her daughter. "Will you see her again?" she asked.

"She said she wants me to meet her tomorrow," said Nova.

"And what does she look like?" asked Zara.

"She appeared to me as an old woman, but as an alien she—"

Her mother nodded. "Tomorrow Zara will collect the water."

"What?" Nova said, confused. Clunk. "But that's my job."

"Pick that up," her mother said. "Find a safe place to hide it… Zara should go and be blessed as well. Just think of the fortune we'll have once both of you have a blessing like this! We could buy our own mines again, we could be among the elite. We could—"

"This is about helping people," Nova said, kneeling to scoop crystals into a bag. "This isn't about riches."

Her mother and sister snorted and closed the door to their mother's room behind them. Nova knew they were planning something. She put all that she had thus far collected under the sink in the kitchen before going to her little room and opening her worn holo-computer. Nova searched the network for information about the governor of the planet. She'd have to go to the capital city tomorrow and tell him of the alien.

However, when she woke, she was the only person in the house. The vehicle was gone, too. Her mother and sister had surely left in search of the old woman. Nova winced, wondering what her sister might say to the woman. Zara was the exact opposite of what the alien had wanted to find in humans.

There was nothing to do but wait for them to return and study the map of the planet. Nova memorized the trek to the closest town with a shuttle to the capital. Her mother and sister would have to beg rides from others to get to the mines, but she was leaving them enough crystals that they could easily pay for the help.

"You!" shrieked a voice. Her mother slammed the door of the chamber without even removing the over-suit. "You lied to us!" Nora blinked, confused, and her mother pointed toward the outside. Zara staggered toward them. She stepped into the pressure chamber but their mother locked the door.

"Don't you dare come in!" she cried.

"What is going on?" Nova asked, alarmed.

"Let me in," sobbed her sister, pounding on the door before shrieking. Nova saw little creatures falling to the floor of the chamber. Nova's stomach turned. The five-legged creature that resembled a spider was known for destroying the first few crops that colonists had planted. They had been driven back as far as humans could make them go. The snake-like creatures were iridescent and reflective—beautiful now, but deadly when deep in the mines where they hid, and they could bite. Other creatures she'd never seen or heard of before started dropping from Zara's mouth as well as she continued to pound on the door.

"There was no old woman," her mother seethed. "A beautiful woman asked us for help, but of course we denied her—we were waiting for the old woman. And so, she cursed your sister. Look at her! I can't let her inside."

Nova stared at Zara. She had slumped to the ground. "I'll go get help," Nova said as the crystals fell around her feet. "I'll send people to help you. There's plenty of fuel for you in the meantime."

She didn't let her mother answer. Nova pulled on her suit and grabbed what she'd packed before dashing around Zara's creatures and hopping into the vehicle. She used some of her fuel to make the vehicle move at a breakneck speed, a luxury she had never had before.

She sent a doctor to visit her home once she reached the transport station. Everyone stared at her as the crystals slipped from her lips. Whispers followed her as she went to pay for a shuttle ticket. No one sat by her in the waiting room, but she could feel dozens of eyes on her. She just counted the minutes until the transport would arrive and take her away.

"Excuse me," said a voice. She looked up and saw a handsome young man. "May I sit here?"

She nodded and he took a seat, studying her.

"I have been told that there is something unusual about the way you speak."

Nova glanced to the side.

"They say crystals fall from your mouth."

She still didn't respond. But instead of walking away, he gave a deep, throaty chuckle. "I do hope it's true," he mused. "After all, I've been waiting for the one who will speak for the planet."

Nova slowly turned to look at him. His eyes brightened.

"Ah, so the rumors must be true. What is your name?"

"Nova," she said, a crystal falling to her lap.

"And I am Thane. My father is the governor of this planet." He shook his head at her. "No, don't look too surprised. I'm not nearly as impressive as that makes me sound. But a creature appeared to me last night and told me that you would come here soon. An alien, after all this time.... Well, it told me that I was to find you and take you to my father."

"And then what?" Nova asked, letting everything fall to the floor. Her heart was beating faster and faster.

"You are going to be the richest woman on the planet," Thane said. "Richer than he is. And that is going to give you more than enough power to sway him from his treatment of the people and the very land. I've tried to convince him to do right, but it's never done any good. But you— Well, Nova. The transport is here, and I hope you'll come with me."

She nodded, smiling brightly, and took his hand.

Before long, Nova and Thane were considered the most influential of the citizens on Soren-10. And while Nova made sure that her mother and sister were cared for, she kept them far away from her so that her true focus would be the planet and colonists—as well as Thane, the man she loved.

---

Cate Parker enjoys sci-fi stories of all sorts, but you'll never find her in a spaceship even if she had the chance. She'd much rather keep her feet on the ground and enjoy life with her husband and children, dreaming about the universe instead of chancing being lost in it. You can learn more about Cate and her projects at cateparker.com.

# THE GIRL WITH THE CYBERNETIC HANDS

## John Donald Carlucci

*Inspired by The Girl with the Silver Hands*

Rathbone "Rat" Grey stared across the diner at his prey. An old man sat at the counter and sipped slowly at his piping-hot soy-caff. His frayed collar and unraveling sweater clearly advertised the social rung of the ladder he clearly clung to desperately. A sour smile crossed the criminal's face as he moved to sit in the seat next to the old man.

"I haven't got any money," the old man said, his eyes registering the fear he felt realizing a situation had developed he was most unequipped to handle.

"Calm yourself, old man," Rat said as he motioned to the decaying robo-unit behind the counter. The squealing of its gears as it slid along the counter edge was enough to set his teeth on edge. The whole diner was a rotting dinosaur from the early 2050s and deserved a mag in the brain to end its misery. Rat doubted any techservers had repaired or cleaned any of the joint's mechs in the last ten years. "What's your name, pops?"

"I said I don't want no trouble," the old man said as he stood to leave. Rat grabbed his arm and yanked the old man back into his seat. The criminal's upper lip twitched as he pulled a small vibroblade from his pocket and ignited the blade. The old man practically stank from the fear and adrenaline coursing through his frail body. Rat enjoyed the genuine terror that paled the man's skin.

"I said I wanted your name." Rat spread the old man's hand on the counter and slowly tapped the counter surface between the elderly man's fingers. Wisps of smoke lifted from where the white-hot blade tip melted the counter top.

"I must ask you to stop destroying private property or I will notify the authorities," squealed the robo-unit's voice from its tinny speaker.

"My name is Peter Davis," the old man said as he yanked his hand free of the ruffian.

"Well, Mister Peter Davis." Rat extended the blade to its full length of two feet and sliced the robo-unit in half. Disengaging the blade and pocketing the handle, Rat smiled another sour smile that revealed his silver teeth. "I have a deal for you and I think you really want to consider it before saying no."

"I've said it already, I have nothing." Peter shivered in his seat as he turned his watery eyes toward the threatening young man. He knew who the Rat was, as anyone living in this neighborhood did. Peter knew he was a ruthless thug who ran all of the rackets in Old Steel district. He'd also heard the rumors that Rat's business ventures had been hemorrhaging money. No one knew how or why, but Rat had his wireheads searching everywhere for the syndicate wireheads brave enough to screw with him.

Whispered wire had it that Rat was rolling snake eyes.

"You have a Think-Box, don't you?"

"Everyone does, it's the law." Peter was confused. His Think-Box was connected to his home service unit and allowed him to do everything from communicate with his daughter Ashley, to receive his corp-script, to voting. It was a silly question, but the realization of what Rat wanted froze his guts like an icy wind.

"I want to buy it," Rat said as he fanned out an array of corp-script in a variety of colors and values. It was enough to feed his daughter and himself on real meat for years. No more of those bland soy steaks the corps provided. Peter's hand twitched as he tried not to grab the script from Rat's hands.

"Why do you want it? You know the trouble I will get in if I file a replacement claim? The corps will just turn it off when I do."

"I don't care what you do, old man. I just need what's behind your system firewall for one night and I will pay greatly for it," Rat said as he added more script to the pile.

"Take it," Peter choked out as he grabbed the script. He knew nothing about firewalls or networks. That was his daughter's domain. All he knew was a small fortune had dropped in his lap. He was about to thank the Rat when red and blue lights began streaming down the street at the same moment wailing sirens split the silence.

"That shitty robot waiter must have gotten off a 9-1-1 before I killed it," Rat said as he grabbed Peter's arm and yanked him toward the door. "We've got some work to do, old man."

While not a wirehead, Rat did possess considerable skill as a hacker himself and he quickly opened the log on the old man's Think-Box. The criminal hastily reviewed what had been happening on Peter's home network. Rat's wireheads could have penetrated that network without Peter's Think-Box, but Rat liked to compartmentalize things. His crew had given him the general location, but Rat had handled the surveillance himself. No use in letting those junkies get close to a new idea of how to rip him off. He wanted to plug that hole. Rat paid the auto-car when they arrived at Peter's building and tossed the Think-Box back to the old man as they exited the vehicle.

"See, now you don't even have to file a complaint."

"But I still keep the script?" the old man asked shakily.

"Just shut up and take me upstairs," Rat demanded as he pushed Peter toward the squalid building.

"We didn't talk about this." Peter practically squealed from fright.

"Should we talk about this?" Rat asked as he flashed his vibroblade. Peter said nothing as he realized the terrible mistake he had made in accepting Rat's money and led the criminal into the building.

* * * *

Ashley sat at her holotab and scanned the spreadsheets she had just found. Her holotab was a scavenged unit she had customized herself from discarded tech she'd found while foraging in the Old Steel district. The tablet was voice-activated or a holographic keyboard could be projected out. She couldn't stand the idea of, nor afford to become a wirehead. Supposedly, wireheads were more proficient hackers since they were mentally wired into their equipment, but the tech caused them such pain they became addicted to the drug Blue Smoke. It killed the pain until their systems adjusted to the dosages and the wireheads took more and more of the drug. Ashley shivered at the thought and remembered watching her mother wither away from the drug's ravaging dosage increases.

Ashley's tech talents were natural, as was her wish to help the hospices where the wireheads eventually wound up after Blue Smoke turned their brains to mush. Help that could only be found by stealing script from the accounts of people who couldn't care less about the Smokies. Ashley had been draining the particularly plump accounts of a criminal named Rathbone Grey, when she noticed something odd.

Her father's Think-Box had accessed the house logs a few minutes before. She had not wiped those yet because her firewall had been secure, and she would have done so in a few minutes. She was confused because her father couldn't record a vid without screwing up the broadcast settings. He wouldn't even know what a log contained, let alone access one. It was just as she realized what had happened when the door of the meager apartment burst in.

"Dollface, just sit there or I kill poppa here," Rat yelled as he flashed the vibroblade he held at Peter's throat.

"Oh, Dad," she whispered as she slid back from the holotab.

"I'm sorry, Ashley." Peter looked impossibly smaller as he visibly shook with fear. Life had broken her father and the loss of her mother had completed the job. "He offered me so much money."

"Kiddo, you have had a hell of a ride on my coattails," Rat said as he moved over to where she sat. He glanced at the screen and smirked. "Christ, lady, you're still milking me dry!"

Ashley said nothing as she defiantly stared up at the criminal.

"Okay, enough chitchat. I want my money back," Rat said as he looked around the clean, but empty unit. "It isn't like you spent any on a nicer shit-hole."

"It's gone," Ashley said.

"What do you mean, little girl?" Any lingering cordiality had disappeared and only the ugliness remained in Rat's voice. He leaned in as he extended the vibroblade again to its full two-foot length. "I'm not playing games. Return every last piece of script to my accounts."

"You've donated all those funds to charity, just like these now." Ashley said as she reached out her hands to hit the last holokeys to transfer more funds. Rat screamed as he slashed the vibroblade down and severed Ashley's arms mid-forearm. The blade was so hot that the wounds were cauterized immediately, and it took a shocked few seconds for the pain to punch Ashley hard. Her shrieks were almost as loud as her father's and she tumbled from her seat to the floor.

"Aw, shit," Rat muttered as he slid the blade back into his pocket. Despite being useless, Peter moved quickly to his daughter's side and lifted her from the floor. His eyes flared with anger and violence, but that slipped away as the old man realized he could do nothing in the end. Rat slid two cards onto the table. "Take her to the DocBox at the end of the hall and use this credit voucher to get her fixed up."

"Right," the old man barked as he leaned down to snatch up the cards. "What's the other one?"

"The name of the man and company your girl is going to steal from to make up for my losses. She's good, better than my wireheads. I want twice what she took and she can keep whatever else she finds as compensation. She shouldn't have pissed me off. I get angry and can't help myself sometimes. We could have worked this out better."

"How the hell is she supposed to code without hands?" Peter pleaded.

"She can still talk, can't she?"

\* \* \* \*

Ashley could only remember bits and pieces from the incident three days before. She had been asleep much of the time while the nanotech bandages from the auto-DocBox accelerated the healing in her stumps. Peeling the deactivated wraps from her arms with her teeth, Ashley could see the burnt tissue had been replaced with smooth pink skin. Her arms ended beneath the elbow and Ashley knew there was nothing like a transplant or biomech replacements in her future. That kind of credit and access was available only to the cloudwalkers in their thousand-story high-rises. Without Rat's voucher, she would only have received bare minimum medical attention from the DocBox. Aspirin and bandages were the best sprawlers like her could expect.

Too bad it was Rat who had created the situation he paid for in the first place.

It took twenty minutes for Ashley to get her tablet set up on the table and Rat's card next to it. Peter had left hours before to hide in one of his coffee shops or bars. Ashley was fine with not staring into his guilt-ridden face anymore.

She had work to do.

"Tabitha02," Ashley said as the tablet activated. It was comforting to name her tech after her mother and it felt like Ashley was speaking to her at times. "Activate handicapped mode."

Even though she had cobbled her equipment together from scraps, Ashley was proud of her tech and smiled broadly as a holographic keyboard appeared floating in air above the tablet.

"Expand keyboard by 300 percent," she said. The keyboard grew in size, so each key was now five inches by five inches. "Perfect."

Ashley started typing slowly by hitting each key with her right and left stumps. She grimaced at both the pain, as the pain-killers could only handle so much, and the awkwardness of typing with essentially two fingers. Curious, Ashley entered the card information. Her father had explained what Rat's expectations were, and began to research her so-called target.

Jason Pear was the CEO of a boutique pharmaceutical and medical research and development company with new civilian and military contracts. An up-and-coming firm that had recently gone public after a successful human trial of an inhibitor for Anderson's (wirehead) addiction. Ashley became intrigued and spent the afternoon learning more about

Pear and his vision.

* * * *

Rat stared at his screen, cloned to Ashley's tablet, and studied what she studied. While he wanted his money back, Rat was growing more interested in Ashley. She was magnificent in her endurance and her will-power. He regretted losing his temper as he had, but Rat was feeling a great need for her growing in his belly. When he felt that need, he had no qualms about taking the object of his desire. No one just gave you anything in this world.

* * * *

Ashley sat on a bench near the modest thirty-story building that served as the headquarters for Pear Industries. She fully realized how risky and just plain silly it was to break someone's code directly outside their building, but Ashley didn't care any longer. She was faced with an ugly choice offered by an even uglier man and she just did not care. Besides, it was a lovely evening and there was a delightful pear tree sitting majestically on the grounds of Pear Industries. She smiled lightly as she began to type again with her holographic keyboard.

* * * *

The buzzing of his com shook Jason Pears from his thousand-yard-stare. The boredom of his infinite number of reports frequently caused Jason to fall down a rabbit hole, but it was rare he was interrupted at this time of night.

"Go ahead," Pears said as he pushed the com button.

"This is Harris in security and we have a breach."

"Harris, just be concise."

"Sir, sorry, we have a breach into the financial division. A low priority account is being diverted."

"Really? Our security systems are good. I know, I pay for them."

"Yes sir," Harrison said with a slight gulp, but enough of one to make Pears smile. "We're tracking the penetration and the wirehead seems to be right outside the building. We're dispatching security now."

"Have you tracked the transfer?"

"Yes, that's the weird part, sir."

"Weird?"

"The money has been transferred to a hospice that cares for Blue Smokers and wireheads."

"You mean Anderson's Addiction, don't you?" Pears said with an edge to his voice.

"Sorry sir, slip of the tongue."

"Tell security to contain the area, but don't approach."

"Why not, sir?"

"Because I'm bored and heading downstairs myself."

* * * *

Pears leaned against a light-post and watched the young woman pinpointed by his security team. He was amazed that although she was missing most of her arms, she had still managed to get by his top cyber team and their wares.

"Hi there," he shouted at the startled girl. He walked briskly over to her and smiled. "Calm down, I won't hurt you."

"I know you," she smiled with her eyes clouded in sadness. "You're Jason Pears, aren't you?"

"Guilty as charged." He winced at his stupid joke.

"Yeah, I looked you up before coming here tonight. I did a great deal of research on you, actually."

"Really?"

"Yeah and I suppose your corporate goons are waiting in the shadows to apprehend me."

"Goons," Jason shouted at the shadows. "Be off with you."

Ashley stared at the handsome, but tired man with the quirky smile. "Are you for real?"

"Are you? I understand you raided one of my building maintenance accounts and diverted the funds to a hospice for Anderson's Addiction. You understand full well that my company is losing script on and for the treatment of said disease, but diverted those funds assuming I wouldn't care if discovered. Am I close?"

"Spectacularly so, but I don't know why you would incur such a loss. Corps and cloudwalkers don't have hearts," Ashley said, clumsily folding up her holotab.

"This one does," Pears said quietly.

"Why?"

"Because my grandfather, on my mother's side, was a Blue Smoker. I still remember the stories he told me when I was a child and too hyper to fall asleep. I also listened to those stories as he lay dying, a wire addict, and he couldn't string two solid sentences together."

"Oh." Ashley was embarrassed that her research had not been complete enough.

"Let's discuss it over a drink upstairs," Pears said as he motioned upward to his penthouse.

"You know I had planned on being arrested after I broke in, right?"

"Maybe later, after you tell me your name."

"Ashley."

"Nice, but I still need that drink."

\* \* \* \*

Rat screamed in fury. He was prone to random and intense fits of anger and Ashley was the source of his ire. Rat had nearly had a stroke when Ashley transferred the money she was supposed to steal for him to those smokers! Now she'd been out of his reach for weeks while she stayed with that cloudwalker Pears.

However, Rat had an idea on how to deal with Ashley.

\* \* \* \*

"What is this?" Ashley asked as Pears laid a long box on her lap.

"I'd tell you to open it and see, but…" He motioned at her stumps.

"Ass," Ashley laughed as he opened the box to reveal two silver and high-tech prosthetic hands. They were delicate and beautiful. "Oh, Jason."

"I run a medical corp. Who is better suited to helping you than I?" Pears said as he helped Ashley slip on the hollow prosthetics. He watched as the silver hands started responding immediately to Ashley's mental commands and smiled.

"They are magnificent! I can feel with them, Jason," Ashley said as tears streamed down her face. "I can't possibly thank you enough."

"Maybe you can figure out something when I return from New Chicago."

"I don't want you to go," she whispered.

"I know, but think of how much fun we'll have when I get back." Pears said as he kissed her and left his new love with a heavy heart.

\* \* \* \*

Hours later on the bullet train, Pears was surprised and sickened to receive an email he'd never expected. Harris was notifying him that additional thefts had just occurred from more accounts at Pears Industries. The transfers had occurred within the building and Ashley Davis was assumed to be the culprit.

Harris was a thorough and exceptional security officer. Pears trusted his judgment, as he would his own. Pears had been wronged in the past, but never betrayed like this. Pears dashed off an email telling Harris to escort Ashley from the building and bar her access. The cyber team was to shut down outside access to the accounts until he returned, He wanted a complete audit of security and options when he got back.

Damn her.

* * * *

Rat laughed his ass off.

He had spoofed the security email information and sent the message to Pears from Ashley's access through her holotab in the corps' network. He captured and leaked Pears' responding email back to Ashley and his spies outside reported her fleeing the building.

Rat figured he would let her stew a bit before making his move.

* * * *

Ashley had known things were too good to last between a sprawler and a corporate one-percenter like Jason Pears. She couldn't believe he had lost such confidence in her after the first sign of trouble.

"What's wrong?" her father asked as he opened the door to find her crying in the hallway. She threw her arms around him and just let go. She cried so hard, she forgot how much her new prosthetics made her stumps itch.

* * * *

Four days later, Pears walked into the security office for an update from Harris concerning the system audit. Negotiations were long and tough with Gene Corp in New Chicago and he did not have the time to speak to his people about the transgression. He trusted them to do their jobs until he returned.

The man looked bewildered at his boss.

"I have no idea what you're talking about, sir. Our systems have been fine with no reported incidents."

"I got your email about the thefts and Ashley," Pears said.

"I'm sorry sir, but I still have no idea about any emails or security breaches." Pears looked at the man with a sickening realization.

"Is Ashley in the building?"

"No sir, she checked out of the building four days again and has not returned."

Pears turned and left the room quickly.

* * * *

Still miserable, Ashley had not left her father's apartment since flee-ing Pears Industries. Her prosthetics were itching horribly. She knew she couldn't afford any adjustments she needed to stop the irritation and was just about to remove them. With slim hope, Ashley rushed to the door.

"Jason?" she cried as she yanked the door open, only to find Rat smiling at her.

"No, my little bird," he said as he pushed her back and entered the apartment. "Ah, I see your cloudwalker has given you new wings."

"What are you doing here, Rat?"

"Taking what is owed me."

"Weren't my arms enough for you?" she snarled as she tried to slap Rat. The criminal caught her silver hand in his own and examined the gleaming prosthetic.

"Fine workmanship," he said as he twisted her arm and Ashley fell to the floor. "I want the script you were to steal for me twice. I guess we have to work out some other arrangements."

"You forged those emails, you pig," Ashley spat back at the crime lord.

"You stole from me twice, gutter-bitch. I had to get you away from your corporate keeper somehow, didn't I? His trip came at the perfect time to divide and conquer," Rat said as he reached for the woman. Pears burst into the open apartment and grabbed Rat from behind.

"Get off her!" he yelled with the full intent of saving his love, but cloudwalkers like him were not trained combatants. They hired security forces to protect them and never left them behind when planning to be a hero.

It took only an elbow and two punches to Pears' face for Rat, a street trained fighter, to take down the would-be savior.

"Okay, arsehole, we play for real," Rat said as he pulled the vibro-blade from his pocket and extended it to full length. Pears closed his eyes as the thug swung the blade at his face faster than the cloudwalker could imagine. He heard the sizzle of the blade for longer than he expected and opened his eyes.

"What the hell are you doing?" Rat asked as he stared at Ashley, holding the vibroblade inches from Pears' face.

"Damn, those really do have a high melting point," Pears said with considerable relief.

"You're lucky I'm such a forgiving person when it comes to ass-holes," Ashley said. She yanked the blade from Rat's hands and shattered the control unit. Before the criminal could say or do anything else, she punched him square in the face. Not realizing how strong the prosthetics were, Ashly ended up knocking Rat out. "That's for taking my arms."

"Before you punch me with those, can I apologize profusely?"

"How about you fix the connections on this thing and we call it even? They are itching like crazy."

"Well," said Pears as he hit a series of buttons on each limb, "there is good reason for that. See, I kept an additional function of the prosthetics a secret for when I got back. These are a prototype unit going to market soon. Not only do they function as limbs…"

"What?" Ashley gasped in surprise as both prosthetics unfolded and dropped to the floor. In their place were two freshly grown and bright pink arms, ending in hands.

"But they grow back replacement limbs within three days." Pears smiled sheepishly back at the crying woman as she hugged herself. "Surprised?"

"What are we going to do about him?" Ashley asked. She pointed at the unconscious criminal crumpled in a corner of the apartment.

"I'll call Harris to get a detail over here and turn him over to the authorities," Pears said as he typed a message into his Think-box for his security chief.

"That's good," Ashley said with a thin-lipped smile. "How did you know I was in trouble?"

"I didn't know. I was coming to apologize and overheard this ruckus coming down the hallway. Do you think I would have left my security team behind if I thought there would be trouble?"

"Do you think I'm not trouble?"

"This is going to cost me, isn't it?"

"Yeah, you're going to need to buy me a lot of stuff."

"I figured as much," Pears said with a smile as he held out his Obsidian card.

"First, let's talk about that hefty donation you're going to make to the Addison's hospice."

JDC (b. 1965) is an American writer and artist who lives and works in PDX. JDC has studied several disciplines ranging from pen and ink, painting, and assemblage art. Recent exhibitions include: Rusty Epiphanies: Darke Ruminations (2013) and Gods and Monsters (2015). He is currently writing an animated H.P. Lovecraft series he is hoping to produce as well as his first full length novel. His clients include Nikki Finke's Hollywood Dementia, *Strange Aeons* magazine, H.P. Lovecraft Film Festivals PDX and Providence, *Astonishing Adventures* magazine, 20th Century Fox International Theatrical Marketing, and LoveCraft Wines. Visit his website at www.John-DonaldCarlucci.com.

# CHOSEN ONE

## Maki Morris

*Inspired by Japanese folklore*

W̶e scurried along the forest edge like a pack of fearful rodents. The night was lit bright by the light of a full moon. We crept and dashed from one patch of shadow to the next, all the while turning our gaze toward the sky in search of the winged hunters in pursuit of their prey.

Our outing was intended to last for no more than three days. A pilgrimage to pay homage to the great Sun Goddess. To beg mercy for our ailing parents, who were struck down by a mysterious illness that had rendered our country without its Emperor and Empress. While the military braced for imminent threat of Mongol invasion, our court officials scattered about the imperial palace like ants on scorched earth.

In such times of uncertainty and dire pandemonium, women were expected to recede into the shadows. Thus my sister, Misaki, and I were cast out on a spiritual journey in the most oppressive time of the year. The summer heat had drained our spirits and burdened us with fatigue. Therefore, when we happened upon a small patch of forest, amidst miles of open road, we all rejoiced in unison and thanked the gods for their protection.

However, such a moment of joy quickly turned into unfathomable horror, when our camp was attacked by a small army of unknown foe. The assailants descended upon us cloaked within a mist. Winged and shadowy creatures, no doubt formed and spit out from Hell, unleashed their attack in eerie silence and with brutal skill. They slaughtered my one hundred soldiers in a matter of a heartbeats' time. No amount of expert warrior training could have saved my men from such an enemy. The soldiers' horrendous shrieks of anguish and pain will forever be the source of my nightmares.

The four of us remaining, who have miraculously survived the massacre, quickened our steps toward the lonely light emanating from a dwelling up the road, glowing and beckoning like fire signals to aid lost ships to a safe harbor.

Colonel Masamoto was first to reach the dilapidated wooden fence that surrounded the house within. He motioned us to a halt with a lift of his hand. He then dropped to one knee in front of my sister and said, "Your Highness, allow me to inspect the house for your safety."

My sister gave her permission with a quick nod of her head.

The Colonel then turned his attention to Sen, a traveler who happened to be passing by when the attack took place. He had single-handedly saved me from becoming a victim of the winged assailant. Although I was grateful for his bravery, the Colonel remained cautious as he said, "At this moment, I have no other choice but to place trust in you. I demand your word that you will protect the princesses and accompany them to safety, should I not return."

My sister took a sharp intake of breath upon hearing the Colonel's command. I have known for many months of Misaki and the Colonel's clandestine meetings. As a royal princess, my sister was to be married off to the House of Minamoto as a token to strengthen their allegiance to my father. However, the heart is a greedy, obstinate organ, especially when it comes to love, as it brazenly feigned blindness toward the edict of duty and obligation.

Sen placed his hand to his chest and bowed his head. "You have my word, sir, that I will give my life to protect the Royal Highnesses."

With a stern glance over at Sen, the Colonel disappeared into the darkness beyond the front gate. The stillness in the air was unnerving. The summer nights are normally brimming with the sound of cicadas and crickets, but this night was ominously silent of any. Even the breeze could not be felt, leaving the night still and silent, as if to forewarn of a hidden danger.

Our attention was focused at the front gate, anxiously awaiting the Colonel's emergence. Time seemed to standstill and my patience was wearing thin, when finally, the Colonel strode out from the front entry followed behind by a small, hunched figure carrying a lantern.

"Here is a good lady of the house come to pay Your Royal Highnesses a proper welcome," exclaimed the Colonel. An elderly woman attired in a faded, tattered kimono scurried forward in front of us. She placed the lantern on the ground and bowed deeply. "My house has never been so blessed as to receive such noble guests. We are profoundly honored to welcome you to our humble home."

When she rose from her bow, she picked up the lantern and raised it high to look us over. The light illuminated the old woman's saggy, coarse skin, and the unsightly lines that etched deep across her forehead and around her mouth. Her cloudy eyes drank in our looks with hunger like a wolf appraising its prey.

Misaki stepped forward and took command. "My good woman, you have the gratitude of my father, the Emperor, for offering us your hospitality."

The old woman bowed low again. "You do us great favor. Please come in and allow us to serve you."

My sister and I followed the woman into the dark house. From what I could make out in meager light, the house was square in shape with a small courtyard at the center, full of dead weeds and rock-strewn bare earth. My senses escalated to a heightened state of alertness when an indefinable scent assaulted my nose, a strange mix of sweet, salty, and metallic.

"Here we are!" said the old woman as she motioned us into the first room on the left. She placed the lantern on the floor and moved across the room to gather up seating mats. She placed the mats before us and said, "Please sit and rest. I will be back in a moment with refreshments."

My sister stood still to appraise the filthy, threadbare mat placed in front of her. With a swish of her kimono, she knelt and sat upon it. Her spine erect and tall, she smiled and lowered her head toward the old woman.

"I shall be but a moment," said the old woman as she disappeared down the hallway.

"Sit!" hissed my sister. I stared at the unsightly mat and swallowed down my revulsion. As I finally yielded to my sister's command, Colonel Masamoto strode into the room. But he came in alone. I did not see Sen follow.

"Colonel, where is Sen?"

The Colonel kneeled and bowed. He then went to grab a mat and placed it on the other side of my sister. He adjusted his sword and scabbard, and sat down. He did not meet my eyes when he said, "Your Highness, I think best that Sen should remain outside."

I was about to protest and demand explanation, when my sister's hand gripped my wrist with such force that I quickly understood that the subject was no longer open for discussion.

My mind whirled with speculation as to what might have occurred between Sen and the Colonel, while my heart ached for Sen's unfortunate predicament.

I took a deep breath for courage as I was about to insist that Sen be allowed inside, when the old woman returned with a tray. Upon entering the room, she placed the tray on the floor before us and bowed again.

She then placed the cups and plates in front of us and said, "I have brought tea and sweets for Your Royal Highnesses and something more palatable for the Colonel." The old woman's eyes seem to glint as she placed a sake pitcher in front of the Colonel.

The Colonel's already beautiful features brightened further when he saw the pitcher. The old woman raised the cup and offered it to him. "Sir, allow me to pour you a cup."

The Colonel gratefully accepted the cup as the old woman poured sake into it.

The old woman then smiled mischievously as she gazed upon the Colonel while he drank it down in one smooth motion. "There is plenty more, so do drink up!"

I knew my sister was as famished as I was, yet as a paragon of noble birth, she leisurely drank her tea and daintily partook of the red bean sweets. While half of a cake still remained on her plate, my teacup and plate were both empty. Poor Sen's plight completely forgotten, I shamelessly tried to catch the old woman's eyes to have her attend to my empty dish.

We all sat in such contentment to have found shelter and nourishment that when the Colonel began to sway violently clutching his chest, both Misaki and I sat immobile. For a moment, our brains doubted what our eyes were seeing.

However, when I saw the look of excitement and triumph illuminate the old woman's features, the hideous image instantly released me from the hypnotic hold. *She had poisoned the Colonel!*

As the Colonel lay flat on his back, writhing like a basin full of eels, my sister reached out to place her hand on his chest and began to say something to me. But strangely, I could not hear a thing. My vision grew blurred, and my head felt too heavy to be balanced upon my shoulders. My hands instinctively extended toward my sister, clawing at the space between us as if I were drowning. But the darkness seized and pulled me under, into a nameless place between reality and abyss.

\* \* \* \*

I slowly gained consciousness to the soothing sound of rustling water nearby. A cool breeze brushed against my cheek. For a brief moment, I was certain that this was a dream. A wonderful dream of napping on the soft, tall grass by the seashore.

"Mayu!"

"Mayu!"

I heard someone calling my name from afar. I tried to focus, but my mind fought to remain within the dream. When the caller's plea grew insistent and frenzied, I forced my eyes to open.

I awoke on a dampened river bank. My eyes were still blurry, but I could make out two large mounds of dry leaves that burned brightly, illuminating the area where the old woman was busying herself over a wheelbarrow.

"You are alive!" whispered my sister. Misaki's porcelain white face glowed like a full moon from the nearby firelight. A beautiful feature known to cause such fierce frenzy amongst the court artists was now marred with dirt covered tear streaks.

"Where are we?" I tried to push myself off the ground, but my hands were useless, bound with thick rope.

"Here, let me help." My sister scooted and wiggled her own bound body close to mine, so I could lean against her to right myself. By the time I had achieved the upright position, I was covered in sweat from exhaustion and a dull pounding in my head.

I had to concentrate to survey my surroundings. We sat on a small clearing by the river that fed into a large lake. Thick wooded forest lay on either side of the river that gave me ideas as to our possible escape route.

I then saw the old woman hunched over at the river's edge, sharpening a menacing looking knife. I felt a chill travel down my spine with frightening thoughts of what she was planning to do with that knife. As I continued to look about me I saw a slumped figure of a man tied to a tree. His face downcast. But the familiar look of the gleaming, black armor told me that the man tied to the tree was our Colonel.

I could not restrain myself when I turned to my sister and said, "Has she killed him?"

"Shh! We must be quick about it!" My sister hissed at my ear.

"I do not understand!" My heart pounded in my chest like a beast trying to free itself from my ribcage.

"There is no time to waste! Make haste and turn around so I can undo your binding. We must get to our daggers and end our lives with honor before that she-devil can murder us both!"

For a moment, it seemed as if she spoke to me in a language I could not comprehend. As a royal princess, I was made aware that we were the descendants of Goddess Amaterasu, divine blood flowed through our veins and thus our bodies and souls were sacred. Therefore, before any possible desecration of our bodies could take place, we were taught from young age to help each other leave this world with honor. A dagger to the heart.

I knew what was expected of me, yet my mind struggled with my sister's morbid scheme. Out of obedience, I turned my back to her. While my sister's hands pulled and yanked at the rope, she whispered, "Once we have freed ourselves, the deed must be carried out quickly. You must not give way to a moment of hesitations, do you hear? If we could just get a little running start toward each other, that will help drive the dagger deep into our hearts!"

I felt queasy and barely able to breathe. In that moment, I not only was unable to divulge the fact that I had lost my dagger during the night's attack, but I was also uncertain that I had the courage to thrust a dagger into my sister. Death with honor was a proper way to leave this world, yet would such an act still be considered murder? My conscience was torn between my obligation to Misaki and the eternal condemnation of my soul.

Then my mind turned to Sen. He was out there somewhere. Surely he could be counted upon to come to our aid. "Misaki, have you seen Sen? He can save us!"

I heard my sister's voice shake with emotion. "Mayu, I fear we are alone without any hope. When he was denied entrance to the house, I'm sure he did not remain long."

I was consumed with panic when I felt someone loom over me. It was the old woman with a knife in hand and a smug sneer. "You have woken just in time!"

I feigned courage. "I-I command you to free us right this moment!"

Instead of complying with my request, the old woman's eyes grew wild with malevolence as she took her knife's sharp edge and placed it beneath my chin. "*You* command *me*?"

My sister pressed her body into my back with a whimper. I do not know where I even found the courage to speak when I shouted, "We are the daughters of your Emperor! You will do as you are told before my army descends upon this miserable place and exterminates you!"

The old woman began to cackle, exposing her mouth full of strange sharp teeth. "Such display of heroics! Little Princess, do not think I am ignorant of what has become of your army!"

The knife against my throat was pressed deeper. "All that fussing and screaming. But in the end, your army was no match for *mine*!"

As if someone had poured liquid metal into me, I felt a kind of reckless hardiness form within my body. Perhaps it was due to the knowledge that I was a hair's breadth away from death itself, and if I could not achieve an honorable death, then at least I would not leave this world as a coward.

"*Your* army? I will wager everything dear to me that you will not be able to produce your so-called army here and now! You are a deceitful fool!"

She could have simply slit my throat and have done with it, but the old woman leered back. "Before I dissect you two into pieces, allow me to grant you your last wish."

The old woman carefully slid the knife back into the scabbard tied around her waist. She then turned and walked a few steps toward the river's edge. She faced the water and raised her arms out. Suddenly, I saw a bright green light appear on her wrists. A light so bright it lit up the old woman's face and body. But while my mind was stunned to have witnessed such devilish sorcery, mist began to rise from the lake. The surrounding air began to vibrate with strange humming sound that shimmied the water's surface and made leaves on the ground shudder. It was as if a huge legion of locusts was descending upon us.

I felt Misaki working furiously on my binding again. "As soon as I get you freed, you must run! Run into the forest and do not look back!"

As the cord fell from my wrist, I instantly began to work on Misaki's bindings. But my sister yanked her wrist out from my grasp. "Go! Go and save yourself now!"

"I am not leaving!" I reached for her bound hands again, but this time I grasped it tighter. My sister protested but I was determined to set her free.

I had successfully unwound the last bit of rope from her wrist when I noticed that the mist had formed into a wide column above the lake. And what emerged from there nearly struck me dead from fright.

Nearly twenty winged, dark creatures flew out from the misty column like a swarm of wasps fleeing their nest. Images of the assailants, I thought I had espied from the night of the attack, did not even come close to the horror my eyes were seeing at that moment. These creatures were made of black, dull metal, resembling the skeletal shape of a half man, half spider with rotating sword-like blades that kept them afloat in midair.

I felt Misaki yank my arm, but I could not move nor look away. My eyes were seized by the effortless manner in which the creatures soared through the air, with the dexterity of birds with glowing green eyes, as they circled above our heads like filthy flock of buzzards impatient to pick through our bones.

The old woman now stood before us with triumphant glee. "You should have taken heed to your nursemaids' cautionary tales to be wary of strangers. Especially those that seem innocent and readily accommodating!"

Her vice-like fingers grasped my chin and lifted my face up to her. "Your little band of escape artists may have slipped past me once, but this time you will not get away from me again!"

Her next maneuver came so swiftly, I had no time to react. The old woman's knife was out of her scabbard and up in the air, ready to strike. I heard my sister scream as the airborne creatures descended into a tight dark mass just above our heads.

Then all of a sudden, there was an unexpected flash of light so bright, it temporarily blinded me. I was prepared to meet my death, yet in the very next moment, I saw the old woman's head roll across the river bank. As a royal personage, I have witnessed beheadings and it is always a very messy business. But this decapitation was nothing like I had observed before. There was no blood at all. Instead, bright sparks flew out from the cleft neck of the old woman as if her head was made of fireworks powder.

"Princess, are you unharmed?" Sen shouted, as he rushed to our side. He had with him the Colonel's sword that he had no doubt used to remove the old woman's head.

Misaki turned her gaze to him and said, "Sen, I am very glad to see you! You are a man of your word to save us from that she-devil!"

Sen bowed his head. I saw his mouth move as if he was about to say something more, when all of a sudden, the flying creatures began to drop from the sky. It was like being caught in the middle of a severe hail storm. Creatures came crashing down, hitting the ground with dull thuds. One by one, I saw their eye-like green lights extinguish upon impact.

My sister and I at once clung to each other and shielded our faces. I felt Sen's weight over ours, to protect us from falling debris. The dreadful racket of metal plunging into the riverbank seem to go on for eternity. All the while, I feared that one of them was sure to fall on our heads and kill us all. But finally, after silence had prevailed, we felt safe enough to unfurl from our huddle to survey the aftermath.

The winged assailants had lost their fearful appearance, as they were now earthbound and mere misshaped metal haphazardly lodged in the soil. Seeing that the old woman's body and head remained lifeless, we rushed to where the Colonel was still bound to a tree.

My sister's eyes were brimming with tears as she held his hand. While Sen worked to remove the rope around the Colonel, I peered into his face, but it was difficult to decipher his current state from mere moonlight.

"I must move him closer to the fire!" said Sen.

He then hoisted the Colonel over his shoulder and placed him on his back near the pile of burning leaves. The fire was slowly dying, so I ran into the woods to gather up as many sticks as I could carry.

As I headed back to fuel the balefire, I heard a bubbling sound coming from the lake. The sound of belching and gurgling grew louder, as if the lake was boiling.

From the murderous she-devil to pestilent winged creatures made of metal, I was convinced that this was a most frightening nightmare from which I did not know how to wake. As the lake continued to churn with such force, I feared that we were all doomed with no salvation in sight.

Sen tore his attention away from the mysterious movement of the lake to lower his ear above Colonel's nose and mouth. "He still breathes, but barely!"

My sister placed Colonel's hand to her cheek as she quietly wept.

Then the sound of something large emerging from the lake caused all of us to turn our gaze toward it. From the tremendous cascading sound of water, I imagined a ghost ship or a mythical monster had emerged. So I strained my eyes and surveyed the darkened lake, yet nothing seemed amiss.

"Do you see anything out there?" Too much had happened on this night and I no longer trusted my own eyes.

"No, I do not see a thing! How can this be?" uttered Misaki, as she too stared intently toward the lake.

Sen picked up his sword again and ran toward the lake. When he reached the water's edge, something utterly incredible happened.

A door opened, a glowing opening that hovered just above the water's surface. It was as if someone had cut out an opening between two worlds. Next came a long ramp, like a protruding tongue of a dragon, extending all the way until it reached the shore. Misaki, Sen, and I were transfixed, and no one dared to move or utter a word.

Then a figure emerged. Woman or man, I could not tell, but the person was glowing with iridescent white light. As the stranger neared the shore, I saw Sen rush forward, sword drawn, ready to obliterate whatever it was.

But before the sword could make contact, the stranger waved a hand in his direction and Sen abruptly froze in mid strike.

Misaki's features were suffused with panic when she said, "We must have committed an unspeakable sin, as Goddess Amaterasu has cast us all to Hell!"

I wished desperately to find a credible explanation to ease Misaki's fears, yet everything that had happened to us thus far could not be so easily clarified or reasoned with. As my mind failed to produce not one solution to aid us out of the current predicament, I felt defeated and spent.

The stranger moved past Sen, still frozen in place with his sword raised high, and leisurely made its way down the ramp to the riverbank. Upon its approach, I could now see that the stranger was a woman dressed in a form-fitting garment. I blushed to the core as she might as well have been bare, as her attire left nothing to the imagination. Her features were pale, with wide eyes set far apart upon her face. Her nose was difficult to see except for the small opening of her nostrils and very pretty small lips. I could not see if she wore her hair in any fashion as her head was completely hidden beneath a head covering that matched her garment. Devil or not, she was beautiful in her own unique way, and I was mesmerized by the way her entire being glowed with such soft, pearl-white light.

"Have you no shame that you present yourself to us thusly attired?" said my sister.

But the stranger paid no mind to Misaki's indignation. She knelt beside the Colonel and placed her hand, with the longest fingers I have ever seen, on his chest.

Misaki slapped her hand away. "Do not touch him! Keep your distance!"

The stranger peered into Misaki's anguished features and stared intently into her eyes. At once, I saw Misaki's whole demeanor relax. She looked as if she had been put under a sorcerer's spell, with her eyelids half closed and her mouth slack.

The stranger then proceeded to place her hand on the Colonel once again. A strange blue light emanated from her palm. Instantly, I saw the Colonel stir and open his eyes.

All this time, absolute fear had rooted me at the edge of the clearing. With Sen and my sister ensnared in such a fixed state, I knew it was up to me to come to the aid of the Colonel.

I forced my legs to move, and in doing so, a snap of the twig beneath my foot caught the attention of the stranger. When our eyes met, I felt a sense of calm come over me. Curiously, I was no longer frightened. I was able to approach the stranger and the Colonel, who was now in a sitting position by the bonfire.

The Colonel behaved as if he had just awoken from a deep slumber. His movement was sluggish and confusion clouded his eyes when he said, "Where are we? How did I come to this place?"

When the stranger moved her hand in front of the Colonel's face, he too fell into a similar trance-like state just like Misaki and Sen.

"Are you here to kill us all?" The question simply spilled out from my lips. Since the night I had lost my army in the woods, the subsequent events have all been leading up to one objective; elimination of our entire party.

The stranger's eerie eyes, a blue-gray in color, stared back at me. Then I heard her speak. Her voice was soothing, like a breeze rustling through the leaves, and calm, like the gentle peal of a wind chime. I heard her voice not through my ears, but in my head. And I was not only able to understand her words but her emotions, as well. When she spoke, I felt as if we were connected as one.

"It has never been in our directive to eliminate the specimens. We were placed here to simply observe the female inhabitants' development on this young planet. Our lab has been hidden here, concealed in the lake, for a very long time. My custodian's duty was to blend in with the populace but also to keep the specimens away from our research facility. Yet something went terribly wrong when my custodian decided to purposely eliminate specimens and launch its own unauthorized experiment. When your male specimen terminated the custodian, the study had to be halted and I had no other choice but to intervene."

While she spoke, I felt her disappointment and uneasiness in the pit of my own stomach. In that moment, when I made the connection with her emotions, all her memories and thoughts rushed into my mind.

Then I understood it all: her ancient heritage, her mission, the other worlds, and most of all, what was at stake for our survival.

"This is too much!" The staggering supply of information left me dazed and terrified.

She gently placed her palm onto my forehead. "There now, do not be afraid."

The warmth of her touch eased my brain. But once the initial panic had subsided, frustration resurfaced again. "What is all this to me? I am but a woman! My lot in life is to be a vessel for procreation and to serve my husband. That is all that is expected of us!"

The stranger's eyes narrowed, and I saw her impatience expressed in a noticeable tremor of her palm. "Thus, our study continues. The female species advances slowly on this planet, not because they are inferior to their male counterparts, but because they are readily made to believe that they are substandard. We have even injected chosen females with nanobots to release ambition and trigger an independent thought process, yet progress is still at a stagnant rate. The test results are utterly disappointing."

Exhaustion of body and mind was too great to conquer when I exclaimed, "What does it matter to anyone else outside of this world?"

"Because the Universe requires balance. There are vibrations and positive forces that are emitted out into the Universe when planetary harmony is achieved. Conversely, if your world is unable to achieve balance, then others have no recourse but to exclude your planet from future contact. Ruined worlds become ripe for takeover by malevolent forces, and there will be no assistance from the rest of the Universe should your world become abandoned. Your planet is so very young, there is still time to create harmony and be worthy enough to be included into the advancement with the rest of the Universe."

My chest seemed to constrict hearing such magnitude of responsibility placed before me. "But I am a mere girl with no special power."

The stranger slowly rose to her feet and looked back toward the lake. "I have spent the majority of my life here on this beautiful planet, and have witnessed extraordinary feats achieved by many specimens. A single seedling, for example, can mature into a towering tree, but it can also provide shelter and food for wildlife, assist climate control, emit oxygen to sustain human life, and all the while, continue to procreate. Such a simple life form can provide so much for the good of others, yet the human species, especially females, limit their own contribution. Just because they believe they are mere girls with no special power."

I felt blood rush to my cheeks; with anger or shame, I could not tell. Her decided observation rendered me speechless, loss for any attempt at contradiction or justification.

The stranger stood before me as she pressed her right wrist with her left finger. In unison, the grounded metal creatures' green lights turned on. One by one, they took to the sky and formed into a tight knit circle. Once all the creatures had joined the group, the dark mass flew into the opening above the water and disappeared.

"Because of my custodian's misconduct, I will be recalled and another will take my place to carry on future testings and collection of data. I will miss this planet with its unique landscape of water and land, and mostly, I shall miss viewing the striking movement of the sun."

She reached out and took hold of my hand. "I wish you well. The Universe waits for your world to join us."

I pressed her hand with mixed emotions stirring within my heart.

The stranger waved her hand in the direction of Misaki and the Colonel. My sister's eyes fluttered as the Colonel reached out to place his hand on her shoulder.

My eyes followed the stranger as she moved up the ramp. When she stepped into the opening, she turned back and raised her hand in a gesture of farewell. The instant the door opening vanished from sight, Sen was released from his fixed state. His raised sword came down in a wide arc slashing through the air.

As I stood dazed and wondered if all that I have seen and heard were a mere creation of my mind, Misaki came to stand beside me with her eyes wide open. "Mayu, you are bleeding!"

I looked down to where Misaki's eyes had settled, and noticed that I had a small cut on my hand where the stranger had touched me.

Then I knew. I was one of the chosen ones.

Maki Morris swore that she would never write an Asian-themed story, yet Japan's Kamakura period with its wondrous folklore and lyrical language would entice her into writing a historical fantasy from that bygone era. By day, Maki is a creative director in Northern California providing marketing services to corporations, authors, and publishers. At night, she escapes into superbly crafted stories written by amazing authors that inspire her to keep on writing. Check out what Maki is up to at makimorris.com, or reach out to her on Facebook at www.facebook.com/maki.morris.

# MERMAID IN MANHATTAN

## Melanie Kinder

### Inspired by The Little Mermaid

Deep down in the sea lived Rori, a mermaid fascinated by all things human. She loved shipwrecks, where she found the best items for her collection of valuables. Her father, who had a grand distaste for humans, could never find out where she stashed her prizes.

One day, she saw an enormous shadow looming overhead, and she swam carefully to the surface to investigate. It was a cruise ship with windows galore. She peeked inside and gasped. She'd never witnessed humans dancing, only seen them on the finternet, where everyone could watch anything.

Once technology had made it possible to tap into the airwaves of human satellites, Rori was able to observe humans. She loved listening to them speak—and watching them dance.

Inside the ship, one woman's dress flowed magically as her partner spun her around. What Rori wouldn't give to have legs. Hours passed as she watched, enthralled. Then, she remembered her sister's birthday party. *Oh no*, she thought. *Father is going to kill me.*

Hastily, she swam home. With arms crossed, her oldest sister scowled at her. The rest of her family wore masks of disappointment. She didn't want to imagine her father's face. When angry, he could bore holes down to the soul.

Sandi the star fish crawled up to her, "Where have you been, my dear?"

Rori had to be careful how much she told her. Although she was a great friend, she had a big mouth and could easily get her in trouble.

"Sandi, can you dance?" she asked.

"Oh yes, I love to. Why do you ask?"

"I would like to learn how."

"But you possess no legs. I have five."

Rori went to her bedroom and spent the day dreaming about how life would be if she could somehow acquire legs—to walk on land, run in the sand, and bask in the sun. She pulled an old photo album out from under her bed. It had waterlogged wedding photos of humans dancing. She held it to her chest, shut her eyes, and began twirling around the bedroom. It just wasn't the same.

Her oldest sister, Rachele, caught her in the act. "What are you doing?"

"I'm trying to dance but I can't, not with this stupid thing," she said slapping her hips. "I need legs."

"Do you realize what the humans would do to us if they knew we existed? They would capture our people, experiment on us, or worse, take our tails for dinner."

Rori winced. "You don't know that."

"I've seen enough of their movies to know. Sister, you're beautiful the way you are. You have so many talents."

Rori cried. "Just go," she said.

"But Rori!"

"I said go." She continued to sob. "You know what? I'll go." She stormed out of her bedroom and out of the house.

She had been so angry she didn't realize where she was. It appeared to be some sort of coral forest.

Something brushed against her. It was a shifty-looking tiger shark with red eyes.

"I heard a rumor," he said.

"What rumor?"

"You want something you cannot have."

"Oh. Everyone wants something they can't have. It's called life."

"Yes, but what if I knew a way you could obtain anything you dreamed of?"

"I'd say you're pulling my fins," she told him.

"Have you heard of the sorceress, Seehexe?" he asked.

"I don't know any sorceresses, and I don't like the sound of this. I had better go."

"Fine. I guess you'll never experience what it is like to dance."

Rori turned sharply. "How did you know about that?"

"My master perceives many things, little fish."

"What are you saying? That she can give me legs?"

"Yes."

"Well, I don't believe you." Rori's stomach did a twirl. Curiosity gnawed as it often did, but she had to hold her ground. Or did she?

"I can see that you do," the shark said. "If you want to find out the truth, follow me to her lair."

* * * *

The witch's lair was dark. Harmless sharks, eels, and puffer fish made their homes there. Rori's skin grew colder the moment she reached their territory and saw their eyes looking back at her. Then, she passed the largest flat-screen shellevision set she'd ever seen. An episode of "Sharkville" played.

A large bionic seahorse of a woman swam out behind a bed of coral. "Ah, child, I'm glad you came."

Rori shivered. The sorceress was beautiful in an ugly, slithery sort of way. Her red glowing bionic eyes shifted their focus.

"The shark said you can grant me anything I want."

"Yes, child. At a price, of course."

"I don't have anything to offer."

"Oh, of course you do. You have a soul, don't you?"

"Well, yes, but…I want legs, so I can walk among the humans."

"Don't you mean dance?"

Rori wondered how the witch could know such things when she herself discovered that wish just hours earlier. "Yes, I'd do anything if I could dance."

"And I can give you that."

"I don't want to give away my soul."

"A compromise then," the witch said. "I'll grant you legs for three days, and if you win a dance competition, you can keep them forever. But if you fail, your soul is mine."

Rori's head was spinning. Could three days be enough to learn to dance, much less win a competition?

"Oh, come on, dear. Don't you want to experience what that is like? You'll never know until you try. And there is only one way."

"I'll do it."

The witch's bionic eyes funneled in, out, and back in. "Very well, dear."

"Wait. But what if I want my tail back?"

"If you win the competition before sunset on the third day, and you wish to receive your tail back, so be it. But you must win the competition first."

Rori considered for a moment and then nodded.

"I need you to repeat the terms of our agreement, so I am sure that you comprehend," the witch said. "And please understand that your words are binding."

She did just that.

The witch handed Rori a large pearl. "Hold this, and step inside the teleportation machine. You'll appear in Manhattan in a beautiful dress perfect for dancing. I'll even toss in a matching bag, a hotel key, and enough currency for you to get around. If you find you're lacking something, just hold the pearl and ask. It isn't just magic, but it has a built-in transponder. If the request is reasonable, it will be granted. It is the least I can do for putting your soul on the line."

\* \* \* \*

The machine transported Rori to a busy city street. Her sea-green dress matched her eyes and complemented her thick, blue hair. The garment ruffled in the summer breeze, and the sun warmed her bare shoulders. She pulled the hotel key out of her bag and observed the logo. Then she looked up the Manhattan street and realized the hotel was right in front of her.

A front desk clerk wore a name badge that read, "Merriam."

"Hi. I'm looking for room 73."

"Down to the end of the hall, take the elevator up to the third floor, and it'll be the third door on your right."

"Great. Thanks. Also, do you know where I might find dancing?"

"You mean, like a dance club?"

"Yeah, a dance club."

"The Rave-n is about a block up the road on the left."

Rori went to her room to drop off the luggage provided by Seehexe. Wasting no time, she headed to the Rave-n.

\* \* \* \*

The music boomed so loudly outside the venue that Rori wondered how bearable it was inside.

After a few moments, she got used to the volume of the music. And what interesting music it was. It sounded like dubstep, if she remembered correctly. She was happy to see she wasn't the only one with blue hair. The DJ had spikey, black, red-tipped hair. He was the most attractive boy she had ever seen, and although she wanted to watch the people dance, she kept glancing back at him. When their eyes met, her cheeks heated, and she looked away. She sneaked another glance and gasped. His gaze was still locked on her.

Since leaving her fins behind, Rori had a deep thirst. She went to the bar and sat down. Another new experience.

A man said, "Buy you a drink?"

When she turned, she found it was the handsome one with the red-tipped black hair. "If it's not too much trouble, I'll take some water."

"I'm Dominic."

"Rori."

"Well, at least let me buy you something to eat."

"I am quite hungry. What do you recommend?"

"Oh, they make good hamburgers here."

"All right, then. A hamburger."

The man behind the bar was half-man, half-machine. The right-hand side of his body looked like solid chrome. "You want fries with that?" he asked.

Rori glanced at Dominic, who shrugged. "Sure," she said.

When the food came, the smell made Rori's belly grumble. Thankfully, the music was loud enough to drown it out.

First, she tried a fry. "Yum."

"Here," Dominic said. "Put some salt on it."

With that, she shook the white granules onto her fries.

They tasted heavenly. The salt reminded her of home. Now she knew why her water had tasted so strange. So she shook some salt in it, too.

Rori watched out the glass wall to the dance floor. She wanted to be out there and knew she'd better be if she didn't want the witch to collect on the bargain.

"You want to dance?" His smile was heartbreaking.

"I don't know how."

"Well, I think I know what you need," Dominic said. He signaled the bartender. "A strawberry margarita, please. And two shots of your best tequila." He smiled at Rori. "I noticed you like a little salt with your drink, and you could use some liquid courage." His laugh was even better than his smile.

He showed her how to use the salt and the lime, and she did as he instructed, feeling her face contort. Wow. The sensation on her tongue and in her throat was sharp and sour. She wasn't sure if she hated it or liked it. The margarita was much better.

"Drink it slowly," Dominic said. "You don't want to get brain freeze."

Dominic was right; just as she finished the beverage, she no longer feared going out onto the dance floor. There again, she had to follow what he did. His body moved fluently like a fish.

Her head began to swim with euphoria. This is what she had come for, and the freedom was every bit as glorious as she thought it would be.

After a few songs, they went back to the bar, where they talked for hours. Both lost track of time. He offered to call her a taxi. She declined because the hotel was only a block up the road. He did not let her walk alone.

The next day, Dominic and Rori strolled through Central Park. People walked alongside various breeds of dog. Some rode on what Dominic referred to as bicycles.

Rori pointed to them. "I want to do that."

Dominic's eyebrows raised. "I've got an even better idea."

The bicycle he rented had two seats and two sets of peddles. Rori giggled with delight as she got on the back. "I don't know how to do this."

"That's okay," Dominic said, "Neither do I."

They wobbled at first, but in no time, they were peddling together. There were a couple of close calls as they turned a sharp right. They coined it, "the turn of death" and laughed about it all five times they passed through.

When she saw hoverboards skating by, she decided that was what she wanted to do next. Dominic suggested they wait until tomorrow.

"Besides," he said, "it's time I get to the Rave-n. I'm on again tonight. You should come. There's something I want to show you."

When they got to the club, he walked her over to a machine with flashing colored lights that said: DANCE DANCE REVOLUTION.

"What's this?" Rori asked.

"It's DDR. It shows you what spots to step on, and you try to keep up with it. It teaches you how to dance. Sort of. Well, it's a start." He pulled a green piece of paper similar to the one the witch had given her out of his wallet, stuck it in the machine, and told her to give it a try. "Now, I have to get ready," he said. "I'll catch up with you later."

Thankful the dance machine was on the far end of the club where he couldn't see her, she hopped on the game, and after a couple of hours, she got pretty good. A few people gathered to watch her. And then, more and more. One of the spectators said, "Damn girl, you're good. Are you competing tomorrow?"

"There's a contest?" She wondered if it counted. It had to.

"Yeah. It's sort of a big deal."

"I'm in," Rori said.

Dominic made his way through the crowd. "Making some new friends?"

"Yep." She laughed. "We're all headed to your place."

"Sweet," he joked. "But seriously, what's with the crowd?"

"Well, there's a DDR contest tomorrow, and I'm going to win."

* * * *

The dance competition took place during the day. The race was close but ultimately, she won. Before she confessed the truth to Dominic and made the decision whether to live as a human or a mermaid, he said, "I need to tell you something."

Rori nodded for him to continue.

"I'm leaving town tonight, and I'll never see you again. I can't help but be bummed about it. I want you to know it's not that I don't care."

"Can't you come back?" she asked.

"Not from this." He sighed. "Come on, I'll walk you to the hotel, and we can discuss it."

"No, tell me now. I can't let you just walk out of my life."

"I have to."

"Why?"

"It's crazy," he said.

"Well, if you're never going to see me again, what's the harm in telling me?"

"Yeah, you make a great point." He looked in all directions and then said, "I'm well…uh…I'm a merman. You know what that is?"

She stifled a laugh. "Of course, I do."

"Tonight is my last human night."

Rori's heart leapt with delight. "Mine too, Dominic." She grabbed the pearl and made the wish. "Mine too."

And as merfolk—with access to the finternet—they lived happily ever after.

Melanie Kinder has degrees in both engineering and science and more than six years in Yun Moo Kwan Hapkido. Website: www.redthrice.com, Facebook: www.facebook.com/melaniekinderauthor, Twitter: @melaniekinder

# THE EMPRESS'S NEW APP

### Stacy Renee Lucas

*Based on The Emperor's New Clothes*

Hannah Christiansen was the queen of the halls of Valley High. When she flounced past the walls of metal lockers in her short, pleated cheerleader skirt, the gazes of the students who weren't as cool as she followed. The lower classmen studied the clothes she wore, noted how she rimmed her blue eyes with smoky make-up, and memorized where she got her highlights done. Hannah was so fond of clothes that she spent hours poring over the Insta-feeds of her favorite fashonistas, and it was even rumored that on her school breaks she'd traveled to Paris to have some clothes made by famous fashion designers. Those who had been lucky enough to go to Hannah's house described her two-story closet in detail. When she turned sixteen, her parents gifted her with a convertible, so her ensembles would be visible for all to see.

Of course, Hannah easily won the title of Empress of the Spring Ball. A week before the dance, two girls dressed in black approached her car as she was leaving school for the day. They were known as "the techs," and the only reason Hannah had noticed them at all was that they dressed alike, were always together, and usually listened to music she had never heard while playing on their phones. They had mysteriously shown up as seniors the previous fall. The rumor around school was that they had both achieved a perfect score on their SATs and were set to go to Stanford.

"I'm Jane." The tallest offered her hand. "This is my friend Ashley. We heard about your winning Empress of the Ball next week, and we have an idea."

Hannah looked at Jane's sweater, so worn that it was almost gray. And was that flannel underneath? She needed some fashion help, stat. "I'm not interested."

Hannah opened her car door, but Jane grabbed it. "How would you like to have your own app? Something nobody else has, and everyone will want?"

"You can do that?" she asked.

"We used to go to the technical school," Ashley said.

Jane shot her friend a look. "My dad owns a software company. I can build you something really cool. Then everyone can download it before the dance, and you will have a special filter that will make you look like you are covered in diamonds. Everyone else will be dying of jealousy. But there's a catch."

Hannah leaned in. "What's the catch?"

"Only the coolest kids will receive an invitation to get the app."

"I want it," Hannah said.

"We are going to need some cash to get started," Jane told her.

Hannah opened her Gucci purse. "How much?"

\* \* \* \*

Over the next few days, Hannah watched the girls closely as they huddled over their laptops and tablets at the library, in the computer lab, and in the quad. Twice they asked Hannah for additional money so that they could have access to things they needed online to build the app. By now, the rumor was buzzing around the school that Hannah was going to have her own app that people could download. Hannah wanted to check on their progress, but she didn't want to be seen associating with the two at school, so one day she asked her best friend Paige to talk to the girls as they worked in the cafeteria. Hannah trusted her oldest friend to tell her the truth. She watched from a few tables away.

"How's it going?" Paige asked.

Jane spun her laptop around and revealed her screen, filled with numbers and symbols. "We're just building the code for the app. It's a lot of work."

"Oh, that looks intense," Paige said, but she had no tech background, and it was meaningless to her. "When will it be done?"

"Tell Hannah it takes time, so she has to be patient. The text inviting people to download the app will go out in two days, and only to the cool people."

"So?" Hannah asked when Paige returned to her table.

"It looks like it's coming along great. They said the download invitations will go out in two days."

"Did they say who they are sending them to?" Hannah sighed. "I don't want just anyone having it."

"She didn't give me a list, but she said only the coolest kids would get it."

Hannah clapped her hands together. "I can't wait to see it."

* * * *

In two days as Jane and Ashley had promised, text messages went out to the school's elite, informing them that they could download the app on the night of the Spring Ball with a special access code. Hannah could no longer keep the app secret and told all of her friends about it. On the night of the ball, the techies met Hannah outside the school gym with their phones in hand. Hannah wasn't clad in her usual designer dress, but instead wore a simple black shift.

"I didn't want to ruin the effect of the app," she told them.

Jane and Ashley held their phones up in front of Hannah and gasped. They moved around her at different angles, noting the glittering filter that complemented her tan skin. Paige tried to get a glimpse of her friend through the phone, but all she saw was a blank screen.

Finally, it was time for Hannah to ascend the stage and accept her crown. After it was placed on her slicked blond hair, she signaled for the assembled crowd of students to hold up their phones. As she held up her hands, devices filled the air.

Her stomach dropped as a buzz formed among the crowd.

"I can't see anything," a girl whispered.

"Mine isn't working," said another.

Hannah scanned the room for the techies and caught sight of them heading for the back door. She suspected that the whole thing had been a sham, but there was no way she was going to let those two losers get the best of her. She raised her arms higher, and smiled as wide as she could.

---

Stacy Renee Lucas loves poetry, *cafe au lait*, and haunted houses. While living in the French Quarter of New Orleans, she received her J.D. from Loyola University-New Orleans. She returned to California's Central Valley to practice law. She is currently at work on a thriller set in New Orleans, and she is represented by AKA Literary Management. Find her on twitter at @stacyreneelucas.

# ALICE THROUGH THE SNAPFACE FILTER

## Megan McCord

*Inspired by Alice Through the Looking Glass*

Alice lets her book fall onto her chest, stretching her long limbs, swaying lightly in her hammock. She always keeps a hammock wherever she lives. In this apartment, it's in the living room. Next to the potted palm. By the picture window overlooking the street below. She is bored with this book. She'd rather read a fashion magazine.

Books and magazines are quaint nods to the past. Grandma activities. Reading is passé and holding some grubby book or paper magazine in your hands makes one look ridiculous. Out of touch. Out of sorts. Out of one's mind.

Alice had a grandma who impressed upon her the secret loveliness of a good book. The grace between the pages of a fashion magazine. Gramma Joan would read to her until she could read to herself. Gram said books teach us how to live. Make us smart and empathetic people. Expand our worldview. Teach us what's important. Fashion magazines teach us to appreciate detail and beauty. Artistry. Nobody considers these things anymore. Alice feels silly for doing so herself. What a waste of time. She pinches herself on the arm.

Gramma smelled of Chanel No 5 and Vitabath. She was like no other. She was natural. Nobody is natural now. Gram's words of wisdom wash over Alice like so much blah, blah, blah. She yawns.

Precious time.

Guilt makes Alice want to improve herself by reading literature. But not many people read books anymore; it takes so long. And what's it for? What's it do for you to read about fake people and fake situations? There are real people posting photos of their food, their pets, their darling children, and their perfect partners. Real life is happening. Why hide in a book when you can be amazing online? If Gramma Joan were alive today, she'd understand. It's not about substance.

But Alice knows she's out of place. Alice knows she doesn't fit here. Alice knows she's faking it. She runs her fingers down the spine of the book on her chest, staring out the window at the branches of the tree beyond.

"Maybe we've been here too long, Dinah," she says to the cat.

Dinah does not respond.

"Maybe there's someone else I'm supposed to be." Tears blur her vision. The leaves of the tree metamorphose into a smile. A many toothed smile. On the face of a fat cat. She shakes her head and blinks rapidly. The fat cat fades.

Enough of that today, she thinks. Stop moping. Stop daydreaming.

The plug-in fan is a failure in this summer heat. Dinah is as flat as a cat can get on the hardwood floor and Alice extends her toe to nudge the animal, making sure she's still alive. Dinah opens her left eye a slit, conveying oceans of annoyance, before closing it again. Dinah is quite the sensation on Insta. She has thousands more followers than Alice.

"Fuuuuuuuck," sighs Alice.

She snaps her book closed and drops it onto the floor next to a pile of *Vogue*, *Harper's Bazaar*, *Elle*, *Marie Claire*, *InStyle*, *Glamour*, *Allure*, and yes, *Teen Vogue*. Alice has been a *Vogue* subscriber since the age of ten (a gift from Joan) and her obsession only grew. She'd spent long hours each summer at her family's beach house, shielding her fair skin under a wide beach umbrella, Bullfrog on her nose and shoulders, gazing endlessly at the models in their couture and bathing suits, reading about their model diets and their model skin and their model purse-sized dogs, and their model/rock star boyfriends and their model hot sex and their back in bikini bodies moments after giving birth. It all seemed so wonderful. And so close. She could almost touch it. She could almost be it.

Almost.

Alice still enjoyed turning pages. Hard copy books and magazines are specialty items now, novelties she pays extra for. No one holds paper in their hands in 2029. Just grandmas. And eccentrics. And what could be worse than to be a grandma or an eccentric?

"But having a grandma was rather nice," whispers Alice. More tears.

Alice has no grandma now. And at 28, she feels like the oldest woman in Los Angeles. In Los Angeles, 28 is middle aged. Practically dead. No one admits to being over 30.

Time is running out.

Dinah stretches her arms and legs Superman style, and lets out a squeak as she yawns. She is Alice's everything. There is no man, no babies, and her career is just left of where she wishes to be.

"Do that again, sweet girl," says Alice as she flicks her wrist, clicking open the camera feature imbedded there. Dinah loves to be photographed and happily re-strikes her Superman pose, stealing a side-glance at her momma. "Who's so pretty?" coos Alice.

She selects the best shot, adds a pink filter with a glitter border and posts it to Insta. Dinah, annoyed with losing her spotlight, begins to bathe, hind leg hiked in the air like a cellist's bow.

Alice is a style reporter for *People* magazine. It's not a horrible job. It's in fashion after all. But it's Hollywood fashion. It's Los Angeles. It's not real fashion. It's not *Vogue*. Anna Wintour helmed American *Vogue* by 38. Alice has ten years to make it. Just ten years. Once you're over forty you may as well kill yourself.

* * * *

Church bells chime from Alice's left hand. She flips her palm over and reads the message displayed on a screen located just beneath the surface of her skin.

*It's on.*

The message bubbles indicate more coming from her editor, Reina Rojo. Alice holds her breath in anticipation.

*2:00 today. Her house.*

A Beverly Hills address. Old Hollywood. New Hollywood lives in Silverlake or Venice. Alice rolls out of the hammock, her feet thunking on the floor causing Dina to turn her head and blink once with irritation. "Yes!" Alice has been chasing this interview for months. Reina is ruthless when it comes to snagging a tough interview. Ruthless with everything else too. She expects her reporters to be as pitiless, stopping at nothing to secure an interview with a tough-to-hunt-down star. She is a famous tantrum thrower and screamer in the office, reducing assistants to trembling hedgehogs and firing reporters like a dealer tossing cards from a deck. By some small miracle, Reina likes Alice. She's not sure why but has decided to keep her head low lest she lose it. This interview is a bona fide get. This interview could catapult Alice into a new position in the world. Maybe *Vogue* would notice her.

Alice knows she can't mess this up or it's off with her head.

Gramma Joan kept books on tall shelves at her Laurel Canyon cottage. Alice would spend entire afternoons, golden light pouring through paned glass onto the floor as she pulled picture book after picture book down to explore. Thick volumes of photographs of old Hollywood stars entranced her. She'd stare at the black and white photos of Garbo and

Lombard, of Rita Hayworth and Veronica Lake. She was spellbound by the Technicolor shots of Elizabeth Taylor's violet eyes, and Jane Fonda's *Barbarella* curls and *Klute* shag. She dreamed of the world these stars inhabited, the meetings at studios, the costume fittings, the evenings at Mocambo or the Cocoanut Grove, paparazzi snapping away, the drives through canyons to private homes behind walls and hedges.

No star fascinated her more than Neige Lapin. Her films were huge box office in the 1970s. She was a star but also an actress, tall and powerful, and never took any shit. Not from anybody. Ever. She left in her wake brokenhearted men and jealous women, villains and enemies, conquests and true loves, with the toss of her shaggy platinum bob and the flash of her white teeth. Her influence over the fashion world was almost as great as her influence in film. Her style was copied by designers and she was the most photographed woman in the world for a decade. After Jacqueline Kennedy. She encompassed everything Alice adored, fashion and movies rolled into one.

Neige started her career as a model in New York, the sunny California girl in a bikini plucked off the beach by a modeling agent on vacation. She was skinny and tan, almost six feet tall with moon glow hair to her waist and a gap between her front teeth. When she got to New York, her agent told her to fix it, but she said no. It'll be my signature. And it was. The imperfection of her smile heightened the beauty that housed it. When she cut her hair off and bleached it snow white it caused a sensation and a slew of copycats. Every woman between 15 and 35 bobbed her hair.

She signed a Hollywood studio contract, and made film after film, first as an ingénue, beguiling and wide-eyed. She rebelled against this pigeonhole, graduating to more serious parts in films by the heavyweight directors of the '70s. She won two Oscars, put her hand and footprints in cement at the Chinese Theatre, was married three times, was on hundreds of magazine covers. Her iconic status was sealed. At the age of forty-five, at the height of her beauty and talent, she disappeared.

Like a rabbit down a hole.

Gone.

And now, after two years of calls and emails and messages and gift baskets, Alice will interview her.

This golden afternoon.

In Neige's home.

Where no reporter has ever been.

Her heart beats faster. She leaps up to ready herself.

\* \* \* \*

"What filter should I wear?"

Her choice of filter is of the utmost importance. When Alice was a kid, filters were limited to the pictures one posted on their various social media sites. She'd choose kitty ears and whiskers, or giant bows and long eyelashes. She could change the color of her hair, her eyes, her height, her weight. She could have large breasts or small. A pert nose or a wider one. At first it was just for fun. Something she and her friends would laugh over in junior high school. But the technology advanced and society's expectations shifted. One could apply the filter directly to their bodies. The beauty business was revolutionized. Plastic surgery was rendered obsolete. Click your preferences on your imbedded device and you could look like whatever you wanted. You could be whomever you wanted. Or at least look like them.

You may never feel like them.

But you could pretend.

Alice swipes through her saved favorites in "make-believe." She could be a geisha girl. A mermaid. A pirate. She decides it might be better to go more realistic today for her meeting. Neige is, after all, an icon.

She taps on a category she calls "me only better." It contains filters to make Alice's natural features...better. Her teeth straighter. Her hair thicker and blonder. Her finger and toenails perfectly shaped and polished. She's already tall, and if she's having a good day, she can see that she quite naturally falls into the category of beautiful. She could be a model in the pages of the fashion magazines she loves so much. But this perception is always fleeting. On a bad day, or even a regular day, she suspects she is falling short, her flaws exposing to the world the fraud that she is.

She chooses the most enhanced version of herself, taps, and instantly her hair grows longer, falling in soft blonde waves to her waist. Her waist cinches in two inches, and her light blue summer dress hugs her slender curves. She gazes into her looking glass, turning this way and that, inspecting the filter's work. As satisfied as she can ever be, she scoops up her car keys and bag and scoots out the door, blowing a kiss to Dinah as she leaves.

\* \* \* \*

The driveway to Neige's house is hidden by tall shrubs and gracefully drooping tree limbs. If Alice hadn't known where to look, she'd have missed it, as hungry paparazzi had been missing it for decades. No car could fit through the growth and the gate was obscured, blending with branches. As though no one lived there. Or as if the person who lived there wished never to be found. She locates an ancient keypad, its number rusty. She peers closely at it, wondering what to do. "Call" beckons one button. She presses it. There is the old-fashioned sound of a dial tone. Alice raises her eyebrows, thick and arched as the filter makes them. She doesn't know what to do next. She presses the button again.

"Who is it?" A woman's irritated voice under the scratchy sounds of the tiny round speaker.

"Alice Bantam from *People*. I'm here to…"

The gate begins to open, ripping branches and vines as it slowly swings back toward the driveway. At the top of the driveway is a two-story house covered by a thatched roof. Alice walks up the steep hill to another small garden gate. Upon a low stone wall sits the largest house-cat Alice has ever seen. Delighted, she reaches out to pet it, only to draw her hand back as the cat smiles at her, revealing a mouthful of human-looking teeth.

"Oh my," whispers Alice. "I think we've met before."

She hurries past the cat to the front porch, knocking at the door. She sees her reflection in the window and worries her filter is flickering. She's adjusting its settings as the door flies open.

"What?" A petite redheaded woman in a French maid's outfit stands guard as a dish is hurled behind her, crashing into the wall.

Alice instinctively ducks and says, "I'm Alice. I'm the rep…"

"Well, come in then," says the maid, clearly sizing Alice up to be a nincompoop.

"Thank you." Alice steps inside as another dish hurtles through the air, crashing into the fireplace mantle. *Who's doing that?* she wonders.

"Wait here." The maid indicates Alice should sit on the couch. Dishes continue to whiz by, crashing here and there. An oinking piglet in a baby bonnet runs through the room.

Alice's bottom barely touches the couch cushion before she hears "Maryanne! Who is it? Is it that dreadful reporter? Bring her in! Let's get this over with."

Alice swallows hard and stands up. She runs a hand over her hair and the filter blurs and buzzes. She puts her hand down quickly.

"This way," smiles Maryanne and Alice follows her through a long dark hallway. The hallway walls are covered in photographs of Neige. Neige from her early modeling days, when her face was still a little round from a swiftly receding childhood. Neige's first cosmetics campaign, when her hair was still to her waist. Neige in her infamous white-blond bob, the icon fully formed. Neige kneeling over her star on the Walk of Fame. Neige holding her Oscar.

"Hurry up. We'll be late. We must never be late for Ms. Lapin. Only Ms. Lapin can be late," scolds Maryanne.

Alice quickens her step following Maryanne further down the endless hallway. At last a door appears. A tiny door.

"I can't fit through," says Alice.

"Adjust your filter," commands Maryanne.

"To do what?" says Alice.

"To make yourself smaller."

"But it's just a filter. It doesn't actually change who I am," explains Alice.

Maryanne rolls her eyes and the tiny door expands to normal size. With a twist of the knob, she pushes it open and a voice within the dark room asks, "Then what good is it?"

Alice looks at Maryanne who gestures she should go inside with another eye roll.

"What good is what?" asks Alice, blinking in the darkness.

Maryanne follows her in, throws open the drapes, and light inundates the room. She curtsies and leaves, pulling the door shut behind her.

There is silence.

Alice's eyes adjust to the sudden brightness, brightness that almost serves as camouflage for her elusive subject.

Almost.

An image materializes.

Neige Lapin sits before Alice at a table set for two. For tea. There is a teapot and tiny cakes upon which is written *eat me*.

"Join me, won't you?"

Alice draws her breath in, Neige coming into focus. Alice can't quite place what's wrong. Something is strange about Neige. She doesn't look like a person should. She looks old fashioned. She looks like Gramma Joan. She looks... Alice's giant filter eyes widen.

*She looks old.*

"Don't be so shocked," laughs Neige. "Sit and join me." She pats the seat next to her. "Did you not think time would touch me?"

Neige sits tall in her chair, regal still, with her white hair in its famed bob, small diamond studs in her ears, sparkling only somewhat less than her blue eyes. She smiles as she consults a pocket watch.

"We only have a few minutes." She snaps the watch closed. Neige takes in Alice's filter. "That's quite fetching."

Alice doesn't take her eyes off Neige as she sits on the edge of the offered chair. "Thank you," says Alice, fidgeting under her idol's gaze. "There are so many questions..."

Neige interrupts. "Is that even close to what you look like?"

Alice touches her filter hair, sitting back. "I don't know."

"You don't know what the filter looks like? Or you don't know what you look like?" Neige's eyes are ice blue, but not cold or mean. Her eyes shine, offset by the snowy veil of hair surrounding the actress's wrinkled pink face. Alice can't take her eyes off the face before her. So crinkly. So mesmerizing. So full of…

"Look at me," says Neige. "Really look at me."

"Is that why I'm here?"

"What do you see?"

"Reina will kill me if I don't ask you…" Alice flips her palm seeking her recording function.

"Don't look at that, dear. Look at my face and tell me what you see."

Alice drops her hand in her lap and takes a deep breath, squeezing her eyes shut, their long filter lashes grazing her bubblegum cheeks.

She opens her eyes and sees Neige.

She sees an old woman. With wrinkles. And freckles. And a saggy neck.

"I'm sorry," she stammers. "I don't know what you want me…"

"Keep looking." Neige takes Alice's hands in her own.

Alice blinks.

She narrows her eyes, focusing the lens of her filter eyeball on Neige's face. She sees the wrinkles begin to smooth. She sees the freckles shrink into the poppyseed sprinkles of youth. She sees the skin on Neige's neck lift, revealing the cut of her jawline, the fullness of her lips, the blush on her high cheekbones. Alice watches Neige's face transform like a film running in reverse. She is 70. She is 50. She is 35 and then 20. She is a child. She is a baby.

Her face is a story. Like a movie. Only real.

Under the layers of flesh and experience, Alice sees the girl Neige was, on the beach, in the sand, scraping her knees as a wave throws her down. Running in the sun with her brother chasing her, her cheeks red, her nose peeling, and her bathing suit still wet from the ocean. She is laughing and her brother is her favorite. She sees Neige at his funeral, sees the part of her he takes with him disappear forever.

Alice sees Neige in her Oscar gown, clutching the gold statue, giving her controversial speech about equality. She sees Neige daydreaming with a film script in her lap, an artist creating a role, a dreamer becoming a character. She sees Neige in bed, curled into a ball, unable to move in the aftermath of her first husband's death in a plane crash. Her only true love. There were never babies, just characters and adoring fans, then solitude. She sees her writing. She sees her lovers. She sees her eating and bathing and crying and laughing and fucking and shitting and picking her nose.

Alice lets out a cry.

She is so real it hurts.

"What do you see?" asks Neige.

A tear rolls down Alice's filter cheeks.

"I see you." She gulps for air. "I see what beauty is."

"What is it?" prods Neige.

"It's...living. It's not perfect. It's true." Alice shakes her head. "I don't have the right words. But it isn't this," she says, tapping her filter face.

"Show the world. Show my face to the world."

"Are you sure?" Alice clutches Neige's bony hands. "No one looks like you now."

"But they do. Underneath it all, they do."

"They do?"

"Indeed." Neige kisses Alice's forehead. "You are beautiful, too."

"I am?"

"Don't you ever look at yourself? When you turn your filter off?"

"I try not to. I don't like what I see." Alice looks down.

"Why not?"

"I'm not... I don't look like I should. I don't look right." Another real tear rolls down her unreal cheek.

"Let me see."

"What?"

"Let me see you."

Alice pulls her hands away. "Ms. Lapin, I came here to do an interview with you. One you agreed to and one my editor is expecting."

"This is the interview. This is the point." She lifts Alice's chin with her bent finger. "Turn it off. Show me who you are."

Alice stares at her palm, sliding her fingers over the buttons imbedded there. They control everything about modern life. They are the keys to being real. At least that's what she thought. Now she's not so sure. She looks at Neige and with a few taps of her fingertips, the filter turns off.

* * * *

Alice bursts through her front door, dropping her bag on the floor as she runs past Dinah to the full-length looking glass at the end of her hallway. A curtain is draped over it so Alice doesn't have to see herself. She rips it down and stands close to the glass, close enough to fog it with breath, close enough to see her eyes. She slowly walks backwards taking in more and more, revealing her features. She sees herself for the first time in years. She walks close to the looking glass again, staring into the blue of her eyes. She sees the thoughts that lay beyond. She sees the mind at work. She sees her core. She sees her dreams. She sees herself.

Her real self.

Alice smiles. Two of her bottom teeth overlap. Imperfectly. It's beautiful. Dinah winds around Alice's legs.

"Are you hungry, my dear?"

Dinah purrs and follows Alice into the kitchen. Alice puts Dinah's plate of tuna next to her water dish and gives her pats on the head. "I love you, little bear." Dinah flicks her tail.

Alice fishes out a teacake she stashed in her pocket at Neige's.

*Eat me,* it says.

So she does.

Megan McCord is a writer of short fiction and has an MFA from Antioch University, where she teaches writing in the Undergraduate Studies and Bridge Programs. A native of Los Angeles, she engages in stereotypical activities like teaching yoga and driving a hybrid car. She enjoys writing about the city, and lives there with her man and a tiny, bossy cat. Her website is at www.meganmccord.com.

# LOS AHOGADOS (THE DROWNED)

**Kathleen Alcalá**

*Inspired by the legend of La Llorona*

She woke with the ocean breaking gently against the walls of her room, the bed beginning to rise upon the tide.

She reached out for the baby, but could not reach him, and kept reaching until she opened her eyes. The room was dry, the breeze gently blowing the curtains in from the summer-soaked yard.

Tiza sat up, then got out of bed. She touched her stomach with her fingertips, drew on her jeans from where they lay on the floor from the night before. The floor was dry, her clothes dry, everything dry except the dream.

Tiza drove into town, where she met Mark to drive out to the job that day. They were house painters with Homer & Sons. Always epic, she tried to joke, but nobody ever got it. Homer was just Homer Scranton, and as far as she knew, Tiza and Mark were the closest people he had to sons.

They painted in near silence. Ever since Mark had hit on her last Saturday in town, and Tiza had refused, things had been a little tense. She hoped he would get over it, a married man with kids at home. The last thing Tiza needed was some tangled affair in a town with three stoplights.

She had moved here a year before, bagging groceries for a while, pumping gas. The painting job offered an apprenticeship, which sounded slightly better, although the pay was about the same. There was some state money for training, so she took it. Homer was nice enough, an old Dutch country farmer who had taken up house painting as a more reliable source of income.

They wore white jumpsuits over their regular clothes to paint, even though it was hot. Homer insisted that it made them look more professional. On the worst days, Tiza wore shorts and a tank top, but now she didn't want Mark to look at her. Why did it always end up this way?

Tiza looked up at the low hills that flanked the town. Instead of green scrub rising to a modest forest, Tiza could see the profile of a giant baby just over the crest, floating on its back in a lake or ocean. It waved its hands, but did not seem distressed. Tiza turned her back on it and climbed the ladder to paint under the eaves of the house.

It wasn't too hard to hide her pregnancy. She stood behind a counter most of the time, and didn't encourage people to become overly familiar. A few people guessed, she figured, when her blouses got more and more billowy, but Tiza didn't think they had told anyone. Still, after the birth and signing the papers at the hospital, she decided to move away for a fresh start. She never told the father, an amiable cowboy she saw a few times in Pendleton. Cute, but not too bright.

She had really looked at the baby just once, a good, long look, and saw how he would grow up and have the same winsome smile, the same stiff, black hair and long, lanky arms and legs.

Maybe they would find each other someday, she mused later, father and son, wondering what it was that drew them together. The baby had regarded her with her own copper-colored eyes, waiting to see what she would do. She had handed him to the social worker and turned away to sleep.

Tiza climbed down off the ladder to move it. She pulled the respirator off over her head to gulp some fresh air. By now the giant baby had drifted farther away, and she saw that a little ship was sailing past it. She hoped the baby would not grab it and hurt anyone.

\* \* \* \*

They finished up with the spray painting and got ready to go back to the shop. Tiza and Mark would return tomorrow to do touch up with brushes, and strip off the masking tape. Mark drove while holding his cigarette out the window. Tiza opened her own window and let the breeze cool the side of her face.

"Everything good?" asked Homer when they got back to the shop. He sensed their unease, the lack of joking and talking.

"It's fine," Tiza answered. "It'll be done tomorrow."

Mark hung up the keys and switched his painter's cap for his regular one. "I'm gonna grab me a cold one," he said on the way out. An invitation? A warning?

Tiza returned to her little rental, stopping for a dozen eggs and a head of lettuce on her way home. Omelets and salads were easy.

She had thought about names during the pregnancy. Robin. Jaden. Finally, she had settled on Alza. She liked the brevity of it. with a 'z' like her own name. She didn't care if it wasn't a real name, since she told no one. She imagined him drifting away from the hospital, going from town to town. Not looking for her, she hoped, but finding a good life with a couple who were thrilled to adopt a healthy baby. Maybe he wouldn't have to know, although in this day and age, she found that unlikely. No matter where you lived, DNA was gonna find you. She prayed that she would be old by then, too old for him to expect an answer to the inevitable 'How could you?'

Tiza reached into her refrigerator for a jug of cold water to wash down her medication. Once a day, without fail. It made her feel light, detached, like a balloon that was about to drift up and away.

Post partum depression, they called it, when she could not get out of bed, did not care if she ate or not. She had not begun to see Alza until starting on the meds. Before then, he had just been a presence, someone else in the room who did not say anything at all.

Tiza turned from the refrigerator to see the kitchen table afloat, the paperbacks in the low shelf beginning to soak through and warp. Tiza closed her eyes, and when she opened them, the table was still, and she set the egg carton upon it. She did not look at the floor to see if it was dry.

Kathleen Alcalá is the author of six books of fiction and nonfiction. She has contributed to numerous anthologies, including the recent *Latin@ Rising* from Wings Press. Her most recent book is *The Deepest Roots: Finding Food and Community on a Pacific Northwest Island*, University of Washington Press. Praise from Ursula K. LeGuin: "This is a book of wonders. Each story unfolds with humor and simplicity and perfect naturalness into something original and totally unpredictable. Not one tale is like another, yet all together they form a beautiful whole, a world where one would like to stay forever." More at www.kathleenalcala.com.

# BLUEBEARD

## Kitamu Latham-Sampier

*A reimaging of the Grimm Brothers' Tale*

Year 2167.
Planet Pluto.
On Vidus, an Alien/Human Settlement.
Home of The Lazarus Indigo Medical Research Lab & Hospital.
Who is Lazarus Indigo?

Dr. Lazarus A.G. Indigo is a Master Surgeon, not only trained in Human physiology, but one of the few surgeons in the galaxy skilled enough to save alien lives as well. He's received countless awards as well as the nickname "BlueBeard," a double entendre that not only references his rumored ties to a royal family from Earth but his strange physical reaction to his first Alien corpse. His original raven black hair transformed into an eerie and otherworldly blue, with matching eyes. His appearance is very unnerving for some, alluring to others. Though highly successful, he failed when it came to love.

Dr. Indigo is a widower, who has lost five wives. Women of many different species, they met their ends through accidents or illness according to the Doctor. Though the doctor suffered many loses, he's never given up on finding love again. The doctor has fallen in love yet again. Will this relationship have the same ending?

\* \* \* \*

He had met his new love when one of his researchers, a green mantis-like female alien was giving a tour at his lab, In the tour group, he spotted two sisters. The two women were in awe of his laboratory. While they marveled at the technology around them, Dr. Indigo kept his eyes locked on them, but focused mainly on one. The ladies were twins, equally lovely, but the twin with the piercing amber-red eyes captivated him. She was the one asking about every minute detail of the lab with such passion, revealing that her mind matched her beauty. The young lady was so engrossed in everything that she failed to see the doctor and slammed right into him and landed backwards, butt first. She seemed to be a bit frustrated!

"Oww!! What heck!! Oh!"

She looked up to see what, or who, she had slammed into, A very tall pale-skinned man in a tailored jet-black suit underneath a white lab coat, she dropped her jaw at the sight of his iridescent blue goatee and haunting azure-colored eyes. She knew instantly who he was.

"Dr. Indigo! Oh my god, I'm so sorry I bumped into y—"

Before she could finish, the doctor reached for her hand and gently helped her up. His eyes locked with hers.

Indigo: "No. I should apologize. I was admiring your love of my laboratory that I didn't realize I was in your way! My apologies!"

The doctor then lightly bowed his head towards her, still holding onto her hand.

Indigo: "Allow me to formally introduce myself. Dr. Lazarus Azul Ghede Indigo. At your service! And you are?"

The woman was about to answer when the researcher giving the tour quickly stepped in.

Luton: "Sir… This is Dr. Pandora Lyon! The herbalist you invited to speak at the Innovator's Ball tonight. And this is her sister Dido."

The doctor's eyes widened at the discovery that this beautiful creature was the brilliant herbalist whose research had caught his eye! They'd never met face to face before but her advances in herbal medicine had contributed to huge strides in field medicine.

Indigo: "Ah, Dr. Lyon, it's truly an honor to have you both in my facility! Thank you for coming. Dr. Luton, I'll take over their tour, you can take a break."

Dr. Luton nodded and happily went to lunch. Dr. Indigo gestured for both ladies to follow him and continued their tour. Pandora listened intently to the doctor, while her sister kept an eye on the doctor. She could tell he desired her sister and she wasn't sure she liked it. The pair explored the enormous building, which was as much a museum as it was a lab. The ceiling was glass and the bright sunlight shone through reflecting prism-like colors. Hanging crystals from the skylight spiraled downward. It was almost hypnotic.

* * * *

Hours soon passed and the Doctor managed to charm Dido as well as Pandora. Dr. Indigo then revealed he would like to extend his invitation to the Ball to include Pandora's sister and brother. Pandora revealed she and her family were staying in a sad motel on the outskirts of the city. As brilliant as she was, she wasn't very wealthy.

Dr. Indigo then shocked the sisters further by offering them room and board in his home. Before Pandora could hesitate, Dido jumped up and accepted. Dr. Indigo then escorted them out the building where a luxuriously appointed limo was waiting. The doctor promised to notify their brother and deliver him soon.

And with that, the two sisters were sped off towards BlueBeard's amazing home.

Pandora, still dumbfounded by everything, wasn't sure if she should be excited or scared.

Pandora: "Dido, why are we doing this?! You were leery of him before."

Dido: "True, but what if this is an opportunity? I mean, he's very much interested in our research…among other things!"

Pandora: "Dido!"

Dido: "Come on, you've seen the way he looks at you, and although the beard is a bit weird, he is still quite a hottie!"

Pandora: "I'm not hooking up with him! I'm not a mistress!"

Dido: "Who said just hook up? I'm talking work your way down the aisle!"

Pandora: "*Marry him*?"

Dido: "Yeah! Do you realize how much money you'd have access to, all the technology, and the number of lives we can save with that? I mean…what have we got to lose?"

Pandora: "But…"

Dido: "Sis…those rumors about his wives may be just that, rumors. If he was doing something suspicious don't you think this planet's government would have investigated him?"

Pandora: "Still…"

Dido: "Look, sis, just get to know him, I mean… He may be someone you can like…maybe love."

Pandora was dumbfounded. She didn't know what to think. Part of her was obviously attracted to the doctor but something in the back of her mind was telling her to second-guess that feeling.

Those thoughts quickly subsided once she looked out the limo window to see a huge, sprawling mansion. It almost looked like a hybrid of a Las Vegas casino and a Royal Palace. It was truly a sight to behold.

As the limo slowly pulled up the driveway, Pandora was wondering what her next move would be. She had never been so confused and terrified all in the same moment.

The two sisters soon walked through the front door into an amazing entryway with two staircases spiraling in opposite directions. The stairs were ivory, trimmed in gold.

The crystal chandelier danced with the natural light from outside shining on every crystal. It was almost like an aurora borealis was enveloping the whole room.

Dido was practically drooling at the artwork hanging on the walls. Not only that, but there were beautifully sculpted statues near the main entryway. The doctor seemed to collect pieces of art from different parts of the Galaxy.

As both the sisters gawked at this amazing house, they were startled by a disembodied voice.

Simon: "You must be the young ladies staying with us this evening."

The ladies turned to see an android with luminescent skin and electric-blue eyes, dressed in a dark blue tux.

Simon: "Greetings. My name is S1-M0N 9, but you may call me Simon. I am Dr. Indigo's personal manservant."

Pandora: "Oh… You startled us. I didn't realize the doctor had access to robo… I mean, a butler."

Simon: "I do apologize for startling you. Now if you will follow me I will show you to your quarters for the evening."

The robot butler gestured toward a corridor leading farther into the house. The ladies followed him while still admiring the rest of the house.

Soon they arrived at two rooms. They were amazed at how beautiful they were. They were truly rooms fit for a queen.

Pandora noticed a huge bouquet of Martian Sunset orchids. She couldn't help but smell them. As she enjoyed their sweet scent she noticed a small note, which read:

My Dearest Dr. Lyon,

Please accept these orchids as a token of my affection. I've also left some clothing that you and your family can wear for the Inventor's Ball tonight. I am truly delighted that you have honored my home with your presence. I eagerly await seeing your lovely form do this dress justice.

My home is your home, so please, enjoy.

Till tonight!

Lorenzo A.G. Indigo

Pandora: "Lorenzo…"

Pandora wasn't aware that a slight smirk had appeared on her face as she read the note. However, her sister was staring right at her with a huge grin. Pandora looked unamused by her sister's expression.

Pandora: "Shut up."

Dido: "You likey!"

Pandora: "Knock it off!"

Dido: "Well, don't just stand there! Let see what the good doctor left for us. I see a package on your bed!"

Pandora rolled her eyes but begrudgingly opened one of the packages left for them. Their hearts dropped when they looked inside. Dido reached into the box and pulled out a stunning floor-length gown in the most vibrant shade of crimson. It was beaded to perfection with what appeared to be ruby-toned Swarovski crystals. With a heart-shaped plunging neckline and more crystals draping at the shoulder line, the dress looked like it belonged to royalty.

Dido quickly thrust the dress into her sister's arms and ordered her to put it on. About a half an hour passed before Pandora came out, and the dress fit perfectly.

Dido was screaming with delight at how beautiful her sister looked, but realized she had a gift too and ran out the room to go get it. Pandora couldn't help but walk toward the mirror and admire herself.

Pandora: "I don't think I've ever had anything so beautiful."

As she admired herself in the mirror, she heard her sister squeal. She quickly walked towards her sister's room and smiled.

Dido was wearing a beautiful, flowy, floor-length dress. Layered in ruffles, the fabric was light lilac with flecks of gold. With a halter top and a plunging neckline, her little sister looked like a vision.

Dido: "Man, this guy has good taste!"

Pandora giggled. She hadn't seen her sister this happy in a very long time. They'd lost their parents years ago, so it had only been them and their big brother since then. The more she thought about their loneliness, the more the doctor didn't seem like a bad guy; especially if he had this to offer.

Happiness.

With that on her mind, Pandora kept her thoughts to herself as the two sisters finished getting ready and made their way back to the entryway.

They were already excited but that was elevated when they saw their big brother standing at the doorway. Like them, their brother Aegis had crimson hair and piercing amber eyes. He was dressed in a tailored charcoal gray tuxedo with a slight golden shimmer. Although he wasn't the hugest fan of formal wear, he really liked the suit. And he was in awe of his two sisters.

Aegis: "Damn, you two clean up good!"

Dido: "You don't look half bad yourself, big bro."

Pandora: "You do look very handsome."

Even Simon was impressed by how lovely the two girls looked.

Simon: "Now that everyone's here and ready to go, the limo is waiting outside."

Pandora: "I still can't believe this is all real!"

Dido: "Why not? After all the struggles we've gone through, maybe this is God's way of saying 'Hey you earned this!'"

Pandora: "Hmmmmmm…"

Dido: "Just once, let's live it up, regardless of what happens tonight."

Pandora nodded in response, agreeing that they should enjoy this once-in-a-lifetime happening.

Everyone got into the limo and head to The Vidus Amphitheater. The place was lit up like a Hollywood awards show. Dozens of scientists, doctors, surgeons and inventors filled the theater. Some of the universe's greatest minds were there, and Pandora was one of them.

The evening was truly magical, Pandora spoke to the other scientists, absorbing every bit of knowledge she could. Hours flew by as the night wore on. Soon it was time for Pandora's speech. All the tension from earlier disappeared as Pandora confidently spoke before her peers.

As she spoke, Dr. Indigo looked on from the shadows, hanging on her every word.

Once she was done and had received a standing ovation, the doctor swiftly made his way toward her and her siblings, who were congratulating her.

Indigo: "Brilliant speech, Dr. Lyon!"

Pandora turned towards Dr. Indigo, who was in a jet-black tuxedo, trimmed in crimson, complimenting her gown.

Pandora: "Lorenzo…ahhh, I mean, Dr. Indigo!"

Indigo: "Please… I rather like hearing my first name coming from your lips."

Pandora's cheeks flushed as red as her dress. Dr. Indigo then bowed and offered his hand to her.

Indigo: "May I please have this dance?"

The doctor looked at her brother and sister: "With your blessing, of course."

Aegis wasn't feeling his vibe, but before he could say anything, Dido burst in.

Dido: "I'd say, blessing given!"

Dr. Indigo nodded, and Pandora took his hand as they walked to the dance floor. Aegis gave Dido an ugly look, but Dido dragged him to hors d'oeuvres table to distract him.

Pandora and the doctor did the tango so passionately that some of the onlookers started to blush. Pandora wasn't sure if what she was feeling was love or just desire, but she liked it! After the years of being a meek mouse in a lab, struggling to care for herself and her family, the idea of being the center of this powerful man's world was seductive. And she couldn't deny her attraction to him.

As Dr. Indigo dipped her to end their dance, Pandora unselfconsciously, gently, kissed his lips.

This stunned them both, as well as the entire crowd. Aegis was about break them up—and maybe break a few of the doctor's bones—but Dido pushed him back and tried to calm him down.

Pandora: "I'm… I… I'm sorry!"

Dr. Indigo: "W— Wait!"

Pandora panicked and shifted out of Dr. Indigo's arms. Embarrassed, she ran off, trying to find a place to hide.

\* \* \* \*

A half hour passed by the time she found a quiet balcony to try and collect her thoughts.

Pandora: "What was I thinking? Why did I kiss him? I barely even know him!"

Pandora was leaning on the balcony railing, struggling with her thoughts, when she felt a hand on her shoulder. Startled, she spun around to see Dr. Indigo.

Pandora: "Doctor…"

Dr. Indigo: "Lorenzo, please…"

Pandora froze, unsure what to do. So this time the doctor kissed her.

With that kiss, Pandora gave into her emotions. All her life she had to be the strong sister, the fearless doctor, and the substitute mother to her two siblings. Never did she let herself be normal, because normal wasn't going to save her family from poverty or save the lives of her patients. She had to be focused…but right now, she wanted to lose control. To feel free…wanted…desired.

The kiss lingered until Dr. Indigo break it long enough to say two words…

Dr. Indigo: "Marry me."

Pandora's eyes widened!

Pandora: "You can't be serious!"

Dr. Indigo: "As a heart attack. I know I care for you, no matter how short our time together has been. All I know is I've never known a mind as brilliant as yours; your beauty simply matches it! I doubt I will ever find a woman as amazing as you and I don't want to keep looking.

"Marry me and I vow to make you and your family happy. This I swear!"

Pandora was dumbfounded by his declaration of love. They had barely known each other for a day and now he was offering her everything she could ever want. In any other situation, she'd weigh all the pros and cons, but the only thing she could think of was how happy her sister has been this entire time. And she could save many people with such wealth and tech. So for once…Pandora didn't think…she just reacted!

She softly answered him.

Pandora: "Yes."

Dr. Indigo's eyes lit up. He landed a passionate kiss on her. Pandora gave into the kiss and embraced him. At least it felt right.

With their hands locked within one another's, they walked back towards the dance floor and made the announcement. Dido jumped up and down. Aegis, however, was in shock. All of this happened in one day.

The crowd cheered for the doctor and Pandora, but Pandora heard a faint voice in the back of her head saying, "What have you done?"

\* \* \* \*

Six months later…

Time passed by incredibly quickly. They were married less than a week later after their announcement. It almost seemed like it wasn't real, but Pandora became accustomed to a life as a millionaire surgeon's wife. She received more than enough funding for her research and developed new methods for treating soldiers' injuries during battle.

She was sending her little sister to med school to further her own research, and her older brother joined the Earth Alliance Air Force Squadron. Pandora had gained more respect among her peers for her research and received glowing recommendations from her new husband. She seemed to be the happiest she had been in a very long time, all because she had taken a chance and reacted, instead of overthinking every situation.

She still wasn't sure if she would call her feelings towards the doctor love, but there was definite passion and many sleepless nights. She kept telling herself "if love isn't there right now, eventually it will be. We're already married, all we have is time."

He never mentioned his previous wives, only said that the past is the past and their relationship now was all that mattered. But that didn't make her any less unsure at times.

These women might have been his past, but they were still ever-present. Their portraits still hung in their home and they seemed to be almost leering at her. She felt like they were watching over her shoulder, almost telling her that she needed to leave.

With everything going well, why does she have this feeling?

Pandora: "Something is starting to feel really wrong, and I don't know why."

* * * *

As the months passed, she noticed one area of the house she has yet to enter. One room. One room with a huge crimson door. It was the only room in the entire house that the doctor would not allow her to enter.

Other than that, she had access to everything else in the home even the lab, but not this room.

For months this has irritated her, and she asked herself: "Why can't I enter this room? Why am I so consumed with what's behind this door?"

Her husband seemed to be very free with everything but information about his past. Could that have something to do with what's behind this door? The idea started to consume her and one day the Pandora who took a chance to marry a stranger instantly disappeared, leaving behind the true meticulous and inquisitive Pandora she had always been. She had to know what was behind that door.

Another month passed and it all seemed to still be well. Then her husband had to go away on a business trip to a nearby planet.

Doctor Indigo: "I'll only be gone a short time, my love. I won't be away from you long. But there is something I want you to do for me."

Pandora noticed his tone was a little bit colder than normal, icy even.

Doctor Indigo: "Here is the key to the red door, I want you to keep it safe. But as I've said many times, never enter this room. Because if you do I will know."

Pandora got a slight chill down her spine. He'd never spoken so coldly to her before.

The doctor then quickly pulled her close and kissed her, but something was off with the kiss.

It started to feel more possessive, not passionate.

Where did this slight shift in personality come from?

And with that the doctor departed on his trip, leaving his wife alone in their huge empty home. Well not completely alone—she did have Simon, who had grown quite attached to his new mistress. He answered every question she eagerly asked except what was behind the red door.

He claims his database does not have any information on the door, yet when she looks into his robotic eyes she can see something that looks almost like fear. For someone made of wires and metal, he seems more human than her husband sometimes.

As cold as her husband had slowly become, the robot was the most human companion she had in the entire house. Her little sister was away at school and her brother was out in the field.

If it wasn't for Simon, she would feel like she was in a prison, albeit a beautifully built one. All she had when she wasn't working was the empty house, a robot companion, and that one room that kept taunting her.

She had to know. She was going to enter that room.

So later that week, with her husband gone and Simon in the farthest part of the mansion, Pandora finally walked towards the red door, pulled out the matching colored card key her husband had given her, and opened the door.

Suddenly a horrifying stench wafted into her nostrils. She almost threw up. But the room was pitch black, so she couldn't see anything.

As she slowly walked through the room trying to find a light switch, she could hear her own steps. They sounded wet. *What has spilled on this floor?*

She noticed that the red keycard was glowing and matched a glowing light at the end of the room—the key switch? She managed to shuffle through the dark room, bumping into objects until she eventually reached the end and hit the switch.

Once the light slowly rose she was horrified at what she saw. She looked at the ground and saw blood—human blood, alien blood, of various colors—spilled all over the floor. Body parts hung on meat hooks above her. They had been severed with surgical precision. She walked around the room and realize she was in a laboratory. She could see multiple jars of various organs from all types of beings, but the key commonality was all these parts came from females.

As she walked through the room she noticed a head sitting on a table with wires going to the skull. The head looked like it belonged to a female the same species as the doctor who given her and Dido their first tour. Then it dawned on her; she was looking at the head of his last wife. She knew she wasn't mistaken. She'd seen the woman's portrait in this house for months. As she continued to walk around the room, she noticed a wall with niches containing more jars.

They contained the remaining heads of Dr. Indigo's other four wives. Pandora was near the brink of panic. *Who the hell did I marry?* she asked herself. And she noticed all the books surrounding the room. They each had something to do with galvanism. It suddenly dawned on her: he's trying to bring these parts back to life in one woman.

Pandora: "Does he think he is Frankenstein? He's trying to build his own woman. He… He… He murdered these women just so he could have parts to play with? I have to get out of here, I have to tell the police."

With that, Pandora quickly shuffled her way through the blood-stained room back to the front door. But she slipped and dropped the card key on the floor. Blood stuck to it.

Pandora: "God dammit!"

She quickly picked it up, walked out the door, and locked it behind her. As she did, she could hear a car pulling up to the front of the house. She quickly ran down the corridor to peek through the main archway.

Pandora: "Oh my God, he's home!"

Pandora quickly ran back to her room to change her dress. She threw the key into her pocket and prepared to greet her husband. If he discovered that she had disobeyed him and found out his secret, it would not end well. She knew that after what she'd seen.

Before she met her husband, she made sure to send a message to her sister and her brother telling them that something was wrong, and they needed to get help. If something happened, Pandora was not going to go down without a fight. She headed to the kitchen and grabbed a knife and hid it in her other pocket. She took a quick, deep breath and walked to the front door. She fixed a gentle smile on her face and opened the door.

Pandora: "Welcome home, my love!"

When her husband didn't respond, Pandora looked at him.

He looked terrifying. She'd never seen his expression so malevolent before.

He quickly pushed his way through the door and locked it behind him.

Doctor Indigo: "So your mind got the better of you, I see."

Pandora: "What are you talking about?" She tried not to panic.

Doctor Indigo: "You wouldn't listen to one simple request. You could have just found something else to keep yourself occupied with. But you couldn't let it go, could you? My dear wife, with all the technology I possess, what made you think that I wouldn't get an alert if my room was entered without my permission?"

Pandora's heart dropped and tears started to well up in her eyes. He knew she had gone into the room.

Doctor Indigo: "The blood-stained key in your in your pants pocket is a giveaway. I thought you would be different, I thought you could easily be distracted enough to stay. But no, you're just as flawed as the others. Well…looks like you'll have to join them."

Pandora: "Sweetheart, please wait…"

The doctor grabbed her by the neck and began to squeeze. He was abnormally strong and in his fury, the man Pandora thought she had married disappeared. The man who stood here before her was a killer, and if she didn't do something quick, she was going to be his next victim.

Doctor Indigo: Why couldn't you just be a good girl and do as you're told? As brilliant as you are, you become very stupid when you're curious. I did my research on you, hoping you would be the perfect one. But as I see you're flawed, just like the previous ones."

Pandora choked and struggled to speak. "What do you mean?"

Doctor Indigo: "In layman's terms, I was stalking you. Long before we met face-to-face, I invited you here to win you over, to make you mine, because I thought you were perfect. I knew your financial circumstances would help me convince you. I thought you'd be The Perfect Bride, but I was wrong."

The doctor let his free hand trace the line of Pandora's bosom.

Doctor Indigo: "So perfect... But apparently what we had was only physical. Your mind is still flawed. And I need perfection in order to carry on my line."

Pandora was crying and confused and struggling for air. As she dangled from his hand, the doctor began to walk towards the Red Room. Once in there, he roughly slammed her onto the bloodstained operating table, his hand still clapped to her neck.

Doctor Indigo: "After a little encounter years ago with my first alien corpse, my physiology started to change. I discovered with my first wife that I'm unable to produce a child. And unfortunately, making love to her slowly poisoned her to death. I soon realized that in order to find a mate and create an heir, I would either have to find another like me, or I would have to create one. So, I took what remained of my first wife: her womb!"

Pandora's eyes grew huge and she struggled even harder.

Doctor Indigo: "I remarried, and she proved flawed, too. I salvaged her heart. I married again, gaining blood with unique properties. And again, a strong nervous system. Even a few mistresses in between proved useful. I kept trying, hiding my research from the eyes of those who would not understand. Bit by bit, I sliced each to find a piece to build the biological system a female would need to bear my child. A few sacrifices for the gift of life!"

Pandora: "You sick bastard!"

Doctor Indigo: "Hmmm.... I thought as a doctor you would be intrigued. Another flaw. But your body is Perfection."

He raised her shirt to expose her stomach, and smoothed his hand over her womb.

Doctor Indigo: "Just a few internal replacements and you will be completely perfect! A little mental fix as well: just a little death before your rebirth!"

He loosened his hold, and Pandora managed to pull out the knife from her pocket and slab Doctor Indigo in the neck. She quickly broke free from his grip and jumped off the table and ran out the door.

Doctor Indigo managed to get up, the knife buried in his neck, indigo blood pouring out. He ripped out the knife and gave chase.

Pandora ran to the front door, but it was locked, so she headed up the stairs. She ran into the office, where Simon was cleaning, unaware of what was happening.

Pandora: "Please, help me, Simon."

Simon: "Yes, my lady! I will… Will… Eck!"

Simon started to glitch out and spasm, and shut down.

Pandora: "Simon? *Simon!*"

Doctor Indigo: "*Damn robot!*"

Pandora turned to the office door and saw Dr. Indigo fidgeting with his bio watch.

Doctor Indigo: "I knew giving that bucket of bolts an AI was a bad idea. Good thing he has an off switch. Now, where were we?"

Pandora: "No, please!"

Doctor Indigo: "Time to remake you!"

Pandora knew her brother or sister would come, and that she just needed to buy some time. She got an idea: she started unbuttoning her shirt and walked towards him.

Pandora: "If this is my last night, then at least grant me one final request."

Dr. Indigo's lust for her made him freeze.

Pandora: "If my body is perfect, then worship it one last time. Give me one last night of pleasure. Grant me that… Please, Lorenzo."

She moved his hand, which still clutched the knife, and rubbed her hands over his shoulders. Dr. Indigo dropped the knife and pressed his mouth to hers.

Pandora knew now their relationship had never love, just lust at an animalistic level. He stood, pulling on her clothing and nuzzling at her neck. She looked upward, terrified despite the fog of lust. Eventually she looked towards the office door. Her brother and sister stood there, gesturing for her to not alert him.

Dr. Indigo mumbled, his face buried in her chest: "I don't look forward to disassembling this body, but a couple of stitches won't remove its perfection. You're mine, either way."

Pandora pulled his face up to hers: "I belong to me, every part! You own nothing!"

She pushed him away towards her brother, who grabbed him in a choke hold. But Dr. Indigo flipped him over and grabbed Dido's neck. Pandora helped Aegis up and started to move toward her husband.

Doctor Indigo: "One more step and I'll break her windpipe!"

The siblings froze.

Doctor Indigo: "Maybe I don't have to use you, after all. Twins are identical, down to their DNA. Maybe she'll be more obedient!"

He began to squeeze.

Pandora tackled him to the floor, where he fought with her. Aegis kicked the blood-stained knife to Pandora.

Pandora grabbed it and stabbed her husband. Dr. Indigo screamed and rolled over onto his back. Pandora quickly jumped on top of him and plunged the knife deep into his heart.

Vibrant indigo blood gushed from his mouth, splattering Pandora's face. He struggled for a moment, stretching his hand towards Pandora's face, and then went limp. But Pandora kept stabbing and stabbing…until Aegis grabbed her hands.

Aegis: "It's over. He's dead. He's gone!"

Pandora, hands still gripping the knife, panted hard and started to sob.

Her brother and sister huddled together. Dido kept repeating she was sorry, over and over. Her voice was slowly drowned out by the sounds of people and sirens.

Aegis cradled both of his siblings.

It was over.

* * * *

Five months later…

Since Dr. Indigo had no heirs, Pandora was the sole beneficiary of his entire fortune. Many people still didn't believe the truth about the doctor, and many called Pandora a murderer. But the police officers who saw the Red Room knew who the real monster was.

With her newfound fortune, she furthered her own research and tried to give some closure to the families of the women who died at the doctor's hands. She created the Academy of Gaia in honor of those same women, many who had been great scientists and inventors.

Her younger sister experienced a major change after this ordeal. She was no longer so consumed with the finer things in life, but with living it to the fullest, rich or poor. Dido excelled in her studies and started to intern at the labs, which were renamed The Lyon Laboratories and Medical Center.

Eventually, Pandora found love again with an ambitious but kind-hearted robotics expert named Joka Logan. Joka was able to repair Simon and give him full free will. No more remotes!

Pandora offered Simon his freedom, but he refused. Pandora had saved him, yet he couldn't help her when it counted. Simon vowed to be her personal guard…and best friend.

With all the past events, good and ill, Pandora learned to never doubt her intuition again. She also learned to take more chances, and to stand strong in her beliefs.

She hoped to leave a positive legacy and to erase the pain and darkness Dr. Indigo left behind.

---

Kitamu Latham-Sampier is a 34-year-old illustrator based out of Los Angeles, CA. She's been drawing since age five and writing since age thirteen. Her interests are in subjects like subcultural and international themes, legends, mythology, and different eras. Her motto is: Creating Art has always been and will always be my first love, but creating worlds or my characters to live within is another, that is my true passion. Regardless of where life leads me, I plan to do what I love. Because I can't see being happy doing anything else. Instagram: @MarkedLotusInk; @Sankofarida; www.klsart.com

# THE FROG PRINCE

## Stephanie Vega-Gonzalez

### *Inspired by The Princess and the Frog*

Once upon a time, in a distant future, lived a girl name Aricia. She was beautiful and very intelligent. She had gotten her doctoral degree in zoology with an emphasis in herpetology. She was consistently fascinated by all types of amphibians and reptiles, but mostly by frogs and toads. Even though Aricia was a beautiful woman, she had a difficult time finding someone to love. She has had plenty of possible suitors, yet her heart was not set on just any kind of man. No. Her deep yearning was to be with someone who enjoyed and loved her world of herpetology, and not many eligible men worked in this field.

While in her lab one day, she discovered a new frog in an empty terrarium. She named him "Leafy" because he looked like a Yellow-eyed Leaf Frog. He soon became her favorite frog.

She made her way toward his frog terrarium and studied the environment she had created for him—a miniature rainforest, both vibrant and soothing. She had specifically placed ferns, plenty of moss, a piece of driftwood, a fog mister, and a miniature waterfall just for him.

"How perfect would my life be, Leafy…" Her breath fogged up the glass as she leaned closer. "If only I could find the one who truly understands me and my passion."

As if he could understand her, Leafy hopped on top of his driftwood, nodded, and puffed his chest in and out.

"I am smart," she continued. Even though the frog could not talk, in Aricia's mind she believed he did. "You're right!" she said. "I will create a serum that will allow you to truly talk, and possibly turn you into a good friend."

Aricia was determined to create a serum that would do as she wished. For days and weeks she did not leave her laboratory. She worked for many hours testing it on different frogs, but never on Leafy. Many of her experiments turned fellow frogs purple, bright blue, neon green, and even yellow. She even got one to walk on its hind legs, but never did one of her experiments make a frog talk.

Was her dream too farfetched? She glanced over at Leafy, who was sitting by his waterfall. He blinked and nodded, as if telling her to carry on, and she remembered her father's words.

"You're right," she responded. "My father might not be here, but he always taught me to never give up and follow through." Aricia sat down, and then she remembered. "Why didn't I think of it before?" she said, as she stood. Then she rushed to her locker and took out her bag. She opened it and pulled out a round, golden flask, shaped like a ball. "I still haven't tried one element. Gold!"

On that very day, she began to mix the ingredients and placed them in a beaker. She turned her Bunsen burner on low, and heated the liquid until it turned blue. Aricia waited until it cooled, then placed her golden flask on the table. Placing the stirrer bar in, she then carefully poured the liquid into the flask.

"Leafy," she said as she secured the flask onto the clamp and placed the stopper. "You may not know this, but my father gave me this flask. It has been one of the greatest gifts I have ever received." She turned on the magnetic stirrer and adjusted the speed to low.

After a time, the serum was finished. She unclamped the flask and used a dropper to take some out. For the first time, the serum had turned into a colorless liquid.

"Leafy. I believe I finally got the serum right." Her body began to tremble as she placed the dropper down and reached for the flask. The thought that this bottle could hold the key to her dreams made her weak. Aricia ran toward Leafy's tank while holding the flask. Even though she knew the basic rules of laboratory safety, her excitement got the best of her. Not watching where she was stepping, she tripped over a box. The round, golden flask slipped out of her hand. Aricia fell to the floor and was not aware that the flask hand landed on top of the tank screen. The liquid poured in, showering Leafy.

Aricia stood, her breathing rapid. "Leafy. What have I done?" She ran to the tank and picked up the flask. It was empty. She leaned in and studied him, but he had not turned purple, bright blue, neon green, or yellow. She waited for a while, to see if he could stand. But Leafy did not.

"Oh, Leafy. I had thought my new serum was the one, but I guess even I cannot make my wish come true." She laid her head on the table and cried.

\* \* \* \*

After a few hours, she was awakened by a low knocking. Aricia stood and looked around the lab. "Who is there?" she said. No one answered, yet she heard the knocking again.

"Down here," a low, hoarse voice called. She looked down and saw Leafy seated on his driftwood. She leaned closer.

"Leafy, was that you?" she asked, not getting her hopes high. He nodded. This had to be her imagination. "I have to give up my silly dream." She sat back down.

"Now why would you do that?" the hoarse voiced called out again. "Aricia. Why won't you reply? For it is I."

Hearing this, Aricia looked up. "Is it true? Did it work? Can you talk?"

"Yes," Leafy said. "All your hard work and failed attempts have finally paid off, my dear Aricia."

She froze, not believing what she had just heard and seen. Seconds passed as she held her breath.

"I have so many questions for you," Aricia began to breathe easily. She sat next to the tank. "Will you be so kind to answer them?" she asked while attempting to hold herself together and not jump off the walls.

"I will do as you wish, but first you must promise me something." Leafy jumped closer to the wall of the tank. He placed his small hand on the glass.

"Anything for you," she said.

"I will guide you in making a new serum—and with the help of your golden flask, I believe my serum will work. Will you please make it for me?"

Aricia's eyes widened—she was holding a conversation with Leafy. Not wanting to upset her new friend, she nodded her head without questioning him.

* * * *

Leafy and Aricia began to work on making many serums, none of which worked. Three days had passed, and both frog and woman had started to become restless. Leafy persuaded her to do one more experiment. Once she was done, she used the dropper to remove some of the serum, which was a goldish color.

"That's it!" Leafy hopped around his tank. "Please take me out and place me on the floor. Then pour the liquid over me."

She did as he requested. She held the golden flask ball steady, and poured the liquid on Leafy. As it touched his green skin, a flash of light filled the room. Aricia looked away. After the light had died down, she glanced back were Leafy had been. But instead, a tall, handsome man in matching green pants and shirt stood before her.

"Who are you?" Aricia said, while scanning the floor for Leafy.

"Do I not look familiar?" The man's hoarse voice slowly turned normal. "It is I." He took a step toward her.

Aricia shook her head. "How is this possible? It cannot be."

"My name is Deras Royce," he said.

"Wait a minute." That name sounded familiar, but it couldn't be. "Did you used to work in the lab?" Aricia said.

"Three months ago," he said, "and you never noticed me." His voice was calm and even as he stared directly into her eyes. "I worked on my own experiments, hoping to gain your attention. Somehow throughout the process, something went wrong, and I turned into a frog," he said. "That was when I saw and felt your admiration for herpetology—the same admiration I felt for it…and for you."

Aricia was breathless. She stared at the man's eyes, and in them she saw the exact twinkle that Leafy had. He extended his hand to her, and she took it. The coolness of his skin put her at ease.

"Before I turned into a frog," he said, "I received a full grant to study them in Central and South America. The only thing missing was a research partner who shared my passion." He pulled her close. "Aricia, you are the perfect partner. Please give me the opportunity to prove myself to you."

Aricia was thrilled that her wishes had somehow come true. "Yes. I will join you," she said as she embraced Deras in a hug.

Before she knew it, eight white equipment boxes were packed, she was waiting in line to board the airplane. She held her first class ticket tightly as she stood behind Deras's friend, Henry. He was the analyst of their research team, and Deras's loyal friend. He had been searching for Deras during his disappearance, and was glad that he had reappeared.

* * * *

Both Aricia and Deras explored the wonders of Central and South America. Their love for each other and frogs grew with each sunrise and sunset. And they lived, as you would expect, happily ever after.

Stephanie Vega-Gonzalez holds a master degree from California State University, Fresno with an emphasis in early childhood education. In addition to learning about children's growth and development, you can always find her writing stories filled with magic and adventure. She found her passion of storytelling at the age of eleven. Ever since then, she has never stopped writing. On any given day you can find her reading, painting, or visiting the public library with her daughter. Stephanie's motto is to stay positive and happy, work hard and never give up hope. You can contact her at Stephanievvega@gmail.com and follow her on Instagram and Twitter at @SGVega1.

# BEAST

## Christine Pope

### *A Gaian Consortium Story Inspired by Beauty and the Beast*

Author's Note: Although this story is set in the Consortium universe, it takes place roughly a hundred and fifty years before the events of *Blood Will Tell*, et al., at a time when the Consortium was just beginning to expand into the galaxy outside Gaia's solar system and hadn't yet developed the star-spanning empire seen in the series' other books.

\*

"You remember the protocols?" Lt. Lopez asked, partially blocking the double steel doors that opened onto Dr. Killian's wing of the research complex.

"Of course," Nora replied. Despite her best efforts, some of her irritation slipped into those two simple syllables. Did the man—second in command here at Triton Base—think she was an idiot? All right, she was a postdoc researcher with a newly minted Ph.D. and not a hell of a lot of real-world experience, but still. Raymond Killian had asked for her specifically, which meant she'd beaten out hundreds of other contenders for this position. Praying that her expression was more neutral than her tone, she added, "I've read all the briefings. Twice. You have nothing to worry about."

"Oh, I'm not the one who's worried," Lopez said. He looked her up and down in a way that could only be described as offensive, and Nora bristled again. To her relief, however, he swiped a card over the reader next to the entrance, then handed the transparent piece of plastic to her as the doors retracted into the walls, revealing a long corridor painted an institutional gray. If she hadn't known better, she would have thought she was back on Gaia in one of the labs where she'd done her doctoral work, rather than an outpost on Triton, Neptune's largest moon. "I'm not the one who almost pulled your authorization."

"Excuse me?" She probably should have held her tongue, but this was the first she'd heard of Dr. Killian having any second thoughts. It might have taken Raymond Killian a while to make up his mind, but once it was made up, he'd expected her to jump—and fast. "Where did you hear that the offer might be rescinded?"

A shrug. "That's the rumor. The good doctor doesn't confide in the likes of me. Better go in," Lopez added. "He doesn't like to be kept waiting."

No, she supposed he didn't. Nora tucked the key card—tiny chips glowed within the plastic, like fireflies embedded in a matrix—into a pocket of the utility vest she wore. "Thank you, Lieutenant."

He gave her a nod rather than a salute. Well, her background was scientific, not military, so she supposed he thought she didn't rate a salute.

Irritating as Lopez might be, she was almost sorry to hear the doors to the lab complex hiss shut behind her, leaving her alone in the corridor. She had no idea what to expect from her new supervisor.

The story had been all over the news five years earlier. Head down in the first year of her graduate studies, Nora hadn't paid a lot of attention. Of course she knew who Raymond Killian was—even if she hadn't already chosen cybernetics as her particular field of study, the brilliant scientist was a media favorite, combining groundbreaking work on limb replacements and neural networks with a crowd-pleasing appetite for extreme sports, whether those sports involved stratospheric diving or asteroid obstacle courses.

It was during one of the latter races that disaster struck. Killian had been piloting an experimental craft specifically designed for the insanely fast pace and tight maneuvering of asteroid racing. Arguments still raged about the exact cause of the accident, although most people believed that it had to have been mechanical breakdown, rather than pilot error. Since the tiny vessel had broken into millions of component parts, a postmortem of the ship's wreckage was never performed.

Miraculously, Raymond Killian survived. Or rather, he was somehow still breathing when the rescue ship picked him up. His body was nearly as shattered as his ship, however, and no one expected him to live for very long. Somehow, though, he clung to life, and eventually recovered enough to leave Gaia and set up shop here on Triton, where a rudimentary research station was expanded to his specific instructions.

No one ever saw him, though. He gave no interviews, did not allow outsiders to visit the facility, whereas before the accident, every new advance had been announced via media spectacles. The rumor began to circulate that he was forever disfigured, that even his own inventions couldn't save him.

Nora had dismissed those rumors as simply tabloid gossip, nothing to concern her. Actually, since Dr. Killian had stopped publishing in scientific journals, she hadn't thought much about him…until she received a communiqué only a month ago, a transmission apparently from the elusive scientist himself. He had seen her paper on strategies for combating rejection in neural networks, and wanted her to join his team. At first, she'd been flabbergasted that a near-mythical figure like Raymond Killian had reached out to her. After the shock had worn off, she found herself torn. While the opportunity tempted her, she didn't much like the thought of moving to the research facility on Triton, a place so remote that she knew she wouldn't see Gaia again for a very long time. The invitation had been open-ended, so she didn't know how long Killian expected her to stay.

In the end, though, she agreed. Curiosity drove her, along with an understanding of what such an experience could do to enhance her resumé. If, after six months or so, she found herself going crazy from the isolation, she'd find a way to gracefully remove herself from the position. Although she had family and friends who would miss her, they also understood what an amazing opportunity had fallen into her lap. And she also didn't have any romantic entanglements to worry about; while she'd had a few short-term relationships as an undergrad, she hadn't been serious about anyone since. How could she, when she had to focus all her intentions, all her drive, on getting her degree?

All those decisions had seemed eminently logical at the time. Now, though, as she strode toward her first meeting with the reclusive scientist, Nora found her mouth dry and her pulse quickening. Lopez's words echoed in her mind.

*Do you remember the protocols?*

Yes, she did…and now she couldn't help wondering once again at the need that drove them. Beyond the doors she approached now was a clean room. She would pause there to be sprayed down with an antibacterial, antiviral, antistatic mist. Once that was done, she would be allowed into the sanctum. Her interactions with Raymond Killian were to be rigidly controlled: Don't speak unless spoken to. Don't make eye contact.

And above all, never, ever touch him.

Not that she saw any reason why she would do such a thing. She was here as his research assistant, nothing more. All right, if they were in the commissary together, and he began to choke on a sandwich, she supposed she would administer the Heimlich maneuver to save him, but from what she'd heard, she rather doubted Dr. Killian would ever make an appearance in the commissary, much less share a meal with his support staff.

She came to the entrance to the lab, and began to reach in her pocket for the key card Lt. Lopez had given her. However, before she could retrieve it, the doors hissed open. Despite herself, she jumped slightly.

*Damn it,* she thought. *He'd better not be the type who enjoys playing mind games. I don't have time for that kind of crap.*

Chin up, she entered the clean room. As soon as she'd cleared the doors, they shut again. Nora could feel her mouth compress, but she remained where she was, held her arms up as the sprayers extended from the walls and coated every square inch of her face and body. Even though she knew intellectually that the spray wouldn't affect the light cosmetics she'd applied or the clothes she wore, she had a hard time preventing herself from flinching, although she did keep her eyes tightly shut. The literature she'd read had informed her that the spray would not harm the delicate surface of her eyes, but she thought she'd rather not find out the hard way.

After approximately thirty seconds had passed, the sprayers retracted into the walls, and a second pair of doors opened before her. The mist coating her already dry, Nora advanced into the space, noting the various workstations with their heads-up displays, the large metal table in the center of the room with a partially constructed network lying upon it, micro-tubes gleaming under the harsh overhead lights.

The place appeared completely empty, even though it clearly had been built to accommodate a team of five to ten people. She glanced around, saw a door cut in the wall opposite the spot where she stood, although the lock beside it glowed red, indicating that it was sealed.

Should she go to that door? Or should she wait where she was? It was disconcerting to stand here in this empty lab, her satchel with her computer and other necessities slung over one shoulder. Not that she had been expecting to be welcomed by a brass band, but this was the first time she'd ever arrived at a new post and not had someone there to greet her.

Ignoring the other door and its warning red light, she walked over to the worktable and set her satchel down on it, then went over to inspect the network that lay on the table's surface. It was far more intricate than anything she'd seen before, a lattice of interconnected chips and frail, opalescent tubes barely a micron thick. Beautiful in a strange and alien way, like a jellyfish washed up on some forlorn shore.

"Don't touch that."

Nora's hand jerked back, even though she'd had no intention of touching the network. She straightened and turned toward the source of those harsh words…and stared for half a second before she remembered the protocols that had been drilled into her, and dropped her gaze to somewhere around the midsection of the apparition who now confronted her.

His body was covered by a loose dark robe over a close-fitting black jumpsuit. Dark hair fell in a wild and unruly mane to his shoulders. And his face—well, Nora couldn't see his face at all, since it was hidden by an articulated composite-metal mask, something that seemed to shift with his expressions, judging by the way the raised ridges of its brows drew together as he confronted her.

"Dr. Killian?" she managed. The words came out with an underlying tremor, and she inwardly scolded herself for allowing her shock to reveal itself in her voice. Trying to sound steadier, she went on, "I'm Nora Whitaker."

"I know who you are, Dr. Whitaker."

The roughness in his voice wasn't merely impatience; she could tell he must have suffered some damage to his vocal chords in the same accident that had shattered his face and body. "Well, then," she said briskly. Yes, his appearance had startled her. No wonder he'd hidden himself away here on Triton, had avoided even audio-only interviews. But none of that should matter to her. She was here to work…and learn. "Since you hired me, Dr. Killian, you should know that I'm not so inexperienced that I would ever handle an uninstalled neural network without the proper equipment, even if I have been half-drowned in an anti-contaminant spray first."

He came closer. The metal plates around his mouth shifted slightly in what she guessed was supposed to be a smile…or a smirk. "My apologies. I tend to be rather…protective…of my work."

"It's nothing," she said. She shifted her attention from him back to the network. "If I'd built something so delicate, I'd be protective, too. This is light-years ahead of anything I've seen back on Gaia."

"No need for flattery, Dr. Whitaker."

"I don't flatter," she told him. "I only comment on what I see before me, Dr. Killian."

"Raymond," he said. "We can dispense with the formalities."

"Of course…Raymond," Nora replied, although she didn't know if she'd ever feel comfortable addressing him by his first name. Or being around him at all. She didn't know quite what she'd been expecting, only that it certainly hadn't been a figure out of a dark fairy tale, face hidden by a metal mask, his clothing more suited to the Brothers Grimm than a modern laboratory. "Speaking of work, what would you like me to start on first?"

"Not this," he said, one gloved hand indicating the network that lay on the table before him. "I've sent my latest research to your account on the facility's intranet. I think it best if you familiarize yourself with what I'm doing before digging in...so to speak."

Such precautionary measures only made sense, although Nora couldn't help but experience a small stab of disappointment. She'd had visions of working alongside Dr. Killian—Raymond—from the get-go, but it appeared he wasn't willing to give her free run of the lab just yet. "I'll get right on that," she said.

"I have no doubt you will." He hesitated, then continued, "Have your quarters been assigned? Has someone shown you the rest of the facility?"

"Yes. Lt. Lopez gave me a brief tour."

Brief, indeed. She'd been guided to her new apartment, which was small and cramped but adequate enough. It wasn't as though she'd been expecting luxury accommodations out here on Triton. All she really needed was a bed, a bathroom, a small kitchen space for those times when she didn't wish to eat in the cafeteria, a sitting area for relaxing. Lopez had also shown her the commissary, the infirmary, the largish space that could be used for showing films or converted to a bar and nightclub—"We try to be social at least once a week," he'd told her with another of those almost-but-not-quite leering looks—and also the airlock where you could take a suit and go out to explore the surface of the frigid moon.

She had a feeling she'd pass on that particular attraction. If past experience was any indication, she'd be so busy helping Raymond with his research that she wouldn't have time to catch a film, let alone spend the hours necessary to get her suit rating so she could go wandering around on Triton's surface. From what she'd been able to tell as the shuttle descended toward Neptune's moon, there wasn't a whole hell of a lot to see out there anyway.

"Then you might as well go to your quarters," Raymond Killian said. The planes of his mask didn't shift at all, so she had no idea what he was thinking right then. Relief that he wouldn't have to give her a tour? No, she got the distinct impression that he rarely left the lab...if ever. "You have a great deal to get caught up on. Once you've absorbed everything, you can contact me through the facility intranet. You'll find the code in the directory. Have a good day."

That was it? After traveling millions of miles to get here, all she got for her trouble was a five-minute interview and a pile of reading material?

Nora hesitated, but knew she wouldn't bother to protest. This was what she'd signed up for—to be Dr. Raymond Killian's assistant, no matter what that might entail. If only she'd been able to detect some hint as to whether he was even glad she was here. But that strange articulated metal mask was completely still now, and the roughness of his voice did a good job of concealing his emotions. Maybe after she'd worked with him for a few months, she'd be able to pick up on his tells. For now, though—

"You too, Raymond." She picked up her satchel, slid the strap over her shoulder. "I'll contact you as soon as I feel ready to help with the project."

"I look forward to hearing from you."

That, it seemed, was that. Nora turned away from him and retraced her steps, went through the clean room and back out into the main hall-way, over to the bank of elevators so she could head up to the fifth floor of the facility, which was where all the personnel apartments were located. As she entered her own living quarters, she couldn't help but wonder where Killian resided. Somehow she couldn't imagine him rubbing shoulders with the rest of the support staff here. Did he have an apartment of his own by the lab? Maybe that was what lay behind the locked door on the other side of the large workroom where they'd met, how he must have entered the chamber, although she'd been so engrossed in examining the neural network, she hadn't noticed exactly how he got in.

She doubted she'd get to see what was behind that locked door any-time soon.

* * * *

As she delved into Raymond Killian's research, Nora began to see why he had been in no hurry to have her jump in and start right away. It wasn't simply that he'd taken the standard research on the topic of cybernetics and advanced it to a new level—he'd dragged it kicking and screaming to an entirely new plane of existence. If what she was reading was true, then he was very close to creating an individual cybernetic organism, the holy grail of this line of research, and one that had continued to elude scientists, even as the Consortium made great strides in finally perfecting a star drive that would propel them beyond the limits of Gaia's solar system.

Was Killian playing God? Maybe. Right then, Nora didn't much care, as long as she was able to work with him on this project.

After five grueling days of poring over his electronic papers and notes, of pausing again and again to make her own annotations to his research, she thought she had a good enough grasp of what he was doing that she should be able to offer some valuable assistance. She sent him a note using the code listed on the facility's intranet, and waited.

And waited.

Several hours passed, and nothing. Was he so busy with his own work that he hadn't paused to check his messages? Possibly. She checked the chronometer in her apartment, saw that it was past nineteen hundred hours. Might as well get something to eat, and hope that he would respond to her message sooner rather than later.

Nora eased herself out of her desk chair and headed down to the cafeteria. To her dismay, after she'd selected a few dishes for her evening meal, she saw Lt. Lopez waving her over to a table where he sat with several other men and women, all of them wearing the uniforms of the facility's Gaian Defense Force detail.

There wasn't any way to ignore him without being obviously rude, so she smiled and nodded, and came over and took the empty seat next to him. She told herself it could be worse; at least the group at the table included both men and women, so if Lopez had intended to use this as an opportunity to hit on her, he was out of luck.

"Haven't seen you around much, Dr. Whitaker," Lopez commented as she spread her recycled-fiber napkin in her lap.

"I've been busy," she replied. "I had a lot to get caught up on."

"Secrets of the universe, huh?"

Several of the people seated at the table chuckled. Nora noted how Lopez hadn't bothered to introduce any of them, and doubted the omission was an innocent oversight. Forcing a chuckle, she lifted her shoulders. "Oh, I don't know about that. But the research is interesting."

"Want to give us a hint? Killian could be building a bomb in there for all the rest of us know."

Nora waited until she'd put a forkful of noodles and chicken in her mouth, chewed, and swallowed before she answered. "It's not a bomb."

"So what's he up to?"

"I'm afraid that's classified."

Which was only the truth, and of course Lopez—and his companions—probably knew that as well as she did.

"But you're a cyberneticist, right?" asked one of the other guards, a woman with shining coal-black hair and skin, and a lilting West African accent to match.

"Yes, that's right." Nora offered the woman a small smile to go with that reply. It couldn't hurt to show that she wasn't a complete stone wall. She just wasn't able to provide a lot of answers…partially because she didn't have all that many. Yes, she knew what Raymond Killian was attempting to do. What she couldn't quite figure out was why. The Consortium already had mechs—mechanoids, robotic constructs that took on the dirty work its citizens didn't want to perform, although mechs were still costly to produce, even with the enhancements provided by the friendly alien Eridanis. Killian's research went in an entirely different direction, with the end goal of a synthetic human indistinguishable from the real thing. The implications were staggering…and more than a little frightening. Because if you could create something so close to human it might as well be, what implications did such a creation have for the real humans?

"So maybe Killian wants her to help build him a new dick," said one of the other guards, an oversized hulk of a man whose close-cropped hair only made his shoulders look that much wider. His remark was greeted with laughter around the table.

Nora wanted to scowl at the secondary-school humor, but instead she shrugged. "I'm fairly certain he could manage something that simple all on his own," she remarked.

A few sniggers greeted her comment, and she hurried to put some more food in her mouth so she wouldn't have to say anything else. As she ate, however, she couldn't help wondering exactly how extensive Raymond Killian's injuries actually had been. Bad enough that plastic surgeons couldn't do anything to salvage his face, that specialists couldn't completely repair the damage to his vocal chords. He seemed able to walk normally, but that didn't mean much. For all she knew, he already had cybernetic legs and arms hidden underneath the dark, bulky clothing he wore. Limb replacement was very sophisticated now. Facial reconstruction, though…that field of expertise was much more nuanced and difficult. Yes, miracles were still possible, but rebuilding meant there had to be something left to build upon.

To her relief, the conversation moved to whether the theme for the next nightclub evening should be twentieth-century disco or early twenty-second-century synth trance, and Nora was able to eat the rest of her meal in relative peace and quiet. As she got up from the table, though, Lopez stopped her with a question.

"You dance, Nora?"

At least she could answer that query honestly. "No, I'm afraid not," she said. "Two left feet."

His gaze ran down her body, all the way to her feet in their lace-up boots. "They look normal enough to me."

She'd always hated how some men could make her feel as if she'd been stripped naked, just from a single stare. Color flamed in her cheeks, but she said steadily, "Looks can be deceiving."

Lopez opened his mouth to reply, but in that same instant, her handheld beeped from within her pocket. Holding back a sigh of relief, Nora set down her empty tray so she could pull out the device. On the screen was Raymond Killian's call code. "Dr. Killian," she told Lopez. "I need to take this."

The guard's mouth pulled down in a frown, but he didn't argue. "Later, Dr. Whitaker."

She watched him get up from his seat and exit the cafeteria as she raised the handheld to her ear. "Nora Whitaker."

"Nora. I received your message. Could you come by the lab?"

"Sure." Technically, she could have turned down his request, since it was now well after what was considered normal workday hours. However, after spending five days getting up to speed, she wasn't about to quibble over a few hours. Besides, what difference did it really make what time of day it was? She wanted to work. "I'll be right there."

The dinner crowd had already begun to disperse, but Nora could still feel eyes on her as she left the cafeteria. She had a feeling she hadn't made any friends in that particular group, but she wasn't here on Triton to socialize. It would have been easier if Raymond Killian had an entire team working with him, because of course she'd have more in common with fellow scientists than she did with a bunch of GDF grunts. For whatever reason, Killian had chosen to work alone, or nearly alone. Did he think the project was too sensitive to be entrusted to a large staff? Possibly.

When she got to the lab, she found him leaning over a micro-construction setup, one that would interpret the movements of his fingers and translate them to adjustments on a molecular level, performed by robotic arms too small to see with the naked eye. Since she knew how delicate such work was, she paused a few feet away and gently cleared her throat. "Raymond."

He didn't look up. "Nora. I hope I didn't interrupt your dinner."

Of course he had, but she was glad of the excuse to get away. "I was nearly finished anyway."

"Good. You'll find that I keep rather irregular hours. That won't be a problem, will it?"

"Not at all."

The faintest nod of his shaggy head. "Can you take a look at the incubator over on the counter there? I'm beginning to see signs of rejection. Let me know if you think there's any way to salvage the experiment."

"Of course."

Because she'd passed through the sterilizing spray on her way into the lab, Nora knew she didn't need to worry about donning any protective gear except gloves. She dipped her hands into the self-skinning material, then went over to the incubator. A misnomer, really, because these weren't the old-fashioned kinds of incubators used back in the day for keeping newborns alive or for coaxing baby chicks along, but rather an isolated sterile environment to test how neural networks interfaced with living flesh, whether natural or lab-grown.

As she bent over the incubator and adjusted the device's magnifying lenses to view what was happening inside, she could see at once that the flesh used in the experiment was puffy and unhealthy-looking, although it hadn't yet begun to turn red from infection. Since it wasn't too far gone, she thought she might be able to salvage it with a course of T-cell receptor-directed antibodies and other rejection inhibitors.

She pulled out her handheld and began to make a series of quick notes, listing the possible cures that might be attempted. In fact, she was so occupied that she didn't even realize Raymond Killian was standing next to her until his robe brushed against her sleeve and she started.

It was only the tiniest of jumps, but he jerked back at once. "I'm sorry. I startled you."

"Just a little," she told him. "It's fine. I tend to forget about the world when I'm looking through these lenses."

"Good."

She raised her head from the incubator and swiveled slightly on the stool where she sat so she could face him. He now stood about a foot or so away, arms crossed. Right then he looked like nothing more than a dark, ancient god, come to mete out justice to the local villagers—or possibly offer them praise for a good harvest.

"'Good'?" she repeated. "I'm not sure having my head in the clouds is exactly an admirable quality."

"But it wasn't in the clouds," he said. "It was focused on your work. That is what I need from an assistant." The masked face tilted toward the incubator. "What's your prognosis?"

"I think we can salvage the sample. I'll need to run a course of T-cell receptor-directed antibodies, and if that doesn't work, then possibly some micro-surgery on the affected areas—"

"No," he cut in. "I will allow anti-rejection drugs, as those can be administered easily enough. But a solution that requires constant upkeep through micro-surgery is no solution at all."

His objections made some sense, so Nora thought it better not to argue. "Dr. Killian—"

"Raymond."

"Some clarification, if you don't mind. Most of the research you gave me to read seemed to focus on the development of an independent cybernetic organism, so I'm not sure why you want me to focus on rejection issues. In an entirely synthetic construct, the issue of rejection wouldn't even come up, since you wouldn't be trying to fuse cybernetic components to a biological host."

A long pause. For the first time she was able to catch a glimpse of the eyes behind the mask, a clear, cold blue, like glacier ice. He blinked once, and for a moment she thought he wasn't going to reply at all. Then he said, "Contingencies, Nora. If one solution fails, then I want to make sure that we have a solid backup plan."

"A backup plan for what?"

"All in good time. For now, focus on making sure that rejection of the cybernetic network won't be a problem."

He turned away from her and headed toward the door in the far wall, the one guarded by the baleful glowing red eye of the security system. A wave of the hand, and the light turned green and the door opened. The lighting in the hallway beyond that entrance was much dimmer than here in the lab, and so she couldn't make out much of what was on the other side. Then the door shut, and she was alone.

Interesting. She hadn't seen Raymond hold out a key card to open the lock. It was almost as though he had the security chip directly embedded in his hand. Which, she supposed, wouldn't have been all that difficult to manage, if the limb truly was a cybernetic replacement for the one he'd lost in the accident.

Maybe someday she'd have the courage to ask. In the meantime, she had work to do.

* * * *

Days and days, and then weeks. Nora had gotten used to the way time seemed to grow wings and fly when she was buried in her work, but what she hadn't expected was how soon she grew accustomed to having Raymond Killian as her fellow researcher, how quickly she took his otherworldly appearance for granted. His brilliance couldn't be disputed, and yet he was always open to listening to her suggestions, to trying different avenues when his original solutions failed. What they were accomplishing here could only aid in the betterment of humankind—cybernetic limbs and organs to replace those lost to accident and disease, these new iterations stronger and sturdier, less susceptible to the biological rejection that still continued to be a problem, yet virtually identical in appearance to their natural counterparts.

And she'd also learned to navigate life at the research facility, to choose mealtimes when she knew Lt. Lopez and his compatriots would not be in the cafeteria, or, more often, taking her meals in her quarters. In all this time, she'd never seen Raymond Killian eat. For all she knew, he was unable to consume food normally, and had to resort to feeding tubes and supplements. If that was the case, she couldn't help but feel sorry that he'd lost such a basic human pleasure, but she wouldn't ask. As with so many other things, it was none of her business.

Because he'd been so secretive about his eating habits, she was shocked almost into silence when one day, nearly two months after she'd come to the facility on Triton, he asked her whether she would mind sharing dinner with him.

"D-dinner?" she stammered after a long, awkward pause.

"Yes," he said. "The meal most people consume in the early evening hours."

By that point she'd spent enough time around him that she could detect the ironic edge in his rasping voice. "Dinner would be fine," she told him. "Today?"

"Tomorrow," he said. "There's something I want to show you."

From any other man, such words might have sounded vaguely ominous. But she knew that Raymond must only be stating a simple truth. He had something he wanted her to see, something he'd kept out of the lab, for whatever reason.

"Sure," she said. "I look forward to it."

They settled back into their work as though he hadn't just made a highly unusual request. And though she somehow managed to regain most of her concentration, some part of her mind kept worrying at the problem.

Just exactly what did he plan to show her?

That night she sent her usual weekly transmission to her parents on Gaia, knowing that the message would be passed along to the rest of the family, to her brother and his wife, now expecting their first child, to Nora's aunts and uncles and cousins. While her parents had been proud of her for being chosen to work with the renowned Dr. Raymond Killian, they also worried about having their only daughter living on an outpost on the fringes of the solar system. Sending these transmissions was a way of letting them know she was fine, that all was well, even if she couldn't give them any real details about the work she was doing. And also, recording the video was her own way of reminding herself of her connection to that blue-green planet, which now seemed so very far away. Her own world had begun to shrink down to these cold gray hallways, the recycled air, the ever-present low-level hum of the artificial gravity generators.

And a pair of cool blue eyes, hidden forever behind a macabre composite-metal mask.

She did her best to keep her thoughts from dwelling on her upcoming dinner with Raymond Killian. They would work, and then when Raymond thought they'd accomplished enough for the day, they would go into his quarters and share some food. Certainly nothing for her to get terribly worked up about.

Even so, she took a little extra care with her hair that morning, brushing it back and securing it with a smooth silver clip rather than putting it in its usual messy up-do. The usual lash thickener and lip gloss, but this time accompanied by a hint of brown shadow on her lids. When she was done, she peered at her reflection and wondered if it was too much. True, the cosmetics were so faint that most people would probably never even notice them, but it still might be enough of a change that Raymond could see the difference.

Well, she couldn't do anything about it now, except wash her face and start over, and she didn't have time for that. And when she entered the lab, he offered his usual neutral greeting, his masked face all but glued to a microscope.

So much for him noticing.

The day passed in work and compared notes, just as their days always did. At a little after nineteen hundred hours, Raymond said, "I think we've come to a good stopping place. Are you hungry?"

Nora wasn't sure whether she actually wanted to eat. Right then, she was far more concerned with what he wanted to show her, what his private quarters might look like, than simply filling her stomach. However, it was much easier to reply, "Yes, a little," and watch him nod and pull away from the neural network he'd been working on.

"This way, then," he said briefly, and headed toward the door.

Now she was positive that he had the security chip embedded in his hand, since she'd seen him wave at the lock and barely break his stride as he'd entered his quarters dozens of times over the past few months. Still, she couldn't quite find the courage to ask the question as she followed him into a part of the facility that had so far been kept hidden from her.

The glimpses she'd caught had told her that Raymond maintained a much lower light level here than in the lab itself, so she wasn't surprised by the warm, reddish illumination that surrounded her as she made her way down the corridor. Maybe he'd sustained damage to his eyes as well, and utilized lighting that wouldn't pain them. She could see why he suffered the brighter lights in the lab; they were necessary to their work. But once he wasn't working, perhaps he needed to give his eyes a rest.

This wing seemed quite large, as the two of them passed a dozen doors before they came to an arched opening that revealed a multi-use room, with a seating area and entertainment unit to one side, and a round dining table and four chairs on the other. Unlike the institutional plastic and metal furniture found in the rest of the facility, here were leather and wood, and real rugs of woven wool on the gleaming composite floor.

In fact, the place was so much cozier than she'd imagined, she could only pause inside the entrance and look around in surprise.

"I wanted a touch of home, since I had no idea how long I'd be out here," Raymond said. He moved on into the space, past the dining area, and into a smallish kitchen, complete with a sink, refrigeration unit, and convection and microwave ovens.

Realizing she looked silly hovering near the entry like some shy secondary school girl who wasn't sure whether she was about to get thrown out of the popular kids' party, Nora made herself walk over to where Raymond was now getting a pair of glasses down from the cupboard. "Drink?" he asked as he dispensed ice into both of the tumblers, then placed a thin straw in one of them. Of course—the mask had a small opening where his mouth was located, but it would have been extremely difficult for him to try to pour any amount of liquid through it.

She watched him, somewhat discomfited. Was this some kind of bizarre seduction? She couldn't quite figure out what he was up to, although she had to admit that he hadn't shown a flicker of interest toward her during the past several months—at least, an interest that wasn't thoroughly professional. The cruel joke from one of the guards echoed in her mind. She had no idea whether Raymond Killian was even physically capable of a seduction.

"A drink sounds great," she replied, hoping he hadn't noticed her hesitation.

"I hope vodka is all right," he said, then went to a narrow pantry and extracted an equally slender bottle. "I don't have much else."

"Vodka is fine." In fact, it really wasn't; she couldn't help recalling a fairly spectacular drunk as an undergrad, back when she still thought trying to fit in was a good idea. She'd hadn't consumed a drop of vodka since then, but she decided it was better not to say anything now. Besides, all that ice should help to dilute the alcohol a little. She hoped.

He emerged from the kitchen and handed her one of the glasses. As she took it, one of her fingers touched his gloved hand, and an odd little tremor went through her. In all this time, they'd never touched, not even once.

Was that small brush of finger against finger an accident...or something else?

"To progress," Raymond said, raising his glass. She clinked her tumbler against his, then forced herself to take a sip of vodka.

"To progress," she echoed.

"Sit," he told her, indicating the round table a few steps away from the kitchen. It had been covered with a gray cloth, and two place settings waited for them there. "The food is only a few dishes I ordered from the cafeteria, but it should be sufficient."

"Actually, a lot of what they serve is fairly good," she offered. "Surprisingly so."

"Well, the government makes sure to keep me happy," he said. "It's simpler to order the same thing for everyone, which is why the food is of a higher quality than you might expect."

That remark made her raise her eyebrows. She really hadn't expected him to be quite so frank, although what he'd said only made sense. The support staff here at the Triton facility didn't number more than twenty people, so it would have been wasteful to send one supply of food for them and another for the lab's resident mad scientist.

"Then thank you," she said, her tone neutral. "I know the food has made my stay here more comfortable."

"Is there anything else you need?" he asked. "Is your apartment adequate?"

If he'd worried about such things, one would think he would have asked near the beginning of her tenure at the facility, rather than now, when she'd been living here for almost two months. Or maybe he was feeling awkward as well in this setting, and was trying to find neutral topics of conversation. "It's fine," Nora replied. "And even if it weren't, I spend so little time in my apartment, it would hardly matter one way or another."

Raymond didn't respond right away, making her worry that perhaps she'd been a little too honest, that just because he was in an oddly open mood didn't mean she had carte blanche to follow suit. When he spoke, however, he didn't sound put off. "I do admire your dedication."

Blood heated her cheeks. She'd never been good with compliments, even the ones directed toward her accomplishments or her intellect, rather than her appearance. Even though the days of women having to work twice as hard to prove their worth in the workplace were now centuries in the past, it was still discomfiting to have male colleagues seem vaguely surprised by her looks, as if it wasn't possible to be highly intelligent and attractive at the same time. Not that Raymond Killian seemed to have noticed. His apparent obliviousness had come as a relief; at least she knew she wouldn't have to worry about him making inappropriate comments or even more inappropriate advances.

"This is my work," she said. "And it's an honor to have the opportunity to work on your project."

"Ah." A small silence fell as he lifted his glass and inserted the straw through the mask's mouth opening. Nora did her best not to watch, to try to see if she could catch even a glimpse of the mouth beneath that opening. Doing so would have been terribly rude. He seemed to hesitate for a few seconds before he put his glass back down. Had he intended to say something else, then decided against it? Maybe. Most of their conversations had been strictly limited to subjects germane to the work they were doing, and so it was entirely possible that now they were in a more social situation, he didn't quite know how to talk to her.

That seemed the most likely explanation, especially since a moment later he got up from the table and went into the kitchen. She was surprised to see that he didn't go to one of the ovens, however, but instead to the refrigerator. He pulled out two plates of food and brought them back over, then set one in front of her.

"Vodka travels better than wine," he said. "But pairing food with it can be challenging. However, it's hard to go wrong with smoked fish, or cucumber salad. Cucumbers do very well in the greenhouses here."

"It looks excellent," Nora said. She wasn't simply being polite—the food before her might be simple enough, but it looked fresh and well-prepared.

"I hope you think so."

There wasn't much else to do but spread her napkin in her lap and pick up her fork. The salmon tasted as good as it looked, and the cucumber salad provided a fresh, bright counterpoint to the smoked fish. Even the vodka seemed more palatable now that it was paired with such tempting dishes.

It was impossible not to notice how the lower plates of Raymond's mask shifted out of the way, leaving his mouth exposed so he might eat. Although the room was dimly lit, Nora could see the scarring that cut across his lips, forever distorting their shape. The skin along his jawline was also rough and puckered, indicating multiple skin grafts that didn't quite take.

"I hope my appearance won't disturb your appetite too much," he said quietly.

A rush of pity went through her. She didn't think she'd been staring, but clearly he'd noticed that she'd noticed. "Of course not," she replied. "I'm just glad you're comfortable enough to eat around me."

"I'd hoped…." The words trailed off there, and he shrugged. "It seemed foolish to continue to hide from you when we'd been working together for months."

Considering that his mask still covered around ninety percent of his face, and his entire body was swathed in that long robe, Nora thought Raymond was still hiding most of himself from her. However, she couldn't deny that he'd made himself vulnerable even with that small glimpse. It didn't require a great deal of effort to imagine the scarring that must cover the rest of him.

"Thank you," she said. She wasn't quite sure what else to tell him, but apparently that was enough, because she could see the way he seemed to relax slightly, a certain tension leaving his lean form. They ate in silence for a few moments, bites of fish and cucumber salad interspersed with sips of vodka. Maybe it was the vodka that loosened her up enough to venture, "You said you had something you wanted to show me?"

"After we're done eating," he responded. "It's not going anywhere."

Those words only served to mystify her further. Somehow she made herself eat slowly and calmly, to take measured sips of the vodka in her glass. Even with the food, and with the melting ice cubes diluting the potent alcohol, she could feel its effects beginning to hit her—a loosening of the tension that always seemed to tighten her neck and shoulders these days, a certain warmth flooding through her limbs. She pulled in a breath of air, and wished Raymond had given her some water to drink along with the vodka.

Or maybe that had been his intention. Maybe he'd taken her measure, and realized she was someone who didn't hold her alcohol very well. Maybe this was a seduction after all....

She set down her fork. It clattered against the composite of her plate, and she tried not to wince.

"Finished?" he asked.

"Yes, I think so."

Raymond put down his own fork, even as the planes of his mask shifted back into their usual orientation. How did that work, exactly? Micro-controllers guided by small movements of his facial muscles, she guessed, although she'd never before seen a mechanism quite this sophisticated.

He got up from the table, and Nora did as well, sensing at once that she wasn't quite steady on her feet. Damn. It had been so long since she'd drunk anything except a glass of champagne at a friend's wedding, she'd forgotten how potent the heavier stuff could be.

All right. Deep breath. One foot in front of the other. If she concentrated hard enough, she thought she might be able to conceal just how tipsy she really was.

If he'd noticed her unsteadiness, Raymond didn't show any sign of it. Instead of leading her back out to the corridor and into one of the rooms that lined it, he took her away from the dining area, and into an alcove just past the kitchen. Here was another door, with another lock guarding it. He waved his hand at the lock, and the door opened.

At first she could see very little, as the lighting inside the chamber just beyond the door was even dimmer than the illumination in Raymond Killian's living quarters. As her eyes began to focus, however, she saw that the space was around five meters square, with a display on one wall showing various life support functions.

In the center of the space was a coffin.

No, not a coffin, she realized as she followed Raymond into the room. A pod not unlike the type they used to grow synthetic tissue, only much larger.

The smoked fish she'd just eaten turned over in her stomach. "What is that?"

He moved past her, entered a code into the pod's touch pad. The lid lifted, and she found herself staring down into the face of an unconscious man.

Not any man, either. It took her a moment, because it had been a long time since she'd looked at images of the individual in question, and the vodka still fogged her brain despite her best efforts to ignore its effects.

The man in the pod was Raymond Killian. Or rather, Raymond Killian as he had been before the accident destroyed his face forever. The same dark hair waving away from his forehead, the same strong, level brows. The firm chin and faintly amused mouth. Once he had been a very handsome man.

"How…?" Nora began, then shook her head. "What have you done?"

His masked face swiveled toward her. "What have I done? I've re-created myself. This was why I needed your assistance. Before I had your input, I couldn't get past the problems of interfacing lab-grown tissue and a metal skeletal structure in a construct of this size and complexity. Now, though…now it's ready."

"Ready for what?" Even as she asked the question, she thought she knew the answer.

"Ready for me to transfer my consciousness into it. I can be whole again."

A wave of horror went over her. She didn't even know precisely why the notion should be so appalling, but it was. That thing lying within the pod…it wasn't a man. It would never be Raymond Killian, even if he somehow managed to use the neural networks he'd perfected to move his very essence into the thing he'd created.

"It's not.…" She swallowed, forced herself to go on. "Biological experimentation on this level is against the Oslo Accords. You know that."

He turned so he faced her full on. Now the mask he wore was the stuff of nightmares, rather than an interesting technological puzzle. "I didn't think you were the type to let foolish strictures hold back the advance of science, Dr. Whitaker."

The use of her title was deliberate, she knew. Gone was the casual workplace intimacy they'd shared, replaced by aloof disdain. "The laws contained in the Oslo Accords are not foolish. They were put in place for a reason." Despite her better judgment, she reached out and laid a hand on his arm. He startled, but then went still, as though he didn't quite know what to do about such unexpected human contact. "How can you forget all the people who died because of recombinant DNA run amok? There's a reason why this field of study was shut down."

For a second, she thought he was going to wrench his arm away. She could feel the tension in the muscles under her fingers, even through the heavy fabric of his robe and the jumpsuit he wore beneath it. Instead, though, he moved closer, so close that she thought she could sense the heat of his body. No, that wasn't possible, not with the heavy clothing he had on. It had to be a fancy born of fear and the alcohol still coursing through her veins.

She didn't move.

"All I am doing," he said slowly and carefully, his ruined vocal chords lending a harsh edge to every syllable, "is growing new tissue. That much is allowed, even under the Oslo Accords."

"Growing new corneas and kidneys and skin for grafts is one thing," she shot back. "This—this is something completely different."

"So you will not support my research?"

The threat was implicit in those words. Nora knew she was here on Raymond Killian's sufferance. He had been the one to choose her, out of all the potential candidates for the position. More than that, it was easy enough to see why the powers-that-be had quietly green-lit this research, had set him up here on Triton, in what had once been only a small outpost for celestial observation and not much else. If he could perfect this procedure, the ramifications were staggering.

"I didn't say that. I...." Again she had to stop and consider what she'd intended to say, because her usually orderly and logical thought processes seemed to have gone haywire, like a mech short-circuited by a lightning strike. Was her current mental disarray due only to the shock of learning what Raymond Killian was really up to, or his current physical proximity? She drew in a breath. "All I'm asking is that you think about what experimentation like this could mean."

"And what could it mean, Dr. Whitaker, except freedom from this?"

One gloved hand went up to his mask, wrenching it away from his face. Now she could see how tiny receptors had been implanted all along the edge of his skin, making it a simple thing to have the mask affix itself to his flesh. More than that, though, she saw the ruin of his features, the bubbled scar tissue, the deep gash across the once-proud nose. The eyebrows singed away along with the lashes. She'd already glimpsed the damage to his mouth, but somehow it was so much worse when seen with the rest of his ravaged face.

Still, she didn't move. Again, pity stirred within her, but she knew better than to reveal any of what she was feeling to Raymond Killian. He didn't want pity. He wanted to be whole again.

"I understand why you did it, Raymond," she said quietly. "I know your own motives were pure. But what of the motives of the people who funded this project?"

He glared down at her, his face even more the stuff of nightmares now that the mask no longer hid the damage from the accident. And yet, she thought the perfect face of the simulacrum in the pod behind him was even more frightening. At least this face was real. This face was honest.

"What of my investors? They're only a means to an end. They mean nothing."

"No," Nora said. "They mean everything." She lifted her hand from his arm, but not so she could move away from him. Instead, she reached up and laid her fingers against the side of Raymond's face, feeling the roughness of the scarred flesh against her own skin. "Don't let them control you."

His eyes shut. Was this the first time someone other than a doctor or nurse or tech had touched him since the accident? Nora wasn't even sure why she had done so, except that maybe she hoped she could reach him with a human touch, could show him there was no need for the monstrosity in the pod behind him.

A tremor went through him. Then, incongruously, he smiled, light touching his clear blue eyes. "You are a brave woman, Nora Whitaker."

"I don't think so," she said frankly as she withdrew her hand—but gently, so she could show him that she hadn't done so because she was repulsed by him, but only because it wasn't exactly proper for her to continue touching her superior's face. "I think I drank too much vodka with dinner."

"Bottle bravery?"

"I suppose you could call it that."

A nod, and then Raymond began to lift the mask to his face.

"Don't," Nora said, and he paused, staring at her in confusion. Despite the damage to his features, it was far easier to read him now that the mask wasn't hiding his expressions.

"Don't what?"

"Don't put it back on. Or rather," she added, "I don't see the point in your wearing it now. I've already seen you, haven't I?"

The skin where his brows used to be drew together. "What if I'm more comfortable with the mask on?"

She supposed she should have thought of that. Despite the ruination of his flesh, she couldn't see any obvious signs that the mask chafed or rubbed his skin raw. And after so many years of hiding behind that composite-metallic counterfeit of a face, there was probably a very good chance he didn't want to leave himself open in such a way.

Vulnerable.

"Then go ahead and put it back on," she said. "I think you should do whatever suits you."

"'Whatever suits me,'" he repeated, his tone musing. A long pause, during which he shifted slightly so they no longer stood so close, so he now looked at the simulacrum of his former self, rather than at her. "It would suit me to be like that again."

"But it's not you."

His broad shoulders squared. With anger? Since he wasn't looking at her directly, Nora couldn't say for sure. "It's close enough that anyone who knew me—knew the former me—would be fooled. And that's all I care about."

"You care about fooling people?"

This time he did turn toward her, and there was no mistaking the flash of anger in his eyes. "Are you being deliberately disingenuous, Dr. Whitaker?"

"No, Raymond."

His eyes narrowed at the use of his first name, a direct counter to the way he'd addressed her once again by her title. "Then what?"

How to answer? She honestly couldn't even say for sure why it should matter to her one way or another whether he covered his face with the mask again. The replacement body he'd grown for himself—that was an entirely different proposition. That mattered…a lot. Every test she'd been given since she was a young child had indicated that she possessed a genius IQ, but it certainly didn't take a genius to figure out how such technology could be subverted. If Raymond really did succeed in transferring his consciousness to that new body, in a sense he was giving himself immortality. And if he could do such a thing for himself, then the same procedure could be replicated among those with the money and power to pay for such a thing. No change, no progress, only an increasingly ossified upper class that would never allow the power they'd consolidated to slip from their grasp.

Gaia's government was bad enough already. Raymond Killian's invention would make the situation far, far worse.

Once again she reached out and laid a hand on his arm. This time he didn't flinch, but the wary expression he wore only deepened. When he spoke, his tone was rougher than ever. "Do you pity me? Do you think I can be mollified with a touch here and there, a few scraps thrown to a starving man?"

"I'm not trying to throw you any scraps," Nora protested. In fact, it wasn't at all like her to reach out to someone, to be the first to touch another person. In her few romantic relationships, her companions had always been the ones to pursue her, rather than the reverse.

And what the hell was she doing, comparing her current situation to those past entanglements? She wasn't romantically involved with Raymond. She'd touched him because she didn't want him to think he was alone. Nothing more than that.

But....

She thought of the work they'd shared, the easy way the time in the lab slipped past. If asked, she would have said that was simply because she was engrossed in the research, and admired the mind of the man who had hired her to join him as he sought to expand the field of cybernetic investigation. That wasn't even a lie. She did admire Raymond, even as she realized that his desperation had led him down a very dangerous path.

What if her admiration had begun to transform into something else, something even deeper?

No, that wasn't possible.

And yet....

He continued to watch her, lashless eyes narrowed, as though he was studying a wild animal he hadn't yet determined was inclined to attack him or not. The sensible thing to do here would be to take her hand from his arm, to tell him calmly and sensibly that she feared he hadn't explored all the ramifications of his research, and that they should revisit this in the morning after they'd both had a chance to regain some equilibrium.

Instead, she moved closer to him, went up on her tiptoes. Her hands moved to tangle in his unkempt hair. In the next instant, her mouth was touching his scarred one, his lips rough against her skin. She didn't care, though. All that mattered was the feel of his body against hers, the rush of heat that went through her at their contact. For a moment, he didn't move, didn't even seem to breathe. And then his gloved hands were touching her face, holding her, as his mouth opened to hers and she was able to taste him, her body warm with a sudden, throbbing need.

They stood that way as at least a minute passed, possibly more. Nora didn't know for sure, or care. What mattered was that he had accepted her embrace, hadn't pushed her away. At last, however, he lifted his lips from hers and whispered, "My God."

Were those murmured words an invocation...or a curse? She stayed near him, wondering at the flush of desire that still seemed to permeate every cell in her body. Had a kiss ever aroused her like this before? She didn't think so. In fact, she'd lately begun to believe that she was, if not asexual, at least someone who didn't put the same emphasis on sexual relations that the rest of society seemed to.

Raymond Killian's kiss had certainly put that notion to rest. It wasn't that she was asexual, only that she hadn't found the right partner.

Until now.

"Nora," he said, then stopped. He reached up to push a hand through his hair. Odd that it had somehow survived, when his face was such a ruin.

"What, Raymond?"

"Please tell me you didn't do that simply because...." Another pause, and he released a heavy breath. "Tell me that wasn't done out of pity."

"'Pity'?" she repeated, and shook her head. "No. I wanted to. I wanted...you."

Shock flared in his eyes. "How could you want...this?"

"Because it's you. Because you're Raymond Killian, and I see *you*"—she placed one hand on his chest, above his heart—"not what the accident did to you."

He was silent, as though he still couldn't quite process what she was saying. But at least he didn't try to move away. Nora could feel the hastened beating of his heart beneath her palm, and wondered what she would do if he still rejected her, even after everything she had just said.

At last he said, "It did more to me than this," and touched two fingers to his scarred cheek.

Did she dare ask? Once again the cruelly ribald jokes shared in the commissary flashed through her mind. Better to know the worst, though. Anyway, a single shared kiss with him had shaken her body far more than any sex she'd had before.

"How much more?"

A grim smile pulled at the uneven edges of his mouth. "Not enough to prevent me from making love to you, if that's what you're asking. The flesh is willing and able enough. Only...it will not be pretty."

"I don't care about that."

"You're sure?"

She nodded. What were scars, anyway? Only the body's reaction to stress. Surface damage, nothing more.

Well, as long as those scars hadn't also been inflicted on his soul.

He bent and kissed her again, deeply, his tongue touching hers. Once more that blessed heat flooded through every limb, her very core aching with need. God, she wanted him.

After he took his lips away from hers, however, his next words filled her with disappointment. "Not now, though."

"Why not?" she demanded. They weren't children, after all, but adults with the ability to make their own decisions. And she'd decided that she wanted him, more than she'd wanted anything in her life.

"Because I need some time to come to terms with all this." His gaze moved from her to the artificial body resting in its pod. "And because I need to decide what to do next. Your words angered me, Nora, because I'd had the same misgivings. I buried them because I didn't want to acknowledge their truth. I wanted this new body to be the answer, the cure for my situation. Unfortunately, it has only created a new set of problems."

She didn't ask him what those problems were. Raymond Killian was a brilliant man; he probably knew far better than she the conundrum he'd created.

"And also," he continued, "it was already irregular enough for you to come here and share a meal with me. If you leave now, though, you're still within the bounds of what might be considered a realistic amount of time to spend at dinner. If I were to take you to my bedroom, and love you the way I want to—that will be certain to raise questions. We are such a very small group here, after all."

A fact Nora knew all too well. Although she had done her best to keep herself somewhat apart from the rest of the support staff here at the research facility, she still had a general idea of who was feuding with whom, of who was engaged in a short-term relationship, although technically fraternization was forbidden on stations such as this. If she spent the night here with Raymond—if she even spent an hour or two more—someone would be sure to notice. As matters stood now, all she'd done was share a few kisses with him. Her lack of lip stain could be blamed on the meal she'd just consumed and nothing more.

"I understand," she said. "I hate it, but I understand."

His gloved hands cupped her face again, the touch of the smooth synth-leather strangely erotic. His lips brushed against hers before he spoke. "It will not be too difficult, my dear. After all, we do spend ten to twelve hours together every day. Who's to say all those hours must be spent in conducting research?"

The promise in those words made her smile. "You're right, of course. Then I suppose I'll see you in the lab tomorrow at 0800."

The gleam in his eyes made her flush with need all over again. "I look forward to it."

\* \* \* \*

She left soon afterward, smoothing her hair and trying to look calm and composed, as though nothing had passed between her and Raymond during the time she'd spent with him except some dry conversation pertaining to their research. After she left the elevator and turned the corner toward the wing of the building where her apartment was located, however, she had to keep herself from startling and taking a step back.

Standing there in the middle of the corridor was Lt. Lopez, an unpleasant smile pulling at his lips.

"You're out late, Dr. Whitaker," he said. "Rumor is that you had a hot date with the Beast."

Nora had heard the scornful nickname before, of course, but had chosen to ignore it. Now, though, she could feel the blood rush to her cheeks as she retorted, "I'd hardly call a quiet dinner with a colleague a 'hot date.'" Against her better judgment, she added, "And his name is Dr. Killian. Since he's in charge of this facility, it might be a good idea if you showed some respect."

To her annoyance, Lopez's smile didn't fade. If anything, it only grew broader. "You're quick to jump to his defense, aren't you? A little too quick, I think."

"What you think isn't relevant. Now, could you please get out of my way? It's been a long day."

Lopez didn't move. He only stood there, arms crossed, surveying her with the same undressing glance that had made her flesh crawl since the moment she came to this facility…and which hadn't improved over the intervening weeks. "I think your problem is all work and no play. I can help you with that, you know."

Had he been drinking? He wasn't standing close enough that she would be able to smell alcohol one way or another, but she couldn't figure out why else he would suddenly be acting so bold. Or maybe her dinner with Raymond had fired up Lopez's jealousy, made him come here to seek her out.

For the first time, Nora could feel a thin trickle of fear begin to edge its way down her spine. Before now, she'd always viewed Lt. Lopez as more of an annoyance than anything else, a pebble in her shoe that she could generally ignore. But this section of the facility seemed so empty; her apartment was one of four in its wing, but she was the only one living there, as if the station had been built to include a larger complement of scientists, even though she was Raymond Killian's only assistant.

"I don't need any help, thank you," she said crisply, hoping that her matter-of-fact tone would shake some sense into the man who stood before her. "As I said, I've had a long day, and my work has to start all over again tomorrow morning. So I'd appreciate it if you would step aside."

The guard's face twisted in anger—and then Nora realized he wasn't looking at her, was instead staring past her shoulder, down the hallway toward the elevators. She followed his gaze, experienced a flood of relief as she saw Raymond approaching, his mask back in place, dark robes billowing behind him as he strode closer, like some ancient god of vengeance seeking his prey.

When he spoke, however, his words were innocuous enough. "Dr. Whitaker? You left your handheld in the lab." From a pocket on the interior of his robe, he produced the item in question.

"Oh, I hadn't realized. Thank you." She stepped away from Lopez and went toward Raymond, let him put the device in her hand.

He glanced past her to the man who stood a few paces from them. "Lopez? Is everything all right?"

Now looking simultaneously angry and hangdog, Lopez nodded. "Sure thing, Dr. Killian. I was just doing a last sweep before I went off shift."

"It all looks fine here."

"Yes, sir. I'll just be going. You have a good night."

Thwarted rage practically radiating from every pore, he brushed past Raymond and Nora, and got into the elevator. She waited for the doors to close before she said, "Thank God. I didn't know how I was going to get rid of him."

Even though he must have also heard the elevator doors shut, Raymond didn't reach out to touch her. Instead, he remarked, "He does seem to have an unhealthy interest. It's probably best if you go straight to your apartment."

"But—"

He shook his head, his mask tilting upward ever so slightly. Nora followed his gaze, realized he was looking at the fingernail-size security camera mounted to the ceiling. The devices were so small, and so ubiquitous, that she'd mostly forgotten they were even there. But they were, recording every word spoken, every step taken in the facility. No wonder Raymond had refrained from making any public displays of affection.

"Of course, Dr. Killian. Thank you for bringing me my handheld. I'll see you in the lab tomorrow morning."

A brief nod, and he turned and headed back toward the elevators. Nora went on to her apartment, swiped her key card over the lock and let herself in, then entered the code to secure the door again. As far as she'd been able to tell, there weren't any cameras or other security devices in here, but that didn't mean much. No one had made any effort to hide the cameras in the hallways because they were supposed to be there. Technically, it was illegal to record anyone in their private quarters, but she knew as well as anyone else that the Consortium only followed the rules when it felt like it.

As she put her handheld down on the small table in the dining area, she realized she was shaking. No, she really didn't think Lopez would have tried anything physical…or would he? After all, he was second-in-command of the facility's guard detail. Maybe he thought he could get away with assaulting her, even if the incident ended up being recorded. For all she knew, maybe he actually wanted a record, just so he could watch it over and over again at his leisure. No doubt his colleagues would assist him in covering up the crime…even the ones who'd seemed friendly at first.

A shudder went over her, and she made herself go to the refrigeration unit and dispense some water from the door. A few swallows helped her relax a little—and also helped to dispel the last of the vodka-induced fog from her brain.

Thank God for Raymond. He'd come at exactly the right moment. Coincidence, or had he somehow tapped into the feed from the facility's security cameras? Technically, that wasn't his field of expertise, but she wouldn't be surprised to learn that he had such minor hacking abilities among the skills in his toolkit. Back before the accident that had turned him into a recluse, he'd dabbled in everything from software development to building supersonic cars for racing on the salt flats in the former United States' desert Southwest.

Well, whether coincidence or deliberate intervention—either way, she was safe.

For now.

She hated that interruption by Lopez, though, hated that he'd intruded on her evening in such a fashion. Although he'd been sent packing, the nasty little confrontation had effectively destroyed any remaining afterglow from those kisses she'd shared with Raymond. Now all she could do was get ready for bed, and try to cheer herself by recalling the promise he'd made to her. They would be alone in the lab for hours and hours tomorrow. No one ever came to disturb them there, probably because they knew they'd have to suffer unpleasant repercussions if they interrupted his work. He would kiss her again…and so much more.

Heartened by that thought, she climbed into her hard, narrow bed, said, "Lights out," and forced herself to go to sleep.

\* \* \* \*

Although she couldn't help being tense with worry as she went from her apartment to the lab the next morning, Nora saw no sign of Lt. Lopez. She'd had coffee and hot cereal in her own quarters, and avoided the commissary altogether. Still, those precautions weren't necessarily enough to keep her out of her stalker's orbit. However, he seemed to have made himself scarce this morning…or maybe he was just biding his time, waiting for the perfect opportunity to once more find her alone.

As the doors to the lab closed behind her, she wanted nothing more than to run across the room to the spot where Raymond stood by the worktable, and throw herself into his arms. However, since she didn't know whether this space was also under electronic surveillance, she made herself utter a neutral, "Good morning, Dr. Killian."

Although he wore his mask and she couldn't see whether he smiled or not, the amusement in his harsh voice was clear enough. "It's all right, Nora. No one is watching us here."

She knew she should trust him, but even so, she couldn't help casting a wary eye toward the ceiling, toward the corners where security cameras were most often installed.

"Oh, they're there," he went on. "But I interrupted the feed to display a randomly generated video loop, so they shouldn't suspect anything."

"A what?"

"Footage I've recorded over the last few months. It's set up to show the two of us working, but in such a way that the transitions are completely organic. I suppose if someone sat down and watched it straight through for a month or so, they might notice something off, although I hope we won't need quite that long."

Relief rushed through her, and she went over to him, let him fold his arms around her and hold her close. Odd how not so long ago she would have thought Raymond Killian one of the least reassuring people she'd ever met, and now she couldn't think of anyplace that felt safer than being in the circling strength of his embrace.

"No, I hope not," she said, then tilted her head so she could look up at him. Too bad he was wearing his mask, although she understood why he did. He might have doctored the video feed, but there was still the off chance that someone might come by the lab. Such interruptions only happened when one of the facility's guards needed to deliver something in person, and yet they still needed to be careful. "What do we do now, Raymond?"

He passed a hand over her hair. Such gentleness in that touch, even with his skin shielded by the synth-leather of his gloves. "I've been thinking about that. Come sit with me."

Taking her by the hand, he led her to a small table and a pair of chairs set up in a corner of the lab. Nora had sat there in the past while taking short coffee breaks, although she'd never seen Raymond use the little dining set. Now he did sit down, while she took the other chair and looked at him expectantly.

"I've been transmitting my progress to the GSC," he said, naming the Gaian Science Commission, the body that oversaw all government-funded research. "Part of the agreement I made with them in order to have this facility tailored to my specifications. They don't have my most recent update, but they know enough that I can't stall them forever. They know how close I was…am."

"So we can't stonewall them."

"Not for very long. As I said, they don't know that the simulacrum has passed its final tests and is ready for consciousness transfer. But they know what I've built, and most certainly are already exploring the possible uses of such technology."

Since Nora had already imagined those nightmares, and knew that Raymond had as well, she didn't bother to comment. "They have access to all your research?"

"Most of it. There are some notes and observations I've kept to myself, written down in hard copy so they can't scan the information from my files. Even lacking those data points, they could probably reconstruct the pertinent research if necessary."

Damn. She had been feeling hopeful this morning as she woke and then showered, telling herself that Raymond could probably inform the GSC officials back on Gaia that the project had hit a dead end, and that there was nothing more to be done. Now she realized it couldn't possibly be that easy.

"What do we do?" she asked, knowing she sounded hopeless. "Raymond, they're going to do terrible things with this research."

He reached out and touched a gloved hand to her cheek. Despite everything—her worry, the tension knotted in her stomach, even the fact that they were sitting here in the lab and it wasn't even 0900 yet—a thrill went through her at the caress, her body coming alive at his proximity. God, she wanted him to do so much more than merely touch her face.

"I know," he said. "There isn't much I can do about the information they already have in their hands. However, that data is still incomplete. All I have to do is show that the concept is fatally flawed. But I'll need your help with that."

"Anything," Nora promised, even as she thought of how much she'd changed in the last twenty-four hours.

"I'd hoped you would say that." He hesitated, then bent his head next hers and murmured, "It's killing me to be this close to you."

"I know what you mean." His hair had fallen forward slightly, so that one long strand brushed against her cheek. Again her body thrummed with need, although she knew she had to stay focused. "Maybe we should slip back into your quarters before we do any more planning."

A chuckle emerged from behind the mask, but, to her dismay, he shook his head. "No, I fear we don't have time for that. Not now. We only have one chance for escape, and we need to take it."

"Escape?" What in the world was he talking about? They were stuck in a research facility on one of the solar system's remotest moons. It wasn't as though they could simply procure some forged I.D. cards and hightail it to New Zealand or Greenland, two regions of Gaia that tended to be ignored by the Consortium.

"We'll do our best to make the research appear fundamentally flawed. However, that won't be enough for us to escape inquiries. The Consortium doesn't like its research funds spent on boondoggles."

No, it most certainly did not. If Raymond hadn't been at the top of his field when the accident occurred—if he hadn't provided numerous bona fides as to the eventual successful outcome of this area of research—then he would never have been given this facility and all the resources connected with it.

"They'll be looking for scapegoats," she said, and Raymond nodded.

"Precisely. We have to get away."

"How do you propose to do that?"

"The supply ship will be arriving tomorrow. It's not as fast as the GDF intrasystem vessel that's permanently assigned to this station, but at least it will be adequate to prevent the people left behind from being stranded here until a replacement arrives."

It took a few seconds for the import of his words to sink in. "You want to steal the GDF ship."

"Yes."

"You can fly it?"

"Of course."

He sounded completely unruffled, completely sure of himself. Well, why wouldn't he be? The Raymond Killian of the past had flown everything from asteroid skiffs to stratosphere hoppers. And since he had the highest security clearance of anyone at the facility, he shouldn't have any trouble accessing the hangar where the vessel was kept.

Only....

"Raymond, even if you manage to steal it, that ship's only an intrasystem craft. It doesn't have a subspace drive. Where exactly do you think we can go?"

He reached out with one hand and laid it on top of hers. "Tell me, Nora—have you ever heard of Oort 1?"

The name wasn't familiar. Or rather, of course she knew of the Oort Cloud, the band of star stuff and the birthplace of comets that lay beyond the solar system, but "Oort 1" sounded like a space station of sorts, albeit one currently unknown to her. She shook her head.

"I'm not surprised. Its existence is secret, limited to a few people with high clearances. The government doesn't want the general population to know it's there."

"Why not?" After all, Gaia's system was studded with space stations, some staffed by crews with as many as a hundred people, others completely automated observation outposts.

"Because it's not ours. The Eridanis built it."

In response to that remark, uttered so casually, Nora could only stare back at him. The Eridanis? True, those humanoid aliens had proved to be benign enough; the Consortium wouldn't have progressed as quickly in its subspace drive research if it weren't for their assistance. Even so, she couldn't imagine that the GDF would be very happy to have an alien race build a space station so close to its own home system.

"And that's allowed?"

"Who's to allow it? Right now, Consortium jurisdiction only extends to the outer borders of Pluto's orbit. Everything beyond that is wild space—the open sea, so to speak. Rather like it was back in the day, when anything more than eight miles off the coast was considered international waters."

*The generals in the GDF must hate that,* she thought. *To have aliens lurking out there, close enough to observe what we do, and yet with our military not able to do a damn thing about it.*

"How far?"

"Approximately five hundred million miles. It will take about two weeks. But the ship can handle it, obviously, since it's a much greater distance than that from here on Triton to Gaia."

He sounded so calm about the whole thing, as if it was no very great leap to go sailing out into the darkness, looking for one speck of life in all that sea of nothing. "Do you know where Oort 1 is located?"

"Not precisely. But I'm not worried about that. Once we're outside the solar system, we're free of the Consortium's influence. We'll broadcast on all frequencies, asking for asylum. I have no doubt that the Eridanis will hear us and come to retrieve us."

As simple as that. Maybe it was. While she'd never seen one of the aliens in person, they weren't shy about mingling with humans. In fact, there had already been a few Gaian/Eridani marriages, although it was noteworthy that all those pairings ended up living on Eridani. Not that Nora could exactly blame them. The politics on Gaia had made her wish on more than one occasion that she could escape the Consortium's crushing influence, too.

And now it looked as though Raymond was offering her exactly that opportunity.

"You think they would take us?"

"I'm sure of it. After all, we are two highly trained scientists. Valuable contributors to society, so to speak." He paused there and regarded her for a moment. More than anything, she wished she could see his face, just so she could know something of what he was thinking. "But perhaps I'm asking too much of you? If we do this thing, then you will never see your family or friends again. We would have to start all over again on a completely different world."

A shudder went through her. It was one thing, after all, to say goodbye to friends and family for a finite period, even if it ended up being as long as a year or two. But this wasn't a couple of years. This would be forever.

And yet...how could she do anything else? The Consortium could never get the final pieces to the puzzle of Raymond's research. If the two of them deliberately sabotaged it, eventually their treachery would be discovered. Then all they would have to look forward to was the remainder of their lives spent in the maximum security prison on Titan.

She reached over and took both his hands in hers. "You're not asking too much. We can do this. Just tell me what needs to happen next."

\* \* \* \*

It wasn't precisely faking Raymond's death, but they did make a show of hooking him up to the simulacrum, of making sure the whole thing was recorded. The fault he'd introduced to the system caused the synaptic transfer to collapse on itself, followed by a spectacular shower of sparks.

"Not that it would actually explode in such a showy fashion," he'd said with a grin. "But it will take investigators a while to determine that the system was sabotaged. In the meantime, I thought I might as well give them a light show."

The mini-explosion also gave them an excuse to pretend that he'd been injured in the accident. Nora wheeled over a gurney that had been stowed off to one side of the pod where the simulacrum—now a mass of charred flesh—rested, and manhandled Raymond onto it, making as much of a show as she could for the watching security cameras. Luckily, the infirmary was located in the same general direction as the hangar that was her true destination; their belongings had already been stowed in a locker there, waiting to be transferred to the GDF system craft that would take them away from Triton.

Unfortunately, her path to the hangar wasn't as smooth as Nora would have liked. As she pushed the gurney down corridors that now seemed endless, she was suddenly confronted by Lt. Lopez, who came out of a connecting hallway and blocked her progress.

"What happened?" he asked, his tone sharp.

"An accident," she said briefly. "I'm taking him to the infirmary."

"I'll do it."

"That's not necessary—" she began to protest, but he ignored her and grasped the handles of the gurney, began pushing it down the hall toward the infirmary.

Well, at least he was going mostly in the right direction. She trotted alongside him, praying that her expression reflected fear and worry rather than the annoyance she currently felt. What to do, though? Wait until he actually got to the infirmary, then hit him over the head with a bedpan?

It would be a fitting fate, if nothing else.

However, she wasn't given that chance, because Raymond leapt up from the gurney, one hand peeling away his mask so he could smash it across the guard's face.

Lopez stumbled and crashed into the wall. Unfortunately, the blow hadn't been strong enough to knock him out. His hand went at once to the pulse pistol holstered at his hip, drew it out. Nora had always thought the practice of carrying sidearms on this isolated station posturing at best and foolishness at its worst. Now, though, that inner contempt morphed into fear as Lopez raised the pistol and pointed it at Raymond.

No. This couldn't be happening. No time to think. She let go of the gurney and flung herself at Lopez, crashed into him as the gun went off.

A bright blue energy pulse flashed from the barrel, striking Raymond in the shoulder. He staggered backward a few paces, twisted features contorted further by pain.

"Bitch," Lopez panted. "Traitor bitch. You're both going to fry for this."

"You first," she retorted. Instinct took over, and she drove her knee into his groin, then took advantage of his momentary shock to twist the gun in his hand so it was pointed toward him. Without thinking, she pushed the button on the grip, pushed again.

She couldn't see the pulses because they drove directly into his body, but he slumped at once, his uniform smoking slightly where the energy bolts had driven through the fabric and into his flesh. Was he dead? She couldn't tell for sure. That didn't matter, though. What mattered was getting out of here.

"Nora—"

At once she wheeled back toward Raymond. He had one hand flattened against the wall, as if that was the only thing holding him up.

"Are you okay?" she asked.

His mouth twisted. "Define 'okay.' The bolt missed any vital organs, but it hurts like hell."

Damn. For the first time she saw blood beginning to trickle down from the wound in his shoulder. The ship they were planning to steal would have a basic medi-bay on board, but she needed to get him there first.

"Get back on the gurney," she said. "It's the easiest way to transport you to the ship."

Raymond's mouth opened, as if he intended to protest, but then he nodded. Thank God he was able to lower himself onto the gurney without much assistance; Nora knew that if he passed out, she'd have a hell of a time trying to maneuver his six feet and more onto the rolling metal cart. As it was, she worried that someone had already seen the violent little encounter on the security feed, and that GDF personnel might already be on the way. No time to lose.

She took off at a run, pushing the gurney in front of her. Within a few minutes, she reached the hangar, and stopped just long enough to retrieve their belongings from the locker where they'd been hidden. It wasn't all that much—a duffle bag for each of them, a hard-shell case that contained both their computers and a few peripherals. Definitely not a lot to start a new life on a new world.

*It's enough,* Nora thought as she dumped the items on the gurney next to Raymond. He reached out with one hand to steady them, even though she could see the way his teeth gritted with pain while he did so. *He's really the only thing you need.*

Well, Raymond and the love of discovery they shared. She didn't know much about the Eridanis' level of technology when it came to cybernetics; if they'd shared that information with the Consortium government, it certainly hadn't trickled down to the rank and file. If she and Raymond were lucky, they'd have years to find out for themselves.

The ship didn't look big enough to take on interstellar distances, but it didn't have to. Only the distance between Jupiter and Saturn. That wasn't so very much. She'd covered more miles than that to get here. At the time, she hadn't realized she'd end up traveling farther still.

No one guarded the ship. Who would they be guarding against, in this tiny outpost?

"Gangway control…next to the hatch," Raymond said, every word sounding more labored than the last. "Green button."

Nora located the control panel and slid the protective cover out of the way, then pushed the green button as instructed. At once the gangway began to extend from the underbelly of the ship. She let out a relieved breath, then quickly pushed the gurney into the ship before locking the hatch behind them.

"Help me up," he whispered. "Need to get to the cockpit."

"I need to get you to the medi-bay," she said.

"No. Have to…get the ship out of here. I can do it."

How much did a wound from a pulse bolt hurt? Nora had no idea, because of course she'd never been in a position to get shot at before this. Judging by the way Raymond's jaw was clenched, it hurt plenty. And there was the blood, now staining even more of his jumpsuit as he pushed himself to a sitting position.

"At least let me see if I can find a painkiller hypo-spray—"

"No. I need to stay sharp. I can handle the pain. Help me up."

Yes, she supposed he could. Compared to what he'd suffered in the accident and all the myriad surgeries afterward, a pulse bolt in the shoulder probably felt like a mosquito bite.

In silence, she slid an arm around his waist and eased him off the gurney. When his feet touched the floor, he stumbled slightly, and she clutched him tighter. If he fell, she'd have a hell of a time getting him back up again.

Somehow, though, he didn't fall. The two of them staggered forward to the cockpit, and he fell into the pilot's chair, then immediately began toggling switches, pressing buttons.

Through the forward view-screen, Nora could see several of Lopez's security detail hurrying into the hangar, even as the speaker above her head came alive with a screech of static.

"Dr. Killian, just what the hell do you think you're doing?"

He ignored the voice, fingers still moving over the controls. Nora could feel the ship waking up around them, the low hum of the engines signaling its readiness for launch.

"What if they shoot at us?" she asked.

Mouth tight with pain, he replied, "The pistols they carry aren't strong enough to pierce this ship's hull. Besides, they're going to need to leave this hangar in the very near future."

"Wh—"

The word "why" hadn't even left her lips before he tapped out another series of commands. At once the enormous doors of the hangar began to open, exposing the cavernous space to the near-vacuum of Triton's mostly nonexistent atmosphere. Winds began to howl, and the view-screen showed the security guards beating a hasty retreat for the exit before all the usable air was lost.

"Effective," she said as the ship started to move toward the hangar doors.

"Wasteful." His breathing sounded more labored now, and he slumped against the back of the seat. "But they can't...stop us."

Apparently not. The ship accelerated, lifting off the ground and moving in a smooth arc through the perpetual night that surrounded the research facility. Even now, the outpost had been reduced to a few blocky shapes outlined by lights that remained illuminated at all times, since out here on the edges of the solar system, the sun was little more than an oddly bright star.

Then they were truly away, picking up speed, Triton a bluish disc falling away behind them. Raymond roused himself enough to make a few more adjustments to the controls—altering their trajectory, Nora thought, although she couldn't be completely certain.

"We're safe," she said. "Please, Raymond—let me take you to the medi-bay."

He shook his head, then forced himself to sit upright enough so he could tap out a few more commands, this time on the communications console. "Make our plea, Nora. I don't have the strength to do it."

"I will—if I can take you to the medi-bay afterward."

His eyes shut. "Of course."

Heart tight with fear, she made herself move a little closer to the console, so the built-in microphone would pick up her voice without any interference. "Oort 1, this is Dr. Nora Whitaker and Dr. Raymond Killian, formerly of the research facility on Triton. We are requesting asylum. Our ship is headed into the cloud. We hope and pray that you will find us." She paused there. Was it enough? It felt as though she was painting a target on their backs, although she knew the Consortium didn't have any ships out this way except the sluggish resupply shuttle that even now was heading for the moon they'd just escaped. Perhaps one of the GDF's few precious subspace-drive-equipped ships could be sent after them, but she wasn't sure if they really rated that kind of pursuit.

That task done, she went to Raymond, put her arm around him once again. This time it felt as though she had to lift him almost entirely on her own. She gritted her teeth and maneuvered him out of his seat, helped him stagger past the four tiny cabins and the cramped galley, all the way to the rear of the ship where the medi-bay was located.

Somehow she was able to get him inside, and lying down. Luckily, the bay was programmed for pulse weapon wounds, so once she located that option, she quickly got the healing cycle in process. After that, there was very little she could do except wait.

A metal chair had been built into the wall opposite the medi-bay. She pulled it down and sat, and watched the face of the man she loved.

He didn't move, didn't stir, but the readouts on the bay indicated that his heart beat and respiration were within acceptable normal ranges. Despite Lopez's best efforts, Raymond would live.

Nora buried her face in her hands and wept. If asked, she didn't know if she would have even been able to explain her tears, only that they were a mixture of relief and fear. Relief that she wouldn't be left alone out here, perhaps...fear that the transmission she'd sent would sail away into the depths of space and never be intercepted by the Eridanis. For all she knew, this stolen ship might turn out to be their tomb.

At last she dozed a bit, only to be awakened by Raymond's rough, gravelly voice.

"Nora."

She started, pushing herself upright in the hard metal chair. His eyes met hers, awake, alert.

"I'm feeling much improved," he said. "Can you help me out of this thing?"

"If you're sure—" As she spoke, though, her gaze moved automatically to the readouts on the medi-bay. Everything was still in the normal zone. And as she looked at Raymond, she could see that the wound in his shoulder was neatly patched with synth-flesh. He would have another scar, but what did that matter?

"I'm sure." He sat up and swung his legs over the edge of the bay. At once she hurried to him, helping him stand. Now he felt strong and sturdy, and she really didn't need to support him at all.

"Do you want something to eat? I can check the galley."

"Later, my love," he replied, and reached over with one hand to brush her cheek. "I want to see how we're doing first."

Of course he'd want to check on their progress before anything else. Nora nodded, and walked to the cockpit with him, her arm still around his waist. He didn't need the support, but neither did he tell her to let go. Apparently, he needed the reassurance of her touch just as much as she needed to keep holding him, to feel the strength of his body against hers. That was good. They would only have each other going forward.

Once he'd settled himself in the pilot's seat, he began inspecting the controls, clear blue eyes surveying the readouts on the heads-up displays. It didn't seem as though he found anything that worried him, because he gave a satisfied nod and allowed himself to settle against the seat back.

"We're still on course?" she asked.

"Yes, although that 'course' was entirely arbitrary, since I didn't have the exact coordinates of Oort 1 to work with. But the ship is operating at optimal levels, and there are no signs of pursuit. All we can do now is wait."

*Not for too long,* Nora thought, but she remained silent. A ship like this would have supplies to keep them going for several weeks, but eventually those rations would run out. They would be adrift here in the darkness beyond the solar system. At least they would have each other, until the bitter end that eventually claimed them, but—

A voice came over the speaker, female, calm, with a soft rolling accent unlike anything Nora had ever heard before. "Gaian vessel, this is Oort 1. We have received your transmission. One of our ships is en route and should rendezvous with you in four standard hours. Please stand by."

A smile spread across Raymond's ravaged features. He leaned forward and touched the comm controls. "Oort 1, thank you for the update. We are standing by and await rendezvous." He ended the transmission, then shifted in his seat and glanced over at Nora. "You see? Absolutely nothing to worry about."

"Oh, nothing at all." But the voice of the Eridani woman had reassured her somewhat. An alien, yes, but one who sounded friendly, kind. The universe could use a little more kindness…a little more love.

A smile touched Nora's lips.

"What is it?" Raymond asked.

Did she dare make the suggestion? Yes, medi-bays promoted rapid healing, but he'd been shot less than eight hours earlier. On the other hand, he'd certainly seemed energetic enough as she walked with him up here to the cockpit. And she was so very tired of having to wait.

"Oh, I was just thinking about what we should do with those four hours until the Eridanis get here."

He grinned. The accident might have ruined his face, but his teeth were still strong and white and even. "I can think of a few things."

"Then show me," she whispered.

He lifted her from her seat and kissed her, and led her back to the ship's sleeping quarters, to one of the cramped little cabins, which had certainly never been designed for that sort of activity. Nevertheless, afterward Nora couldn't help but smile as she lay in her lover's arms, knowing that she had made the right choice, that her future lay with Raymond Killian…the man some had called a Beast.

Southern California, *USA Today* bestselling author Christine Pope has been writing stories ever since she commandeered her family's Smith-Corona typewriter back in the sixth grade. Because she's a lover of many genres, her books include paranormal romance, fantasy romance, and science fiction/space opera romance. She blames this on being easily distracted by bright, shiny objects, which could also account for the size of her shoe collection. The Land of Enchantment cast its spell on her while she was researching her Djinn Wars series, and she now makes her home in Santa Fe, New Mexico.

www.ingramcontent.com/pod-product-compliance
Lightning Source LLC
Chambersburg PA
CBHW031429250626
47155CB00004B/1674